Les beaux messieurs de Bois-Doré
Vol. 2

by

George Sand

Les beaux messieurs de Bois-Doré Vol. 2
by George Sand

ISBN: 978-93-61152-76-4

Published by

DOUBLE 9 BOOKS
2/13-B, Ansari Road
Daryaganj, New Delhi – 110002
info@double9books.com
www.double9books.com
Tel. 011-40042856

ABOUT THE AUTHOR

George Sand, also known as the pen name Amantine Lucile Aurore Dupin de Francueil, was a French novelist, memoirist, and journalist. Sand was one of the most popular writers in Europe during her lifetime, more well-known than Victor Hugo or Honore de Balzac in England in the 1830s and 1840s, and is regarded as one of the most notable writers of the European Romantic era, having published over 50 volumes of various works, including tales, plays, and political texts, in addition to her 70 novels. George Sand, like her great-grandmother, Louise Dupin, who she idolized, pushed for women, defended desire, condemned marriage, and resisted traditional society's preconceptions. Maurice Dupin de Francueil and Sophie-Victoire Delaborde welcomed Amantine Lucile Aurore Dupin, the future George Sand, into the world on Meslay Street in Paris on July 1, 1804. She was the paternal great-granddaughter of Marshal of France Maurice de Saxe (1696-1750), and her maternal grandpa was Antoine Delaborde, master paulmier and birder.

CONTENTS

CHAPTER XL 7

CHAPTER XLI..14

CHAPTER XLII..21

CHAPTER XLIII 27

CHAPTER XLIV 33

CHAPTER XLV..38

CHAPTER XLVI 43

CHAPTER XLVII..50

CHAPTER XLVIII..58

CHAPTER XLIX 66

CHAPTER L 75

CHAPTER LI..86

CHAPTER LII 93

CHAPTER LIII..100

CHAPTER LIV..107

CHAPTER LV 114

CHAPTER LVI..122

CHAPTER LVII..128

CHAPTER LVIII 137

CHAPTER LIX..144

CHAPTER LX 148

CHAPTER LXI..152

CHAPTER LXII..160

CHAPTER LXIII 166

CHAPTER LXIV 172

CHAPTER LXV...176

CHAPTER LXVI 184

CHAPTER LXVII..190

CHAPTER LXVIII...197

CHAPTER LXIX 204

CHAPTER LXX...210

CHAPTER LXXI 216

CHAPTER LXXII 222

CHAPTER LXXIII..229

CHAPTER LXXIV..236

CHAPTER XL

Since the Moorish woman had taught Adamas divers Eastern secrets for the composition of cosmetic mixtures, the marquis's complexion, his beard and his eyebrows had really improved. They were proof against wind, rain and Mario's frantic caresses; moreover, their perfume was sweeter, and they were more promptly prepared.

At first the old Celadon submitted to the beautifying process in profound secrecy, at the time when the child left his room for his first play. But, as Mario asked no embarrassing or impertinent questions, the old man gradually relaxed his great precautions, and proceeded to his daily rejuvenation with most ingenuous explanations.

The cosmetics were christened cooling perfumes, and the brilliant coloring was called keeping the skin in condition.

Mario seemed not to know what malice was. But children see everything; and he was not duped by Adamas, only he saw no cause for ridicule. His dear father could do nothing ridiculous. He fancied that these artifices were a part of the toilet of all persons of quality.

So it happened that, as he was more or less coquettish himself, he conceived a strong inclination to have his own face made up *like a gentleman's*. He made that request; and, as he was simply told in reply that at his age such devices were not necessary, he did not look upon it as a positive refusal. So that, one evening, happening to be alone for a moment in his adoptive father's room, and seeing the phials scattered over the table, it occurred to him to *perfume* himself in white and pink as he had seen Adamas perfume the marquis. That done, he thought that he ought to enlarge and darken his eyebrows, and, finding that that gave him a martial mien which delighted him hugely, he could not resist the temptation to draw two pretty little black hooks above his lips and a lovely royale underneath.

As he had no light except a single candle which had been accidentally left on the table, he used the colors too freely, and could not draw the outlines very sharply.

The supper-bell rang; he hurried to the table, well pleased with his bad-boy aspect, and maintaining his seriousness admirably.

The marquis paid no heed at first; but, Lauriane having uttered a hearty peal of laughter, he raised his eyes and saw that sweet little face so strangely transformed that he could not refrain from laughing with her.

But in the depths of his heart the good marquis was vexed and grieved. Mario certainly had had no idea of making sport of him; but the broad, loud way in which he had daubed himself betrayed a little too frankly, before Lauriane, the existence and use of that palette of beauty which he believed that he had kept so carefully concealed in the drawers of his dressing-table and on his face. He did not even dare ask the child where he had obtained the materials for that coloring; he dreaded a too ingenuous reply. So he contented himself with saying to him that he had disfigured himself, and that he must go and wash his face.

Lauriane realized her old friend's embarrassment and uneasiness, and restrained her merriment; but Mario's whim seemed to her all the more amusing, and throughout the supper she suffered from that mad, girlish longing to laugh which constraint transforms to nervous excitement.

The effect on Mario was magical, until at last the marquis mildly said to them:

"Come, children, laugh your fill, since you have such a longing to laugh!"

But he did not laugh himself, and at night he reproved Mario, who was penitent, and promised never to do it again.

This antic afforded much amusement to Monsieur Clindor, who broke a beautiful piece of porcelain in his uproarious mirth. Being rebuked by the marquis, he lost his head and trod on Fleurial's paw. Adamas could not resist Mario's droll aspect, and he, too, laughed! Bellinde was the only one who kept a serious countenance, and the marquis was grateful to her for it.

"That child is very mischievous," he said that night to Adamas, "and everything that he does indicates a playful and most entertaining wit. But we must not spoil him too much, Adamas!"

The next day there was more trouble: one of the phials of carmine on the dressing-table was found to be broken, and the beautiful lace table-cover was stained. It was laid at Fleurial's door at first, but similar spots were discovered on Mario's white jacket. He was surprised, and stoutly denied having approached the dressing-table.

"I believe you, my son," said the marquis, with a sigh. "If I deemed you capable of lying, I should be too deeply grieved."

But on the next day the cosmetics were found to be mixed; the red with the black and the black with the white.

"Zounds!" ejaculated the marquis, "this devil's work continues! Will it be the same way with it as with the noses of my poor statues?"

He scrutinized Mario without speaking; there were black stains on the ruffles at his wrists. It might have been ink; but the marquis had a horror of spots, and begged him to go and change his linen.

"Adamas," he said to his confidant, "the child is mischievous, that is all right; but if he is a liar and abuses my confidence in his word, it will break my heart, my friend! I believed that he was made of a superior substance, but God does not choose that I shall be too proud of him. He allows the devil to make of him a child like other children."

Adamas took sides with Mario, who had just entered the boudoir adjoining the bedroom.

At that moment they heard Bellinde engaged in a warm dispute with the child. He was pulling her by the skirt, and she resisted by saying that he took liberties above his age.

The marquis rose indignantly.

"Libertine!" he cried in despair; "already a libertine?"

Poor Mario ran forward, weeping bitterly.

"Father," he cried, throwing himself into his arms, "she is a wicked girl. I was trying to bring her to you to show you what she has on her hands. She touched my ruff, saying that it was stained, and it is she who puts the stains on it; she wants to make you feel grieved and prevent you from loving me. She takes advantage of the foolish things I do to put other wicked things on my back. Father, she isn't a good woman; she makes you think I am a liar, and, if you believe her——"

"No, no, my son, I do not believe her!" cried the marquis.—"Adamas!"

But Adamas was no longer there; he had run after Bellinde; he seized her on the staircase, tried to drag her back by force, and received for his pains a hearty cuff which made him relax his grasp.

At the sound of this scuffle, the marquis darted out into the hall. Adamas had received a violent blow; he was dazed and was pressing his cheek.

"That hussy must have used her claws!" he exclaimed, "my face is all— Why, no, monsieur," he cried suddenly, overjoyed, "it isn't blood! Look! it's the beautiful rouge from your phials! It's conclusive evidence! Ah! upon my word! this business is clear enough at last. Now I hope that you will have no further doubt of that red-headed girl's malice!"

"Monsieur le comte," said the marquis to Mario with admirable gravity, "I confess that I have doubted your word on two occasions. If I were not your best friend, you would be entitled to demand satisfaction; but I hope that you will deign to accept your father's apologies."

Mario leaped on his neck, and that same evening Bellinde, being paid and discharged without a word of explanation, left the oasis of Briantes and her fine shepherdess's name, to return to the realities of life under her true name of Guillette Carcat, pending the time when she should assume a more sonorous and mythological one, as we shall see in the sequel.

While these tragical events gradually faded from the memory of our characters, Monsieur Poulain did not fall asleep in his zeal.

It was on the 18th or 19th of December, when the abbé, cold as to the nose and feet, but with his brain warmed by the hope of a triumph at which he had long been aiming, arrived at Saint-Amand, a pretty town of Berry, situated in a verdant valley, between two streams, and overlooked by the gigantic and wonderful castle of Montrond, the residence of the Prince de Condé.

The abbé dismounted at the Capuchin convent, whose vast enclosure, shaped like a cross, lay under the protection of the princely abode. He avoided seeing the prior, whose attentions and good offices he dreaded; he preferred to do his work himself and to travel alone. He simply accepted a frugal repast from one of the monks, his kinsman, shook off the snow with which he was covered, and presented himself at one of the wickets of the castle, where he exhibited a passport in proper form.

"Thanks to the works undertaken by Sully, and especially to the improvements made by Monsieur le Prince," who had purchased that domain from the fallen minister, "the castle of Montrond, which assumed more importance at a later date, in the wars of the Fronde, had become a most luxurious abode as well as an impregnable fortress. It was more than a league in circumference; it comprised numerous buildings, an enormous and magnificent château of three floors, a huge tower or donjon a hundred and twenty feet high, the walls of which were crenellated, and which was surmounted by a platform whereon was a statue of Mercury." [1]

"As for the fortifications, they were so abundant, arranged in the shape of an amphitheatre and in tiers, that even one who had scrutinized and studied them for a long time could hardly understand them." [2]

In that labyrinth of stone, that powerful vassal's lair, that significant mystery, dwelt Henri de Bourbon, second of the name, Prince de Condé, who, after three years of captivity for rebellion against the crown, had become reconciled with the court and resumed his post as governor of Berry.

In addition to that office he held those of lieutenant-general, bailiff of the province, and captain of the great tower of Bourges: that is to say he monopolized the political, civil and military power of the whole centre of France, since he enjoyed the same privileges and held the same offices in the province of the Bourbonnais.

Add to this power an enormous fortune, increased by the sums which, *under the form of an indemnity*, each rebellion of the Condés cost the crown, that is to say France; by the almost forced purchase of the magnificent estates and châteaux which Sully possessed in Berry, and which he had no choice but to surrender to Monsieur le Prince at a great sacrifice, by reason of the pitilessness of the time and the *misfortunes* of the province; by the *secularisation*, that is to say the suppression, to the prince's profit, of the richest abbeys of the province, that of Déols among others; by the gifts which the rich bourgeoisie of the cities were compelled by custom, flattery or cowardice to make; by the heavy bowls of gold and silver filled with Berry sheep in the form of gold and silver coins; by the *azure chariots*, carved and decorated with silver satyrs, drawn by six beautiful horses with harnesses of Russia leather trimmed with silver; by taxes, exactions and vexations of every sort imposed upon the common people: money under all names, under all forms, under all pretexts—that was the sole motive, the sole aim, the sole grandeur, the sole joy, and the sole talent of Henri, grandson of the great Condé of the Reformation, and father of the great Condé of the Fronde.

Two great Condés, who were most ambitious and most blameworthy for their conduct toward France, God knows! but capable, too, of rendering noble service against the foreigner, when their selfish interests did not lead them astray. Alas! therein we see the *frightful* 17th century! But they were endowed with courage, grandeur, aye, with heroism; while he who plays a part in our narrative was simply covetous, cunning, prudent, and, people said, something much worse.

His birth was tragic, his youth unhappy.

He first saw the light in prison, born of a widow who was accused of having poisoned her husband. [3] Married himself when very young to the lovely Charlotte de Montmorency, the constable's daughter, he had had for a rival that too lusty and too venerable gallant, Henri IV. The young princess was a flirt. The prince kidnapped his wife. The king was accused of seeking to make war on Belgium for giving her shelter. The charge was at once true and false; the king was madly in love, but Condé, pretending a jealousy of which he was incapable, exploited the king's passion to the advantage of his ambition, and forced the king to take harsh measures against a rebel.

Unlucky in his family relations, in war and in politics, Monsieur le Prince consoled himself for everything by love of wealth, and, when the terrible ministry of Richelieu supervened, he was living very quietly, rich and unhonored, in his good town of Bourges and in his fine château of Saint-Amand-Montrond.

But, at the time when our rector Poulain, after six weeks of manœuvring and intriguing, succeeded in finding his way into his presence, Monsieur le Prince had not renounced all political ambition, and he was still to play his rôle of vulture during the death agony of the Calvinist party and that of the royal power, hoping to rise on the ruins of both.

The rector thought that he was perfectly well aware what sort of man he had to deal with. He judged him by the reputation of a *good* prince which he had made for himself at Bourges; familiar, condescending, talking to everybody without arrogance, playing with the school children of the town and cheating them, very fond of gifts, gossipy, stingy, whimsical and exceedingly pious.

The prince had all those qualities; but he had them in much greater degree than anyone as yet supposed. History declares that he was too fond of the society of children. He cheated from avarice and not simply for amusement; he did not follow the example of Henri IV., who returned the money. He was passionately fond of gifts; was a gossip from envy and evil-mindedness; he was avaricious to frenzy, whimsical to superstition, pious to atheism.

Lenet in his panegyric, says of him most ingenuously, or rather most maliciously:

"He understood religion and knew how to make the most of it, knew every fold of the human heart as thoroughly as any man I ever knew, and could decide in an instant by what motive a man's action was guided in affairs of every sort. He had the art of taking precautions against the artifice of other men, without letting them be apparent. *He loved to gain an advantage.* He undertook few affairs which he did not succeed in carrying through, by temporizing when he could not gain his object in any other way. He knew how to avoid any danger of losing that which was due to him, and to grasp any opportunities which might benefit him in any way. In short," says Lenet blandly in conclusion, "he seems to me to have been a great man and a very extraordinary one."

So be it!

As for the prince's physical characteristics, they are thus described, in a private letter, by a more illustrious pen than Lenet's:

"A face attractive at first sight; somewhat long, but with regular features; nothing of the power or of the marked peculiarity of feature of his son, the great Condé; smiling eyes; a face possessing no slight charm, with its frame of long hair; moustaches turned up at the ends; a long, heavy royale. Uncertainty in the shape of the forehead, which is of medium height, largely developed in the upper portion; some flabbiness in the cheeks. That smiling glance was one of those in which one can detect, with some attention, the lack of dignity and of serious faith, a petty, selfish disposition and much indifference. But that is the second impression; the first is not disagreeable. The best of his portraits bears the device: *Semper prudentia*." [4]

The statue of Mercury, the god of sharpers, standing on the summit of the donjon, is even more eloquent.

[1] Raynal, *History of Berry*.

[2] Memoirs of Monsieur Lenet.

[3] Charlotte de la Trémouille, wife of the first Henri de Condé, was imprisoned eight years, then acquitted, but never exonerated.

[4] Henri Martin. Unpublished letter.

CHAPTER XLI

Monsieur Poulain, while not a physiognomist in the highest sense, was a shrewd observer none the less; but he was at first impressed only by the agreeable side of the prince's countenance.

Monsieur de Condé received him alone in his closet, and invited him to sit. He displayed the greatest consideration for any man who wore a cassock.

"Monsieur l'abbé," he said, "I am ready to listen to you. Pardon me if important duties have compelled me to keep you waiting a long while for this appointment. You know that I have had to go to Paris to fetch Monsieur le Duc d'Enghien; then I was obliged to find another nurse for him, she whom his mother had selected having no more milk than a stone; and then— But let us speak of yourself, who seem to me to be a man of resolution. Resolution is a fine thing; but I am surprised to find you so persistent in appealing to me concerning such a trivial affair. Your clodhopper of—What do you call the place?"

"Briantes," replied the rector, respectfully.

The prince glanced furtively at him, and saw, beneath his humility, an air of assurance which disturbed him.

It is a peculiarity of great minds to seek to fathom and make use of the forces with which they come in contact. The prince was too suspicious not to be timid. His first impulse was not so much to make use of people as to refrain from doing so.

He affected indifference.

"Very good," he said; "your clodhopper of Briantes has killed in single combat, or rather in a singular combat and in a suspicious way, a certain— What is the dead man's name?"

"Sciarra d'Alvimar."

"Ah! yes, I know! I have inquired about him; he was a man of no consequence, and one who fought unfairly himself. The fellows must have been evenly matched. What does it matter to you, after all?"

"I love my duty," replied the rector, "and my duty bade me not to allow a crime to go unpunished. Monsieur Sciarra was a good Catholic, Monsieur de Bois-Doré is a Huguenot."

"Has he not abjured?"

"Where and when, monseigneur?"

"I neither know nor care. He is an old man, he is unmarried. He will soon die a natural death. When the beast dies, the poison dies! I do not see that there is much occasion to worry about him."

"Then your highness refuses to cause this affair to be investigated?"

"Investigate it yourself, monsieur l'abbé. I do not prevent you. Apply to the proper authorities. This comes within the province of the magistracy; I do not give my attention to the offences of the common herd: I should never be done with them."

Monsieur Poulain rose, bowed low and walked to the door. He was humiliated and deeply offended.

"Oh! stay, monsieur l'abbé," said the prince, who was desirous to fathom him without seeming to do so; "if I am not interested in your Monsieur d'Alvimar, I am deeply interested in you, who write an exceedingly well-turned letter, furnish valuable information, and seem to me to be a man of courage and spirit. Come, speak frankly to me. Perhaps I may be able to assist you in some way. Tell me why you desired to see me, instead of applying to your natural superiors, the higher clergy?"

"Monseigneur," replied the rector, "such an affair was not within the jurisdiction of the church."

"What affair?"

"The murder of Monsieur d'Alvimar; I have no other motive. Your highness insults me by thinking that I have made use of that circumstance as a pretext to gain access to you, in order that I may address some personal petition to you; such is not the case. I am impelled solely by the dissatisfaction which every sincere Catholic feels to see the *pretenders* begin anew their thieving and murdering in this province."

"You said nothing of theft," rejoined the prince. "Had this D'Alvimar any property which was taken from him."

"I do not know, nor is that what I mean. I had the honor to write to monsieur le prince that this Bois-Doré had enriched himself by pillaging churches."

"True, I remember," said the prince. "Did you not give me to understand that he had some sort of hidden treasure in his house?"

"I gave monseigneur most precise and accurate details. A part of the treasure of the Abbey of Fontgombaud is still there."

"And it is your opinion that we should make him disgorge? That would be difficult, unless by employing officers of the law; and the tardiness of legal procedure would enable the old fox to put the *corpus delicti* out of sight. Do not you think so?"

"Perhaps Monsieur d'Aloigny de Rochefort, whom your highness has appointed fiduciary abbé of Fontgombaud, might take measures——"

"No," said the prince, with some vehemence, "I forbid you—I beg you to let him know nothing of this. I have already incurred sufficient blame for the favors with which I have rewarded Monsieur de Rochefort's valuable services; people would never cease saying that I enrich my creatures with the spoils of the vanquished. Moreover, Rochefort is accused of being too greedy, and, in truth, perhaps he is so to some extent. I would not take my oath that he would confiscate these things for the benefit of the religion."

"I have touched the tender spot," thought the rector; "the treasure makes him prick up his ears. I must manage it so that monseigneur will be my debtor."

The prince noticed the slightly disdainful inward satisfaction of his visitor. The rector was not thirsty for money and jewels. He was thirsty for influence and power. Condé realized it and kept a closer watch upon himself.

"Moreover," he added, "it would be inadvisable to make a commotion over a trifle. This treasure, hidden in an old chest in a country-house garret, is not worth, I fancy, the trouble that would be necessary to obtain possession of it."

"But it is a living spring which supplies the old marquis's magnificence."

"He has been drawing upon it for a long time," rejoined the prince; "it must be drained dry! I used to know your clodhopper slightly; he was a burlesque marquis, of the King of Navarre's making. He was admitted to *my dear uncle's* intimate circle!"

Condé never spoke of Henri IV. except in an ironical tone overflowing with aversion. Monsieur Poulain observed the bitterness of his tone and smiled in a way to gratify the prince. "The marquisate of Bois-Doré," he said, "is a jest which the old man takes very seriously, and he persists in forcing upon everybody his absurd passion for the late king."

"The late king had some good qualities," rejoined Condé, who considered that the rector went too far, "and this old creature of whom we are talking was not one of his worst creatures. He squandered all his property in absurd finery; he cannot have anything left. He never goes to Paris now, he never appears at Bourges, he lives in a hole. He has an old chariot of the time of the League and a castle wherein I should be ashamed to quarter my dogs. He has laid out gardens where all the statues are of plaster; all this smells of mediocrity."

"These are details with which I did not supply monseigneur," said the rector to himself. "He has been making inquiries, he has nibbled at the bait. — It is true," he said aloud, "that our man is only a petty provincial nobleman. He is known to have about twenty-five thousand crowns of visible income, and people are justly surprised that he spends sixty thousand without running into debt and without leaving his estate."

"Can it be that the Abbey of Fontgombaud still holds out?" said the prince with a smile. "But how do you know, monsieur l'abbé, that this horn of plenty exists at the manor of Briantes?"

"I know it from a very devout young woman who has seen reliquaries and chapel ornaments of great value there. A certain child's bed, all of carved ivory, is a *chef-d'œuvre*, surmounted by a canopy— —"

"Bah! bah!" said the prince, "some old woman's tale! We will look into this matter if you insist, for the honor and welfare of the church, monsieur l'abbé; but it is not a matter of great urgency. I must leave you; but I would like first to know if I cannot serve you in any way. Your archbishop is a very good friend of nine; it was I who procured his translation. Do you desire a better living? I can speak to him of you."

"I desire none of the advantages of this world," the rector replied as he took his leave. "I consider myself well placed wherever I can labor for my salvation and pray for your highness's happiness."

"That is to say," thought the prince as soon as he was alone, "the Bois-Doré's coffers are still full; otherwise this ambitious fellow would have asked me first for his reward. He knows that I shall be satisfied with the result, and he will ask me for more than I have offered him. We shall see."

And the prince issued his orders.

On the evening of that same day, the dwellers at Briantes had just wished one another good-night, and were about to separate, when Aristandre, who was gatekeeper, sent word that a nobleman and his retinue desired shelter and an opportunity to rest for a couple of hours. It was raining and was very dark.

The marquis called for a light, and, wrapping himself in his cloak, went out in person to order the portcullis raised.

"We are— —" began an unfamiliar voice.

"Enter, enter, messieurs," replied the marquis, ever a slave to the laws of chivalrous hospitality. "Come in out of the rain. You may tell your names, if you please, when you have rested."

The horsemen rode in; there was two or three of them, and one, who seemed to be in authority over the others, acted as if he would dismount. Bois-Doré prevented him, as the pavement was very wet.

He walked ahead with Adamas, who carried the torch, and returned to the courtyard, followed by his guest, without noticing an escort of twenty armed men, who, having crossed the drawbridge one by one, entered the courtyard after their master, while he was ascending the stairs with his host.

This large escort surprised Aristandre, who, as his functions included that of receiving the servants of visitors and opening the stables, came forward to offer his services. But they refused to unsaddle, and remained with their horses, some around a fire which was lighted in the courtyard, others at the very threshold of the château.

When the marquis entered the salon with the stranger, he saw a man of some thirty years of age, of medium stature and poorly dressed. His face was almost entirely shaded by the flapping brim of his hat and the wet plumes that fell about it on all sides. Little by little he made out the face, but did not recognize it, or, at all events, could not remember where he had seen it.

"You do not seem to remember me?" said the stranger. "To be sure, it is a very long time since we met, and we have both changed greatly."

The marquis artlessly put his hand to his forehead, apologizing for his failure of memory.

"I will not amuse myself by making you cudgel your brains," rejoined the traveller. "My name is Lenet. I was little more than a boy when I saw you in Paris at the Marquise de Rambouillet's, and it may very well be that you paid no attention to such an unimportant personage as I then was. Even now I am only a councillor, awaiting something better."

"You deserve to be all that you desire," replied Bois-Doré, graciously.—
"But, deuce take me," he said to himself, "if I remember the name of Lenet, or if I know to whom I am talking, although his manner recalls a thousand vague ideas."

"Order nothing for me," rejoined Monsieur Lenet, when he saw that the marquis was issuing orders for his supper. "I go on to another château, where I am expected. I have been delayed by the wretched roads, and I beg to excuse my calling upon you at this hour. But I am entrusted with a delicate commission for you, which I must execute."

Lauriane and Mario, who were in the boudoir, rose when they heard that business was to be discussed, and passed through the salon to retire.

"Are those your children, Monsieur de Bois-Doré!" said the traveller, returning the courtesy which they made him as they passed.

"Neither of them," replied the marquis, "and yet I am a father. This is my nephew, who is my son by adoption."

"Now, this is my errand," continued the councillor, with a benignant air and in a conciliatory tone, when the children had left the room, "I am instructed by Monsieur le Prince, who is your lord and my own, and to whom my family, from father to son, is closely attached, to inquire into an unpleasant affair in which you are involved. I will go straight to the fact. You have caused the disappearance of a certain Monsieur Sciarra d'Alvimar, who was your guest as I am, with the difference that he had no escort with him as I have, to protect my person and my commission; for I must inform you that, under yonder window, are twenty men, well armed, and in your village twenty others, ready to come to their assistance, if you do not receive in a becoming manner the messenger of the governor and grand bailiff of the province."

"This warning is unnecessary, Monsieur Lenet," replied Bois-Doré, with much tranquillity and courtesy. "If you were alone in my house, you would be the safer therein. It is enough that you are my guest, and by so much the more are you protected by the commission of Monsieur le Prince, to whose authority I am in nowise rebellious. Am I to accompany you and account to him for my conduct? I am quite prepared, and entirely undisturbed, as you see."

"That is not necessary, Monsieur de Bois-Doré. I have full power to question you and deal with you according as I find you innocent or guilty. Be good enough to tell me what has become of Monsieur d'Alvimar?"

"I killed him in a fair duel," replied the marquis, confidently.

"But without witnesses?" rejoined the councillor with an ironical smile.

"There was one, monsieur, and the most honorable of men. If you wish to hear the story——"

"Will it be long?" queried the councillor, who seemed distraught.

"No, monsieur; although it seems to me that I am entitled to explain my conduct fully in a matter which concerns my life and my honor, I will take as little of your time as possible."

CHAPTER XLII

Bois-Doré told the whole story succinctly, and exhibited his proofs.

Still the councillor seemed impatient and distraught. But his attention seemed to be caught by one point. That point was the incident of La Flèche's predictions at La Motte-Seuilly.

Bois-Doré, having to produce his brother's seal as the final proof of his identity with D'Alvimar's victim, felt that he ought to mention that circumstance; but, before he had time to explain definitely how little real sorcery there was in Master La Flèche's prophecies, he was interrupted by the councillor.

"Stay," said he, "I recall one charge against you which I had forgotten. You are suspected of being addicted to magic, Monsieur de Bois-Doré. And upon that charge I acquit you in advance, for I have no faith in the soothsayer's art, and see nothing in it but a mental pastime. Will you tell me if it happened that these gypsies predicted anything true?"

"Their predictions were fulfilled in every respect, Monsieur Lenet! They declared that within three days I should be a *father* and *avenged*. They informed my brother's murderer that he would be punished within three days, and these things came to pass as they said; but— —"

"Tell me where these gypsies are?"

"I do not know. I have not seen them since. But it remains for me to tell you— —"

"No. This is enough," said Monsieur Lenet, still maintaining his honeyed tone and smiling expression; "the cause has been heard. I believe you to be innocent; but you were ill-advised to conceal the fact. Suspicions will not easily be effaced; people will wonder as I do, why, instead of making public the chastisement of your brother's assassin as an act which did you honor, you concealed it as you would have done an ambuscade. I shall not be able to make Monsieur le Prince understand."

At that point Bois-Doré was sorely tempted to interrupt the councillor by an indignant exclamation; for it was evident to him that that man, after claiming to have full powers in order to induce him to speak, pretended to be unable to absolve him himself, in order to sell him his influence.

"I agree," he said, "that in concealing D'Alvimar's death I followed bad advice, which was entirely opposed to my own inclination. It was urged upon me that Monsieur le Prince was a devout Catholic and that I was accused of heresy——"

"And that is true enough, my dear monsieur. You are considered to be a great heretic, and I do not deny that Monsieur le Prince is ill disposed toward you."

"But you, monsieur, who seem to me to be less rigid in your ideas, and who declare that you have confidence in my words—may I not rely upon you to plead my cause and to bear witness in my behalf?"

"I will do my utmost, but I will not answer for the result, so far as the prince is concerned."

"What must I do, pray, to dispose him favorably toward me?" said the marquis, resolved to learn the terms of the bargain.

"I cannot say," replied the councillor. "He has been told that you have in your household an Italian, a heretic of the worst sort, who, so it seems, may well be a certain Lucilio Giovellino, condemned at Rome as a believer in Giordano Bruno's detestable doctrines."

The marquis turned pale: he had maintained his tranquillity in face of danger to himself; his friend's danger terrified him.

"Do you admit it?" said the councillor, carelessly. "For my own part, I think that the poor devil was punished enough, and I wish him no other harm than what has already been inflicted on him. You can tell me everything. I will try to divert the prince's suspicions."

"Monsieur Lenet," rejoined Bois-Doré, obeying a sudden inspiration, "the man to whom you refer is not a heretic, he is an astrologer of the most marvellous learning. He has recourse to no magic arts, but reads human destinies in the stars with such extraordinary skill that the events of life seem to abide by decrees written on the skies. There is nothing in his operations inconsistent with the duty of an honorable man and a good Christian; and you know as well as I that Monsieur le Prince, who is the most orthodox Catholic in the kingdom, constantly consults astrologers, as the most illustrious persons in all times, even crowned heads, have done."

"I do not know where you have learned what you say, monsieur," rejoined the councillor, shrugging his shoulders; "I have long lived and still live in the prince's confidence, and I have never known him to resort to such practices."

"And yet, monsieur," replied the marquis with assurance, "I am certain that he would in nowise censure my friend's practices, and I beg you to say to him, that if he will deign to test his skill, he will be highly gratified."

"The prince will laugh at your confidence; but I do not refuse to mention the subject to him. Let us return to the most urgent question, which is to extricate you from this difficulty. I do not conceal from you that I have orders to make a search of your house."

"A search?" echoed the marquis in amazement; "a search for what purpose, monsieur?"

"For the sole purpose of making sure that you have no cabalistic books and instruments; for you are accused of practising magic, not so much for the amusement of reckoning numbers and watching the stars, as for suspicious objects and by virtue of a sort of worship of the spirit of evil."

"Really, monsieur le conseiller, you have kept this for a *bonne bouche*! Is this all of which I am accused? shall I not be required to defend myself against anything worse?"

"Do not blame me," said the councillor rising. "I do not believe that you are guilty of such heinous deeds; that is why I urge you to show me every corner of your house, so that I may be able to state and to take my oath that I found nothing here which was not honest and becoming. Remember that I can force you to obey me; but, as I desire to treat you courteously, I beg you to take a torch and light me yourself, without calling any of your people; for, if you do, I shall be compelled to call all of mine, and it is my present purpose to take only five or six, who are at the door of this room."

A ray of light flashed through the marquis's mind; it was his treasure that was wanted.

He made up his mind at once. Although he loved all those sumptuous toys which he regarded as legitimate trophies and pleasant memories of his exploits of long ago, there was no avarice in his fondness for them, and, however much he might regret being unable to resort to them any longer to the profit of his beloved Mario's magnificence, he did not hesitate between that sacrifice and the welfare of Lucilio, concerning which he was much more anxious than concerning his own.

"Let it be as you wish, monsieur!" he said, with a magnanimous smile. "Where is it your pleasure that we begin?"

The councillor glanced about the salon.

"You have many beautiful and costly things here," he said carelessly; "but I see nothing reprehensible, and I know that you would not conceal your instruments of deviltry in rooms that are open to every comer. I have heard of a closed chamber which you call your storeroom, and to which you do not admit everybody. That is where I should like to go, and I desire you to lead me thither without remonstrance or deception; for not only have I a plan of your house, which is not large, but I have the means to turn everything topsy-turvy, and I should be distressed to have to proceed to that extremity."

"It will not be necessary," rejoined the marquis, taking a torch; "I am ready to satisfy you.—Ah! by the way," he added, stopping at the door, "I have not the keys of that room, and I cannot admit you without the aid of my old servant. Is it your pleasure that I call him?"

"I will send for him," said the councillor opening the door. And he said to his men, who were on the landing:

"One of you obey Monsieur de Bois-Doré.—Give your orders, marquis. What is your servant's name?"

The marquis, seeing that he was entirely in his guest's power and was to be kept in sight, resigned himself to the inevitable, and he was about to name Adamas, without any display of useless anger, when that worthy's face appeared behind those of the pikemen who were guarding the door.

"Adamas," he said, "bring me the keys of the storeroom."

"Yes, monsieur," was the reply "I have them about me, here they are; but——"

"Come in," said the councillor to Adamas.

And, when he had obeyed, he added:

"Give me the keys, and remain in this room."

Adamas seemed overwhelmed. He felt in the pocket of his doublet, and replied to the councillor, with a surprising lack of self-possession:

"*Yes, sire.*"

At that word, the councillor, as if attacked by vertigo, laid aside his suave manner, rushed across the room, and hurriedly closed the door between himself and his men, which had been left open.

"To whom do you think you are speaking?" he cried, "and why do you address me so?"

Adamas stood as if dazed, and his confusion was amusing to the last degree.

The marquis had seen the king too often in his childhood, and the portraits that had been made of him since, to believe for an instant that the personage before him was the young Louis XIII. He thought that his poor Adamas was going mad.

"Answer, I tell you!" continued the councillor impatiently. "Why do you give me the name applied to majesty?"

"I do not know, monsieur," replied the crafty Adamas. "I do not know what I am saying nor where I am. My head is in a whirl with some surprising news which I have just learned, and which I ask your permission to tell my master."

"Tell it! speak! say on!" cried the councillor in an extraordinarily authoritative tone.

"Well, master," said Adamas, addressing the marquis, and apparently not observing the councillor's agitation, "the king is dead!"

"The king is dead?" cried Monsieur Lenet, rushing toward the door, as if to go out without taking leave of anyone.

But he paused, suddenly suspicious.

"From whom did you learn this news?" he said, scrutinizing Adamas with gleaming eyes.

"I learned it from the decrees of destiny. I learned it from heaven itself," said Adamas with an inspired air.

"What does this man mean?" demanded Monsieur Lenet. "Bid him explain himself, Monsieur de Bois-Doré; I insist upon it, do you understand? and if this news of his is false, woe to him and to you!"

"True or false, monsieur," replied the marquis, observant of his guest's excitement, "the news surprises and disturbs me no less than yourself. Explain yourself, Adamas; how do you know that the king is dead?"

"I know it by astrology, monsieur! He showed me the figures, and I know them. I saw, I understood, I read as plainly as possible that the most powerful individual in the realm had just died."

"The most powerful individual in the realm!" said the councillor thoughtfully; "perhaps that is not the king!"

"You are right, monsieur," said Adamas ingenuously; "perhaps it is monsieur le connétable. I do not know the signs well enough. I may have made a mistake; but at all events it is either the king or Monsieur de Luynes; I will answer for it with my life!"

"Where is this astrologer?" said the councillor hastily; "let him come here, I wish to see him!"

"Yes, sire," replied Adamas, still bewildered and absorbed, hurrying toward the door.

"Stay," said Lenet, detaining him. "I insist upon knowing why you call me so. Tell me, or I will break your head!"

"Break nothing, monsieur!" replied Adamas; "I have lost my head; can you not see that? That word comes to my lips, I know not how; as truly as God is in heaven, this is the first time that I ever saw your face. Shall I go to find the astrologer?"

"Yes, hasten! and woe to you all, if there is any trick or snare in all this! I will put the torch to your hovel!"

Bois-Doré could do no more than protest his absolute ignorance of this new episode. He did not in the least understand Adamas's conduct, indeed he was somewhat disturbed by it.

He saw clearly enough that the faithful servant had overheard his conversation with the councillor, and that, to save Lucilio, he was making use of the idea that had occurred to him, of passing off the Italian as an astrologer, knowing, as everybody knew, the respect which the Prince de Condé entertained for the art of divination. But would the serious-minded Lucilio give his assent to that stratagem? Would he know how to play his part?

"However," thought Bois-Doré, "we must rely on Providence and on Adamas's genius! It is simply a matter of getting rid of the enemy without his taking possession of my friend's person and mine; after that we will look to our safety in the future."

CHAPTER XLIII

After a few moments Lucilio appeared with Adamas. He was calm and smiling as usual. He bowed slightly to the councillor, very low to the marquis, and handed the latter a paper covered with hieroglyphics.

"Alas! my friend," said Bois-Doré, "I know nothing about it."

"Speak!" cried Lenet to the mute, who motioned that that was impossible. "Then write!"

Lucilio sat down and wrote:

"I obey no orders here save those of the Marquis de Bois-Doré; I do not know you. Leave this room; I will not write before you."

"*Mordieu*! yes you will!" cried the councillor, beside himself. "I propose to know everything, and you shall answer me."

"Forgive him, monsieur," said Adamas; "like all great scholars, he is very odd and capricious. If you wish him to reveal his secrets, speak to him gently."

"Does he want money?" said the councillor; "he shall have it; let him speak!"

Lucilio shook his head by way of refusal.

The councillor seemed to be on burning coals.

"Come," said he, after a moment of agitated silence, "I will find out whether you are a learned man or a fool! Look at my hand and tell me something."

Lucilio looked at the councillor's hand, rose, turned to Adamas and, pointing to his scrawl, motioned to him to speak in his place.

"Yes! I see," said Adamas. "These symbols say that there is a man, a prince, who wishes to place the crown of France on his head. But where is the man who has that sign in his hand? I do not know him."

Lucilio pointed to the councillor's hand.

"Who am I, pray tell me?" said that personage, exceedingly surprised.

Lucilio wrote three words which the councillor alone read, and he with evident emotion. His face changed and his tone became gentler.

"And the king is dead?" he said, trembling in every limb, with terror or with joy. "You see that you must answer me, now!"

Lucilio wrote:

"The king is well; but Monsieur de Luynes died by the light of the flames on the 15th of this month, at eleven o'clock at night."

The pretended Councillor Lenet had no sooner read these words than, without the slightest sign of doubt, he pulled his hat over his eyes, hurried into the hall, and without speaking except to order his men to follow him, remounted and rode away at full speed with his whole escort, addressing no word of thanks or apology, no promise or threat to his hosts at Briantes.

Adamas, the marquis and Lucilio, who had escorted them in silence as far as the outermost gate, in order to make sure that no suspicious personage was left behind in the château or in the village, returned to the salon, where they found Mario.

They were all so deeply moved that they sat for some moments without speaking.

At last the marquis broke the silence.

"So it was Monsieur le Prince?" he said.

"Yes," said Lauriane. "I saw him at Bourges three months ago, and I recognized him at once when I passed through this room and saluted him. Did you never see him, my dear marquis?"

"Once or twice, when he was very young, at Paris, but never since. However, when he mentioned the Prince de Condé, saying that he was in his personal service, that name fastened itself to the face of the false Councillor Lenet, and I became more and more convinced every moment that I was dealing with the master in person. That is why I was so very patient; and I thank God that I was! But how did it happen that you thought— —"

"Monsieur de Luynes did actually die, of scarlet fever, on the 15th of this month, while the king's troops were pillaging and burning unlucky Monheur, on the Garonne. Here is a letter from my father, telling me the news, which one of his retainers, who arrived just after the prince and his suite, succeeded in sending to me secretly by Clindor."

"This is great news, my children, and the whole policy of the government will be turned topsy-turvy once more. But which of you had the idea— —"

"I, monsieur," said Adamas, triumphantly; "as soon as Madame Lauriane said: 'That stranger who is closeted with monsieur le marquis is the prince and no other,' we all four hid in the little passage that you know of."

"We were worried about you," said Mario, "on account of that big escort of men who had a suspicious, threatening sort of look. Adamas suddenly thought of what he afterwards did and said."

"Master Jovelin was none too anxious to lend a hand," added Adamas; "but we had to save you, there was no time to reflect, and he played his part cleverly enough, didn't he, monsieur? Now he has his fortune in his own hands, and if he chooses to replace, or at least to equal in favor the prince's famous astrologer, who has predicted that he would be King of France at thirty-four— —"

"I noticed," said the marquis to Jovelin, "that you could not make up your mind to give him that promise. You simply told him that he had that ambition. But what shall we do now, my friends? for, as you say, we are basely betrayed, and we are exposed to many perils of which we have never thought."

"We must do nothing, keep perfectly quiet," said Lauriane with decision. "The prince is galloping south at this moment and will not think of us again for some time."

"That is true," said the marquis; "he is off at full speed, in order to reach the king's side first, and to grasp the power that Monsieur de Luynes enjoyed, if not the favor. He will have to fight hard for it! Retz, Schomberg and Puisieux will want their share of the cake, to say nothing of the fact that madame the queen-mother and her little Bishop of Luçon will give them some thread to wind! Bah! our petty affairs have already gone out of our *good* prince's head, and will never enter it again perhaps. If only he did not issue any orders against us before he came hither!"

"No, monsieur, there is no danger!" said Adamas. "He had his eye on your treasure, the amount of which must have been grossly exaggerated to him, since so great a prince does us the honor to call upon us for so small a matter. Now we are warned; we can easily hide our little hoard and leave trunks filled with débris for the satisfaction of the curious. The secret exit from the château will be kept in good condition, and we will be on our guard against people who ask for shelter from the rain. But be assured that, if the prince does not come here again in person, nobody else will think of doing it; for if he has given any orders at all, they are that no one shall come and put his hand on the dish upon which he has placed his powerful paw."

Adamas's reasoning was very sound. He concluded by calling down a thousand maledictions on Bellinde, who alone could have discovered and divulged Master Jovelin's real name, the death of D'Alvimar and the existence of the treasure.

It was decided that they should consult with Guillaume d'Ars as to the propriety of announcing D'Alvimar's death or continuing to keep it secret; and to that end the marquis called upon him the following day, in the afternoon.

Guillaume was absent and was not to return until evening.

The marquis sent a messenger to Briantes to bid them not be anxious if he returned late, and went to pay a visit to Monsieur Robin de Coulogne, who was then making a brief sojourn at his estate of Coudray, a pretty château on the heights of Verneuil, about a league from the château of Ars.

Robin, Vicomte de Coulogne, receiver-general of taxes in Berry and farmer-general of the salt tax, was one of the natural enemies of the ex-salt-smuggler Bois-Doré; and yet they had been the closest of friends since the affair of Florimond Dupuy, lord of Vatan.

Those who know the history of Berry will remember that in 1611, Florimond Dupuy, a fervent Huguenot and a great smuggler, had, to show his detestation of the salt tax, kidnapped one of Monsieur Robin's children. The marquis generously exerted himself to restore the child to its father, at the risk of a rupture with Florimond, who was, according to both friends and enemies, "a very uncomfortable bedfellow."

After this incident, the rebellion assumed such serious proportions, that it was found necessary to send twelve hundred infantry, a company of Swiss and twelve guns, to bring Monsieur Dupuy to terms in his château.

Twenty-nine of his people were hanged on the spot, to convenient trees, and his own head was cut off on Place de Grève. Young Robin was afterward Abbé of Sorrèze. The elder Robin was a grateful and devoted debtor of Monsieur de Bois-Doré, and we may well believe that the marquis owed it to that friendship that he was never molested for his former acts of complicity in the crime of salt-smuggling.

So Bois-Doré opened his heart to that faithful friend concerning a part of the embarrassment with which he was threatened by the prince's visit, and confessed that he was particularly disturbed concerning worthy Lucilio, whose presence in his house the hypocritical zealots of the province regarded with an evil eye.

"Your fears seem to me exaggerated," said the viscount. "Monsieur de Groot, whom scholars call Grotius, and who was sentenced to life imprisonment in his own country, succeeded in escaping, did he not, concealed in a chest, thanks to the courage and adroitness of his wife, and took refuge in Paris, where he is neither tormented nor even annoyed by anyone? Why should not your Italian enjoy the same privileges in France?"

"Because the government of France, which is not at all anxious to offend the Gomarists of Holland and Maurice of Nassau, will be most eager to please the pope by persecuting one of his victims. Twenty years Campanella has been in prison, and although he is esteemed and pitied in France, nothing is done to release him from the hands of his executioners; God knows whether they would give him shelter at this moment, openly!"

"Perhaps you are right," said Monsieur de Coulogne. "Very good; I approve your idea of effecting your friend's escape, at the slightest danger that may threaten your château; but I think that you should select a place of refuge to which he can go at once in case of alarm. Have you thought about it?"

"Yes, indeed," the marquis replied, "and I wish to consult you on that point. You own an old manor-house near by, which seems to be quite inhabitable, although I have never entered it. It is so near my house that a man pressed for time can reach there in an hour. It is also near a small farm-house of yours, and if you should give orders to the farmers to that effect, they would be ready, if anything should happen, to conceal and care for my poor fugitive. Will you do me this service?"

"Ask me for my life if you will, marquis; it is yours. So much the more are my servants, my property, my houses at your service. But let me reflect concerning the suitability of the place you have in mind: you refer to my old manor of Brilbault, do you not?"

"Precisely."

"Very well, let us see: it stands quite alone in its grounds, and the roads leading to it are detestable; so far so good. It is not upon the road to any town or village; another point in its favor. The place belongs to me, and the provost's people would never dare to cross the threshold. Moreover, the house is supposed to be haunted by the most uproarious and discontented spirits in the world, the result being that no marauding peasant is tempted to enter, no passer-by to stop there. This is better and better. Yes, I see that your choice, is a good one, and I will go thither with you to-night, to give the farmer the necessary orders."

Bois-Doré, having reflected in his turn, concluded that it would be better for him to go alone, in order not to arouse suspicion.

"Your farmers are no strangers to me," he said. "They were formerly associates of mine in—you know what!"

"Yes, yes, you villain," laughed the viscount; "they procured their salt cheap through you! Very well, take that road when you return; the streams are not full yet, and you can pass without danger. You can tell Jean Faraudet, the farmer, as if I had taken advantage of your passing to send him the message, to come to see me early to-morrow morning. You can cast a glance at the house and examine the surroundings, so that you will be able to direct your friend; indeed, it will be well for him to go there secretly to-morrow night, in order to become familiar with the roads and the entrances. In that way, if he should be obliged to take refuge there, he could do so without losing his way or making any mistake."

"Agreed," said the marquis, "and pray accept a thousand thanks for setting my mind at rest."

The viscount kept the marquis to supper; after which he entered his carriage just at nightfall, and took once more the road to Ars, which was little better than that leading to Brilbault. His reason for taking that direction was that he did not wish his chariot, which always created a sensation, to be seen in the neighborhood of the ruined manor.

With even more forethought than Monsieur Robin had advised, he alighted about a fourth of a league from the place which he proposed to inspect, ordered his servants to go quietly to Ars, and, taking one of the innumerable little paths in which Monsieur de Coulogne had probably never set his foot, but which were as familiar to the old smuggler as the paths in his rabbit warren, he disappeared in the damp underbrush, after pulling his boots up above his knees.

CHAPTER XLIV

It was a mild night and not very dark, despite the heavy black clouds which the wind drove across the sky, opening long furrows filled with stars, which suddenly closed to open anew in another place.

It is said that our noble or bourgeois ancestors were unquestionably more robust than we are to-day, while, on the contrary, our workmen and peasant ancestors were less so.

Such is the belief of the old men of my province, and it seems to me to be well-founded; well-to-do people were accustomed to an abundance of fresh air and exercise of which modern life deprives us, or which it makes unnecessary. The poorer classes were more poorly housed and not so well fed as in our day, to say nothing of the immense number of unfortunate wretches who were not housed or fed at all. The gentleman, with his régime of fighting and hunting, retained his health and strength to a very advanced age.

Bois-Doré, despite his sixty-nine years and the comparative effeminacy of his habits, still had strong sight, lungs impervious to the cold, and was sure-footed on the bare ground or on wet grass.

He slipped once or twice as he skirted the bushes, but he saved himself by clinging to the branches, like a man who knows how to take care of himself in a locality where the irregularities of the ground vary little over a large extent of territory.

Thanks to the short cut he had taken, he reached the farm of Brilbault in ten minutes.

Knowing the timid and superstitious character of the peasants, he coughed and spoke before knocking; then, as he knocked, he gave his name, and was received without alarm, at all events, if not without surprise.

Although the condition of the farming class was still very wretched, it was much less so, morally speaking, in Berry, which had long been a province of freeholds, than in those provinces where serfdom still existed. Moreover, in that region which is called the Black Valley, material resources have always assured the farmer, whether proprietor or tenant, a relative well-being which has saved him from great disasters and great epidemics.

At this period the leprosy hospitals were already empty; the pest, still so frequent in La Brenne and the neighborhood of Bourges, rarely scourged Fromental. The dwelling-houses, which were filthy and pestilential in the Marche and the Bourbonnais, were, at least in our neighborhood, stoutly built and healthy, as is proved by a large number of old country houses of the sixteenth and seventeenth centuries, which are still standing and easily recognizable by their vast tiled roofs, their windows framed with stone cut in the shape of prisms, and their attic windows surmounted by great sheaves of grain moulded in terra cotta. [5]

The marquis felt no repugnance, therefore, to entering the farmer's house, taking his seat by the fireplace, and chatting for a few moments there.

As everybody loved him, the *good monsieur* could safely entrust to Jean Faraudet and his wife, if necessary, the care of a friend of his who was being prosecuted, he said, for an offence against the game laws; and when he informed them that their master, Monsieur Robin, wished to see them the next morning, to give them orders to that effect, they seemed overjoyed and eager to obey, answering him with the sacramental phrase expressive of zeal and willingness in that country:—"*Il y a bien moyen!*"

Madame Faraudet, however, who was called La Grand' Cateline, could not refrain from pitying the man who should be condemned to pass even a single night at the château of Brilbault.

She firmly believed that it was haunted, and her husband, after laughing at her as a sop to the marquis's scepticism, eventually admitted that he would rather die than put foot inside the building after sunset.

"My friend's presence," said the marquis, "will give you courage, I trust, for I promise you that it will drive away the evil spirits; but, since you are not afraid to enter the house by daylight, I beg you to put some wood on the hearth and prepare a bed in the best room that there is."

"We will carry everything there that is necessary, my dear monsieur," replied La Grand' Cateline; "but the poor Christian who goes there won't sleep a wink. He will hear a terrible uproar and hurly-burly all night, just as we do, may the good Lord preserve us! and as you will hear them yourself if you choose to wait till after twelve o'clock."

"I cannot wait," said the marquis, "and besides, the spirits wouldn't stir, knowing that I was there. I know what cowards they are, for I never have succeeded in hearing the voices that shout at the top of the donjon at Briantes, on Christmas night, nor the doors that open themselves at La

Motte-Seuilly, nor the white lady who pulls aside the bed-curtains at the château of Ars."

"It's a curious thing, Monsieur Sylvain," said the farmer with a knowing air, "that there should be apparitions in our old château. We all know that there may be such things in other châteaux, because there aren't any of them where some great wrong hasn't been done or suffered; and that's the reason why the poor Christians who have been tortured or heartbroken in those houses return to them afterward to complain, as souls asking for prayers or justice. But in the château of Brilbault, which was never occupied, there never has been any good or evil done so far as I know."

"We must believe," said the woman, who plied her distaff busily as she talked, "that the former lord died in a distant land, by violence and in sin; for you know the legend of Brilbault, don't you? It isn't long. A noble had built this château as far as the roof, when he started for the Holy Land with his seven sons. The château was sold again and again, but no one ever fancied it. People thought that it brought families ill-luck; that is why it has never been used except to store crops. They put on a roof which is good for nothing now; but there are still two fine rooms and such a hall! So big that two people can hardly recognize each other from one end to the other."

"Can you let me have the keys?" said the marquis; "I would like to see the interior."

"Here are the keys; but my dear Monsieur Sylvain of the good Lord, don't go there! It is just the time for the deviltry to begin."

"What deviltry, my good friends?" said the marquis laughingly; "what sort of creatures are these wicked devils?"

"I have never seen them, monsieur, nor wanted to see them," said the farmer; "but I hear them well enough, I hear them too well! Some groan and others sing. There's laughter, then yelling and swearing and weeping till daybreak, when they all fly away through the air; for it is securely locked, and no human being can enter without leave or help from me."

"May it not be that your farm-hands go there to amuse themselves, or some thief to prevent you detecting his thievery?"

"No, monsieur, no! Our workmen and servants are so frightened that with all your money you couldn't hire them to go within two gunshots of the château after sunset; indeed, you see they no longer sleep in our house, because they say it's too near that infernal building. They all sleep in the barn yonder at the end of the yard."

"So much the better for the little secret we have together to-night," said the marquis; "but so much the better too, perhaps, for those who play the part of ghosts for the sole purpose of robbing you!"

"What could they steal, pray, Monsieur Sylvain? There's nothing in the château. When I saw that the devil used torches there, I was afraid of a fire, and I took out my whole crop, except a few little fagots and a dozen bundles of hay and straw, which I left in order not to make them too angry, for they say that imps like to play about in the hay and the branches; and, to tell the truth, I found it all tossed about and trampled; it was as if fifty living men had walked over it."

The marquis knew Faraudet to be very truthful and incapable of inventing anything whatsoever to avoid doing him a service.

He began to think therefore that, if lights were seen in the old manor, if voices were heard there, and above all, if feet or bodies trampled and disturbed the straw, there was more reality than deviltry in that state of affairs, and that the château, which the farmer and his wife confessed that they had not dared to enter for more than six weeks, might very well be used already as a refuge by fugitives.

"Whether they be maleficent or congenial, I propose to see them," he said to himself.

And, putting his naked sword under his arm, carrying the keys of the château in one hand and a lantern in the other, he started across the fields toward the silent, ruined structure.

Faraudet, when his wife began to lament the *good monsieur's* rashness, was ashamed to let him go alone and decided to accompany him.

But when the marquis had crossed the bridge, he found that the poor peasant was trembling so violently, that he feared that he should be more embarrassed than assisted by a man in such a plight and begged him to go no farther.

Most of the châteaux in the Black Valley, even those of the primitive Middle Ages, are situated in the depths of the valleys instead of on the high land, as in La Marche and the Bourbonnais. There is a very plausible explanation of this anomaly. In a region devoid of any considerable elevations, the water-courses afford the best means of defence.

At Brilbault therefore, as at Briantes, La Motte-Seuilly, Saint-Chartier, La Motte-de-Presles, etc., the manor-house was built on a winding stream of sufficient size to fill with running water the double circular moat.

The bridge over the outer moat was very narrow and supported upon arches of no definite type, midway between the full arch and the ogive.

The whole château was of a transitional style of architecture; the façade was of a curious shape; the door and the staircase window above it were set in the wall to a depth of several mètres, as if for protection from attacks from without.

The top of the building should have been *mascherolé* at that point; but it was originally left unfinished and was finally surmounted by a roof entirely out of keeping with the rest of the structure, which indicated a scheme of some grandeur never carried to completion.

The marquis went straight to the château as the crow flies; the encircling walls had crumbled to such an extent and sustained so many breaches, the moats were so completely filled in innumerable places, that it was not necessary to go to the gates.

He noiselessly opened the main door, which was small and low, under a rampant arch surmounted by an ogive of carved flower-work.

There he partly opened his lantern to look at the floor at his feet, for the farmer had warned him to be careful of the staircase.

[5] These sheaves, which are rare and much prized by archæologists, have retained a sort of traditional vogue in certain localities; the potteries of Verneuil make very pretty ones after old models. The small urn, with four or six handles on several different levels, and surmounted by birds or flowers, is reproduced in their system of decoration.

CHAPTER XLV

It was a spiral staircase of great beauty, broad enough for six persons and as light as the sticks of a fan. It was built of a friable white stone; many steps had been entirely destroyed by the fall of some portion of the building; but those which remained seemed freshly hewn and bore no trace of wear. At each half turn of the spiral was a step, supported by a grinning face, a fantastic beast, or the bust of an armed man carved in relief on the wall.

The marquis was interested in these figures, which seemed to move in the flickering light of his lantern.

He ascended the stairs slowly, listening whenever he stopped; and as he heard no other sound than that of the wind in the crumbling roof, and as the doors of the rooms that he passed were secured by padlocks, he became more and more doubtful of the existence of any inhabitants whatsoever. Thus he reached the upper floor, where were the two apartments originally intended for the châtelain.

As it was the custom, in the Middle Ages, for the lord of the manor to have his own quarters under the eaves, and, if necessary, to destroy the staircase and sustain a siege in his own apartments, gaps were often left in building stairways, so that the châtelain could reach his nest only by means of a ladder which he drew up after him at night. In other instances the steps of the last flight were purposely made so thin that a few blows with a bar sufficed to shatter them.

The latter was the case at the château of Brilbault; and the gaps for which the marquis had to be on the lookout were caused by accident, as we have said. With his long legs he was able to straddle them without serious danger.

These two rooms being those which the farmer had mentioned as suitable for Lucilio's occupancy in case of need, Bois-Doré's first impulse was to go in and see if they were provided with window-frames, or at least with shutters at the windows; for all of the narrow, deep-set windows in the stairway, with stone benches placed diagonally across the embrasures, admitted violent gusts of wind, from which he had difficulty in protecting his light.

But, as he was on the point of opening those seignioral apartments, of which he had the keys, the marquis hesitated.

If the manor-house was in reality resorted to as a place of refuge by any person, that person was probably in those rooms, and, being surprised in his sleep, would seek to defend himself without awaiting an explanation. His proposed exploration therefore should be conducted with due prudence. The marquis did not believe in ghosts, and was the less disposed to fear living things because he was not seeking them with any evil purpose. If some poor devil were in hiding there, he was resolved, whoever he might be, to leave him there in peace and not betray the secret he had surprised.

But the refugee's first fright might assume the form of hostility. The marquis could have made no appreciable noise in entering and ascending the stairs, as nothing stirred. It was most advisable for him to make sure of the truth unseen and unheard, if possible, or at all events without making his appearance too abruptly.

With that end in view, he entered a room with no door, where the most absolute darkness reigned, all the windows being covered with boards or stuffed with straw. The floor was covered with a layer of dust and pulverized cement, of such depth that one's footsteps were deadened by it as by ashes.

Bois-Doré walked for a long while, hardly able to see where he was going. He had closed his lantern, which was unprovided with glass or horn, but had a half cylinder of iron with three holes in it, according to the custom of the province. He did not venture to open it until he had reached the end of that vast apartment and had satisfied himself that he was in an absolutely silent and deserted spot.

Then he placed his light on the floor in front of him and stepped back to an enormous fire-place which was near at hand.

Standing there, he was able to accustom his eyes little by little to so faint a light in so vast a space, and to make out that he was in a hall which extended the whole length of the château.

He examined the fire-place by which he was standing. Like everything else it was of white stone, and the square bases, projecting from the massive columns, seemed as fresh and new as if they had been hewn the day before; the double fillets of the mantel were neither marred nor chipped, and the same was true of the escutcheon, without coat-of-arms, which crowned the mantel. Even the smoke-flue, and the fire-place itself, which was not sheathed with iron, bore no traces of fire, smoke or ashes. The unfinished building had never been used, that was evident. No one had ever occupied, no one now occupied that bare, cheerless hall.

Having satisfied himself of that fact, the marquis made bold to go to ascertain why a barrier of boards, waist-high, extended diagonally across that immense room at a point halfway between the two ends. Upon reaching that point, he found himself looking into space. The floor had fallen or been cut away, as had that of the lower stories, in quite half of the building, perhaps to facilitate the storing of the crops.

The eye plunged into the darkness of an expanse that seemed as large as the interior of a cathedral.

Bois-Doré had been there for some moments, trying to form a just idea of his surroundings, when, from the depths which his eyes questioned in vain, a sort of groan rose to his ears.

He started, closed his lantern, and concealed it behind the boards, held his breath and listened intently, for his hearing was a little dull and might deceive him as to the nature of the sounds.

Was it a door or a shutter closed by the wind?

He had not waited three minutes when the same groan was repeated, even more distinct, and at the same time it seemed to him that a faint ray of light, very far below him, illumined those depths, which, viewed from his position, were literally an abyss.

He knelt to avoid being seen, and looked between the boards which served him as a balustrade.

The light rapidly increased and soon became bright enough to enable him to see, or rather to divine, in a vague blending of light and shadow, the outline of a room on the ground floor, as large as that in which he was, but evidently much higher before the crumbling of the intermediate floors, as he could judge by the spring of the arched ceiling which rested upon bases embellished with fanciful human and animal figures, much larger and protruding farther than those he had previously seen on the stairway.

The only furniture consisted of several piles of dry forage, and boards arranged as a barrier near one end, with the broken remains of a number of mangers. The room had been used for a long time as a stable for cattle. Among the boards could be seen pieces of yokes and ploughshares. Then all these things were shrouded in shadow once more, and the light, ascending, struck the great stretch of wall which formed the gable end of the building, and which was directly opposite the marquis, some forty feet in height.

This light, now pale, now reddish, came from an invisible flame placed under the ceiling of the ground-floor apartment—that is to say, under that part of it which had not fallen, corresponding to that from which the marquis watched this gloomy, flickering tableau.

Suddenly there was a noise of doors closing, footsteps and voices under that ceiling, and a confused mass of moving shadows, sometimes of enormous size, sometimes stunted as it were, was thrown in the most curious fashion on the high wall, as if a great number of persons were passing back and forth in front of a great fire.

"This is a very strange game of hide-and-seek," thought the marquis, "and it is impossible to deny that this château is filled with wandering, chattering ghosts. Let us hear what they say."

He listened, but he could not succeed in distinguishing a single phrase, a word, a syllable, amid a loud murmur of words, songs, groans and laughter.

The appalling resonance of the arched ceiling, which hurled the sounds like shadows against the opposite wall, blended all the voices in a single one—all the words in a confused murmur.

The marquis was not deaf, but he had the sensitive hearing peculiar to old men, who can hear very distinctly sounds that are moderately loud and words clearly articulated, but whom an uproar, a hurly-burly of voices disturbs and confuses to no purpose.

Thus he distinguished intonations, nothing more: sometimes that of a hoarse, loud voice, which seemed to be telling a story; sometimes the refrain of a ballad abruptly interrupted by threatening accents; and then a loud voice which seemed to ridicule and imitate the others, and which raised a tempest of uproarious and brutal laughter.

Sometimes there were long monologues, then dialogues between two or three, and suddenly shouts of anger or merriment which resembled roars. Indeed, it might be that those people were speaking a language which the marquis did not know.

He persuaded himself that they were simply a band of vagrants or mountebanks out of employment, living by marauding, and waiting under cover of that ruin for the spring to come, or perhaps in hiding there because of some crime.

That laughter, those strange costumes outlined on the wall like Chinese ghosts, those long harangues, those animated dialogues were connected perhaps with the study of some burlesque art.

"If I were nearer to them," he thought, "I might be amused; no man is ever ill received in any company, however bad it may be, if he enters it offering his purse with a good grace."

So he took up his lantern and was preparing to descend, when the conversations, songs and laughter changed into cries of animals, so lifelike, so perfectly imitated, that one would have said that it was a whole barnyard in commotion. There were the ox, the ass, the horse, the goat, the rooster, the duck and the lamb, all braying and crowing together. Then they all ceased, as if to listen to the barking of a pack of hounds, the blast of the horn—all the typical noises of a hunt.

Was it a game? Did it occur to the actors to look at themselves on the wall? They did not seem to be imitating the actions of the beasts whose cries they mimicked.

In the midst of the uproar a child cried out in a shrill voice, perhaps to do as the others did, perhaps because he was frightened in his sleep; and Bois-Doré saw the shadow of a tiny person pass, with gestures like those of a monkey. Next there came a huge head crowned by a sort of plumed helmet, with an absurd nose outlined against the bright wall; then a long-haired head which seemed to wear a priest's cap, and which conversed with a long shadow that stood for many minutes as motionless as a statue.

Then all the noises suddenly ceased, and naught could be heard save a low groaning, which resembled the groaning caused by physical pain, and which Bois-Doré had constantly detected, recurring at intervals, like a doleful chord on an organ, in the pauses of that wild charivari.

The tumult stilled, the shadow of a gigantic crucifix was thrown upon the wall.

The light seemed to change its position, and the cross became very small; at last it disappeared, and its place was taken by a single figure very sharply outlined, while a sepulchral voice recited in a monotonous tone a prayer which seemed to be the prayer for those who are in the death agony.

CHAPTER XLVI

Bois-Doré, who had held his place, detained by the amusement he derived from that phantasmagoric spectacle and those strange noises, was beginning to feel so cold that his teeth fairly chattered when this tedious ceremony began.

This time, although he had determined to go to see what was taking place, he was withheld by the appalling resemblance presented by the last apparition. It became more precise and more unmistakable as the sepulchral voice proceeded with its sepulchral prayer, and the marquis, as if fascinated, could not remove his eyes from it.

That head, so easily recognizable by the short hair, cut *à la malcontent*, by the Spanish ruff in which it was framed as it were, by its sharp and angular, yet refined outlines, and lastly by the peculiar shape of the beard and moustache, was the head of D'Alvimar, thrown back in the rigor of death.

At first Bois-Doré fought against the idea; then it took entire possession of him, became a certainty, a source of intense agitation and insurmountable terror.

He had never believed that he was in any danger from ghosts. He said and he thought that, having never put any man to death from revenge or from cruelty, he was quite sure that he should never be visited by any soul in anger or distress; but he was no more disposed than the majority of sensible men of his time to deny the return of spirits to earth, or the reality of the apparitions which so many persons entirely worthy of confidence described in detail.

"This D'Alvimar is surely dead," he thought; "I touched his cold limbs; I saw his body, already stiff in death, taken from his horse's back. He has been reposing underground for several weeks, and yet I see him here before me, I who have always refused to see anything supernatural where others saw terrible phantoms! Was this man, contrary to all appearances, innocent of the crime of which I accused him and for which I punished him? Is this a rebuke of my conscience? Is it a vision of my brain? Is it the chilling atmosphere of this ruin stealing over me and confusing my faculties? Whatever it may be," he thought, "I have had enough of it."

And, feeling the dizziness which is the precursor of a swoon, he dragged himself out to the stairway. There he recovered himself somewhat, and descended the ruinous spiral staircase with a firm step. But, when he reached the foot, instead of mustering courage to force his way into the apartments on the ground floor, he had no desire to see or hear anything further; and impelled by an unconquerable feeling of repugnance, he rushed forth into the fields, confessing his fear to himself, and ready to avow it artlessly to the first person who should question him concerning it.

He found the farmer, more dead than alive, waiting for him on the bridge.

It was an heroic act on the good man's part to remain there. He was incapable of saying or listening to anything whatsoever, and not until he and the marquis had returned to the farmhouse, did he venture to ask any questions.

"Well, my poor dear Monsieur Sylvain," he said, "I trust you have had your fill of watching their lights, and listening to their bellowing! I thought surely I should never see you come back!"

"It is certain that something out of the common course is taking place in that ruin," said the marquis, tossing off a glass of wine which the farmer's wife handed him, and which was by no means unacceptable.

"I fell in with no evil spirits there—-"

"Ah! but you're whiter than your ruffles, my dear monsieur!" said La Grand' Cateline. "Warm yourself, pray, my lord, so that you won't be sick."

"To tell the truth, I was very cold," replied the marquis, "and I fancied that I saw things which perhaps I didn't see at all; but the walk will quicken my blood, and I fear to alarm my family by remaining longer. Good night to you, good people! Drink to my health."

He paid them handsomely for their eagerness to oblige, and returned to his carriage, which was waiting for him at the place where he had left it. Aristandre had begun to be anxious; but, when the marquis assured him that nothing unpleasant had happened to him, the honest coachman was convinced that Adamas was not boasting when he declared that monsieur still indulged in gallant adventures.

"There must be some pretty shepherdess at that farm!" he said to Clindor as they drove homeward.

He was confirmed in this sagacious idea when his master forbade him to speak of his trip through the fields.

Instead of stopping at Ars, the marquis bade him drive on to Briantes. He was surprised at and already a little ashamed of the momentary panic that had caused him to leave Brilbault without fathoming the mystery.

"If I say anything about it, they will laugh at me," he thought; "they will say under their breaths that I am becoming a dotard in my old age. It will be much better not to mention it to anyone; and, as it makes little difference, after all, whether Brilbault is in the hands of a band of gypsies or of sorcerers, I will look about for some other quieter place of refuge for Lucilio."

As he approached the château, his mind, becoming constantly calmer, questioned itself concerning its sensations.

What impressed him most deeply was the fact that he had been surprised by terror at a moment when nothing had happened which tended to terrify him; when, on the contrary, he had felt strongly inclined to laugh at the whimsical antics of those imps and the amusing oddity of their shadows on the wall.

As a result of his reflections on this subject, he ordered Aristandre to stop at the Chambon meadow and walked the short distance from the road to the cottage of Marie the gardener, called La Caille-Bottée.

That cottage still exists; it is occupied by market-gardeners. It is a tumble-down structure, flanked by a stair-turret built of stones without mortar. The pretty orchard, surrounded by dense hedges and wild bramble-bushes, was, so it is said, a gift from Monsieur de Bois-Doré to La Caille-Bottée.

He found the lay brother there, sharing the convent repast with his mistress, who shared with him the wine and the fruit from her garden.

Their partnership was not avowed, however; they observed some precaution, in order not to be "ordered to marry," and thereby to lose the veteran's privilege enjoyed by Jean le Clope at the Carmelite convent.

THE MARQUIS AT LA CAILLE-BOTTÉE'S

"Have no fear, my friends," said the marquis,
interrupting their tête-à-tête. "We have a secret
together, and I simply wish to say a word to you."
"Present, captain!" replied Jean le Clope, coming out
from under the table where he had taken refuge.

"Have no fear, my friends," said the marquis, interrupting their tête-à-tête. "We have a secret together, and I simply wish to say a word to you."

"Present, captain!" replied Jean le Clope, coming out from under the table where he had taken refuge; "I beg you to forgive me, but I didn't know who was coming to the house, and people make so much talk about me!"

"Very unjustly, I doubt not," said the marquis with a smile. "But look you, my friend; I have not seen you since a certain occurrence. I sent you a slight acknowledgment by Adamas, to whom you swore that you had faithfully carried out my orders. Having an opportunity to-night to speak to you a moment alone, I wish to learn from you some of the details as to the manner in which you did the business."

"What's that, captain? there's no two ways of burying a dead man, and I did a Christian's duty as Christianly as the prior of *my* community could have done it."

"I do not doubt it, comrade; but were you prudent?"

"Does my captain doubt me?" cried the veteran, with a sensitiveness which was particularly noticeable in him after supper.

"I do not doubt your discretion, Jean, but I have a little doubt of your skill in concealing this interment; for Monsieur d'Alvimar's death is known to my enemies to-day, and yet I can no more doubt the trustworthiness of my servants than I can doubt yours."

"Alas! monsieur le marquis, your servants were not the only ones in the secret," observed La Caille-Bottée sagaciously; "Monsieur d'Ars's servants may have told; and besides, weren't you looking that night for a man who had escaped and whom you wanted to catch?"

"That is true; he is the only one whom I suspect. I have not come here to reproach you, my friends, but to ask you where, when and how you buried that body."

"Where?" said Jean le Clope, glancing at La Caille-Bottée. "In our garden, and if you want to see the place— —"

"I do not care about it. But was it quite dark, or had the day begun to break?"

"It was about—two or three o'clock in the morning," said the lay brother with some hesitation, glancing again at the pock-marked old maid, who seemed to suggest his answers with her eyes.

"And nobody saw you?" said Bois-Doré, watching them both closely.

That question threw the lay brother into confusion, and the marquis detected more significant glances between him and his companion. It was becoming evident to him that they were afraid they had been seen, and that, in their fear of being contradicted by a reliable witness, they dared not go into details concerning the manner in which they had carried out the marquis's wishes.

He rose and repeated the question in an imperative tone.

"Alas! my good lord," said La Caille-Bottée, falling on her knees, "forgive this poor cripple in body and mind, who has probably drunk a little too much to-night, and can't say just what he wants to say!"

"Yes, forgive me, captain," added the veteran, deeply affected apparently by the plight of his own brain, and kneeling in his turn.

"You have deceived me, my friends!" said the marquis, determined to force the truth from them; "you did not bury Monsieur d'Alvimar yourselves! You were afraid, or had scruples, or did not like to do it; you notified Monsieur Poulain."

"No, monsieur, no!" cried La Caille-Bottée earnestly; "we would never have done such a thing, knowing that Monsieur Poulain is against you! Since you know that we didn't obey you, you must know also that it wasn't our fault, and that the devil in person had a hand in it."

"Tell me what happened," rejoined the marquis; "I propose to find out whether you will tell me the truth."

The gardener, convinced that the marquis knew more than she knew herself, told her story succinctly as follows:

"When you had gone, dear monsieur, the first thing we did was to carry the dead body into our garden, where we covered it over with a great mat; for I wasn't at all anxious to bring it into the house, and didn't see the use of it. I confess that I was terribly afraid of it, and I wouldn't have consented to receive such company for anybody but you, my good monsieur.

"Jean called me a fool and laughed at me, while he was drinking the rest of his wine, to protect himself from the cold night air, so he said, but perhaps it was to turn his mind away from the dismal thoughts that always come to a body at the sight of a corpse, no matter how hard your heart may be.

"I must also confess that the first thing poor Jean here thought of was to take what there was in the dead man's pockets and in the saddle-bags on the horse that brought him here. You hadn't said anything about it, so we thought it belonged to us, and we were sitting here counting the money on the table, so that we could hand over every sou to you, if you should claim it.

"There was a good-sized purse full of gold, and Jean, who was still drinking, enjoyed staring at it and handling it. What can you expect, monsieur? poor people like us are surprised when we have any of it to handle. And we were making plans about how we would spend that fortune. Jean wanted to buy a vineyard, but I said it would be much better to have an orchard well stocked with bearing nut trees; and here we sat, half laughing with joy to find ourselves so rich, half disputing over the use we should make of our money, when the cuckoo-clock struck four in the morning.

"'Now,' says I to poor Jean, 'I am not afraid any more, and as you aren't very spry with your wooden leg, although you can use the spade a little with your good foot, I'll help you to dig the grave. I never wished ill to any living man; but as long as this gentleman is dead, I don't want him to come to life again. There are people in the world who, by going out of it, benefit those who are left.'

"I shall have to admit my guilt, my dear monsieur, for that's the only prayer that that wicked Jean and I said for the dead man.

"Well, we took the spade, and both of us went back into the garden and took up the mat where we had hidden the body. Who was surprised, monsieur? There was nothing under it; somebody had stolen our corpse! We looked everywhere, turned everything over: nothing, monsieur, nothing! We thought we had gone mad and had dreamed everything that had happened that night, and I ran back into the house to see if the money wasn't a vision.

"Well, monsieur, if you were not here questioning us, we might believe that the devil had been acting a farce for us; for the drawer in which I had put the money and jewels was open, and it had all flown away from the house while we were in the garden, just as the dead man had flown away from the garden while we were in the house."

As she finished her story, La Caille-Bottée bewailed the loss of the money, and the lay brother, who only awaited an opportunity to weep, shed tears too manifestly sincere for the marquis to entertain any doubt as to the strange and twofold theft committed on their premises, of a full purse and a deceased dead man, as the gardener said in a doleful tone.

CHAPTER XLVII

During this duet of lamentations, the marquis reflected.

"Tell me, my friends," he said, "did you see no footprints in your garden, no indication that your house had been entered by violent means?"

"We paid no attention to that matter for some time," replied La Caille-Bottée, "we were too much upset; but when it was daylight, we examined everything as well as we could. There was nothing unusual in the house. They must have come in as soon as our backs were turned; we left the door and the drawer open, and the money in plain sight; we were much to blame for that, alas!"

"In that case," observed the marquis, "the deceased did not go away unaided, and had not only friends to take away his remains, but others to recover his money and jewels."

"I imagine, monsieur, that there were only two of them for the first task, and one for the last, and that one not connected with the others; for we discovered the prints of two pair of feet on our flower-beds, going toward the fence on the Briantes side, and those feet seemed to have had on boots or pattens; while on the gravel in our little yard, there were the marks of bare feet, little child's feet, going toward the town. But, as there was already water in the paths, we couldn't discover anything outside of our own place."

Bois-Doré reasoned thus mentally:

"Sancho, having made his escape, must have followed and watched us. Then he probably went to Monsieur Poulain, who sent someone or came himself with Sancho, to obtain D'Alvimar's body and bury it. That accounts for the denunciation. For reasons of which I know nothing, the rector dared not exhibit the body to his parishioners and denounce me publicly. Perhaps he wished to give Sancho time to make his escape. As for the money, some little reprobate must have noticed the going in and out, listened at the door, and seized the opportunity: that is of very little consequence to me."

Then, having reflected further upon the whole matter and asked various questions which resulted in throwing no new light, he said:

"My friends, when we brought that dead man here across his horse, we left the saddle-bags with you, with no other purpose than to rid ourselves of them and wash our hands of everything that had belonged to our enemy. The next day, however, on reflecting that those saddle-bags might contain papers of interest to us, we sent to you to obtain them, and you told Adamas that they contained nothing except a change of clothing and a little linen— no papers or documents of any kind."

"That is the truth, monsieur," replied the gardener, "and we can show them to you now, just as they were given to us. The thief didn't see them lying on the bed, where we tossed them, or else he didn't choose to burden himself with them."

The marquis caused them to be brought, and verified the truth of her statement.

However, on examining them and turning them over, he discovered a sort of secret pocket, which had escaped the notice of his hosts, and of which the stitching had to be ripped in order to open it. He found there some papers which he carried away, after compensating the gardener and the veteran for the loss they had sustained, and enjoining silence upon them until further orders.

It was after eleven o'clock when the marquis returned home.

Mario was not asleep; he was playing jackstraws with Lauriane in the salon, being unwilling to go to bed until his father returned safely.

Lucilio was reading by the fire, not allowing his attention to be distracted by the laughter of the children, but pleasantly soothed in his deep meditations by that fresh, charming music, to which his loving heart and his musical ear were peculiarly sensitive.

Since he had played the soothsayer in monsieur le prince's presence, the children called him the astrologer, and teased him to make him smile. The good-natured savant smiled as much as they wished without ceasing his mental labor, for his kindly disposition and gentle instincts remained united to his body, so to speak, and spoke through his beautiful Italian eyes, even when his mind was voyaging in celestial spheres.

Adamas, who, despite his adoration for his little count, was bored to the point of melancholy by the absence of his divine marquis, was wandering about the halls and the courtyard like a soul in distress, when he heard at last the echoing trot of Pimante and Squilindre and the grinding of the stones in the road, which were crushed under the wheels of the monumental chariot like grapes in the wine-press.

"Here comes monsieur!" he cried, throwing open the door of the salon as noisily and joyously as if the marquis had been absent a year; and he ran to the kitchen to bring with his own hands a bowl of steaming punch, concocted of wine and aromatic herbs—a cunningly compounded and pleasant beverage of which he jealously guarded the secret, and to which he attributed his old master's excellent health and lusty appearance.

Honest Sylvain embraced his son and greeted his daughter affectionately, pressed his *astrologer's* hand, drank the cordial which his faithful retainer offered him, and, having thus gratified his whole family, thrust his long legs almost into the fire, placed a small round table by his side, and requested Lucilio to read certain papers which he had brought, while Mario translated them aloud as best he could.

The papers were written in Spanish, in the shape of notes collected for a memorial, and were held together by a strap. They bore no address, nor seal, nor signature. The notes were a series of alleged facts, official or officious, concerning the state of feeling in France; concerning the disposition, presumed or discovered by stealth, of divers individuals of more or less consequence from a Spanish standpoint; and concerning public opinion with respect to the policy of Spain; in a word, a species of diplomatic production, very well done, although unfinished, and partly in the shape of a rough draft.

It was very clear that D'Alvimar, whose voluntary seclusion and constant writing during the few days of his sojourn at Briantes they had not been able to understand, had been constantly reporting to some prince, minister or patron, the results of a secret mission; that he was exceedingly hostile to France, and overflowing with aversion and disdain for the Frenchmen of all classes with whom he had come in contact.

His minute criticism was not devoid of wit, nor, consequently, of interest. D'Alvimar had a keen intellect, and was a specious reasoner. In default of connections as exalted and as intimate as he might have desired in the interests of his fortune and of the importance of his rôle, he was very skilful in making the most of trivial incidents, and in interpreting a word he had surprised or caught on the wing: a chance remark, a rumor, a reflection let fall by anybody, wherever he happened to be—everything was turned to some use by him; and one could see in that treacherous yet trivial labor the irresistible impulse and the secret gratification of a heart overflowing with bitterness, envy and distress.

Lucilio, who divined at the first word the marquis's deep interest in this discovery, turned over the last leaves, and soon found this one, which Mario translated fluently, almost without hesitation, turning his beautiful eyes to the beautiful eyes of his teacher at the end of each sentence, to make sure before continuing that he had made no mistake:

"As to the Pr— — de C— —é, I shall find a way to see him personally; I have received certain information from an intelligent and intriguing priest, which may be of use.

"Remember the name of Poulain, rector of Briantes. He is from Bourges and knows many things, notably concerning the said prince, who is very greedy of money and exceedingly incapable in respect to politics; but he will go where ambition drives him. He can be led on by great hopes, and used as the Guises were, for he has nothing of Condé but the name, and is afraid of everybody and everything.

"He is for that reason more difficult to catch than he appears. Personally he amounts to nothing. His name is still a host in itself. In the hope of becoming king, he is prepared to give many pledges to the most holy I— —, reserving the right to retract if his interest demands it. It is said that he would not shrink from making way with the k— — and his brother, and that, if need were, one could strike high and hard by means of that paltry mind and that nerveless arm.

"If in your opinion it is wise to encourage him in this ambition, advise your most humble — —"

"Good! good!" cried the marquis. "Here we have the wherewithal to make trouble between our friend Poulain and monsieur le prince, and between them both and the memory of dear Monsieur d'Alvimar. God knows that my choice would be to let that dead man rest in peace; but if they threaten to avenge him, we will let the kind friends who pity him know him as he really was."

"That is all very well," said pretty Madame de Beuvre, "on condition that you can prove that these notes were written by his hand."

"True," replied the marquis, "without that they will not help us. But doubtless Guillaume will be able to provide us with a letter signed by him."

"That is probable; and you must look to it at once, my dear marquis!"

"In that case," said the marquis, kissing her hand as he wished her good-night—for she had risen to retire—"in that case I will return to Guillaume's to-morrow; meanwhile let us be very careful of our proofs and our weapons."

On waking the next morning, the marquis found Lucilio in his room, who handed him a sheet upon which he had written something for him to read.

The poor fellow proposed that he should go away for a time, in order that the storm which threatened them both might not burst upon his generous friend more quickly because of his presence.

"No, no!" cried Bois-Doré, deeply touched; "surely you will not wound me to the heart by leaving me! The danger is postponed, that is clear enough to all of us; and Monsieur d'Alvimar's notes make me feel perfectly secure so far as I am concerned. As for yourself, rest assured that you have nothing to fear from the prince, having so accurately announced the favorite's death. Moreover, whatever risk you may run by remaining here, I think that it would be much greater elsewhere, and only in this province can I protect you effectively or conceal you, as circumstances require. Let us not worry about the unknown; and if you are afraid of adding to the embarrassment of my position, think of this—that without you, Mario's education is a hopeless failure. Think of the service you render me by transforming a lovable child into a man of brain and heart, and you will realize that neither my fortune nor my life can pay my debt to you, for both together are not equivalent to the learning and virtue which we owe to you."

Having, not without difficulty, extorted from his friend a promise not to leave Briantes without his assent, the marquis was about to start for Ars once more, when Guillaume arrived with Monsieur Robin de Coulogne, the latter greatly surprised by what his farmer Faraudet had told him that morning, the former surprised that he had not received a visit from the marquis during the evening, as his servants had led him to expect.

Bois-Doré made his confession and described faithfully the vision he had had at Brilbault, declaring, however, that, until the appearance of D'Alvimar's profile on the wall, he would have sworn that he had not dreamed of the uproar and the shadows, which might well have been perfectly real.

He had the mortification of detecting an incredulous smile on the faces of his two auditors; but when he had told them what had happened previously at the gardener's cottage, and had shown them D'Alvimar's notes, his friends became grave and attentive once more.

"Cousin," said Guillaume, "so far as these notes are concerned, it will be easy for me to authenticate them and to furnish you with specimens of Monsieur d'Alvimar's handwriting and his signature. Meanwhile, I assure you that these pages are in his hand. Put them with your own papers and wait, before announcing the traitor's death, until you are officially called to account therefor."

Such was not Monsieur Robin's advice. He criticised the policy of keeping the fact secret, the precautions taken to conceal the body, and the prolongation of the mystery at a time when everybody in the neighborhood was prepossessed in favor of the lovely Mario, touched by the story of his adventures, and disposed to curse the cowardly assassins of his father.

Bois-Doré would have followed this advice instantly, except for his unwillingness to displease Guillaume, who persisted in his first opinion.

"My dear neighbor," he said, "I would come over to your views and retract the advice I have given the marquis, except for one thought which has occurred to me, and which I beg you to weigh seriously; it is this: that it is unnecessary for the marquis to accuse himself of killing a man who may not be dead at all."

Messieurs Robin and Bois-Doré made a gesture of surprise, and Guillaume continued:

"I have two strong reasons for thinking and saying this: the first is that a man was carried away from La Caille-Bottée's garden, who, although run through by a lusty sword-thrust, may not have breathed his last; the second is that our marquis, whose courage is not of the sort that anyone can doubt, recognized his enemy's face at Brilbault."

Monsieur Robin reflected in silence; Bois-Doré collected his memories of the preceding night, and tried to disentangle them from the bewilderment that had then taken possession of him; then he said:

"If Monsieur d'Alvimar is dead, he did not die on the field of battle at La Rochaille, nor at the gardener's cottage, but at Brilbault, no later than last evening. He died in I know not what strange and brutal company, but attended by a priest who may have been Monsieur Poulain, and by a servant who must have been old Sancho. There was nothing in the confused shadows which I saw to contradict these suppositions, and the one thing that I saw most clearly and distinctly was a crucifix as sharply outlined as the cross on an escutcheon, and under the right branch of that crucifix the emaciated, fleshless face of Monsieur d'Alvimar. The features seemed somewhat agitated at first, while a voice repeated the prayers for the dying; faint groans, which I had heard throughout the revel, I continued to hear during the prayer. Then the groans ceased, the face became like stone; you would have said that the lines were petrified on the wall which showed me their reflection. The head was no longer bent forward but thrown back, and then — — "

"Then what?" said Guillaume.

"Then," said the marquis, ingenuously, "I became weak and idiotic, and I fled to avoid seeing anything more."

"Well," said Monsieur Robin, "however it may be, and whatever may be there, we will go to examine that hovel and ransack it from roof to cellar, if need be, to see what it conceals, and what sort of people it shelters."

Guillaume advised waiting until nightfall, and taking all manner of precautions, in order to make sure of discovering the object of these mysterious meetings.

Faraudet had given Monsieur Robin precise information as to the hour at which the tumult began, and the moment that it became certain that those strange noises were not a pure product of the imagination of terrified peasants, it was impossible not to see, in their regularity and their persistent recurrence, a deliberately adopted plan to spread terror abroad and turn it to advantage in one direction or another.

Monsieur Robin observed moreover that, according to the farmer, this performance had been going on at Brilbault only about two months, that is to say since the time fixed by Guillaume and the marquis as the period of D'Alvimar's death.

"All this," he said, "reminds me that, on the day that I arrived at Coudray, last week, I met at several places on the road, at varying intervals, groups of evil-appearing people, who did not look like peasants or bourgeois or soldiers, and whom I was surprised not to recognize. Ascertain from your servants whether they have not met similar folk in your neighborhood of late."

Several servants were summoned. Bois-Doré's and Guillaume's agreed in saying that, within a few weeks, they had seen many suspicious persons prowling about in the woods and the unfrequented roads of La Varenne, and that they had wondered how those strangers could earn a living in such lonely regions.

Thereupon they remembered numerous thefts that had been committed in farm-houses and barnyards roundabout; and lastly, La Flèche's face had reappeared, with other outlandish faces, at fairs and markets in the towns nearby. At all events they believed that they could swear that a certain mountebank, an irrepressible chatterer, dressed in various disguises, was the same fellow who had prowled about between Briantes and La Motte-Seuilly for several days, at the time of Mario's recovery.

The result of all this information was that they concluded that they had to deal with the most suspicious and artful genus of vagrants and bandits, and they took measures to obtain possession of their secret without giving the alarm.

They agreed to separate at once; for it was very possible that the wretches might have noticed the marquis's visit to Brilbault, and that they had spies on the watch behind the bushes on all the roads.

Guillaume was to return home, take a considerable number of his servants, and pretend to start for Bourges.

Monsieur Robin was to remain at Coudray with his people until the appointed hour.

Bois-Doré was to lie in ambush in the direction of Thevet, Jovelin toward Lourouer.

CHAPTER XLVIII

At nightfall, the servants and vassals, led by these four gentlemen, were to form a large circle around Brilbault and close in rapidly, as in a *battue* of wolves, each man reckoning the time required to reach the ruin from his starting-point, so that they might all arrive at the time fixed for investing it at close quarters.

That time was ten o'clock. Until then they were to move silently and keep out of sight as far as possible; they were to allow anyone to pass who was going toward Brilbault, but, after the stroke of ten, they were to arrest anyone who should attempt to leave the ruin.

They were strictly forbidden to kill or wound anyone unless they were seriously attacked, the main object being to take prisoners and obtain information.

It was also agreed that each man should start alone from his first position, and the positions were assigned in accordance with the minute strategic knowledge of the country possessed by Guillaume and the marquis.

Thus, Guillaume and his men were to separate at La Berthenoux, and scatter along the Igneraie. Monsieur Robin was to go alone to his farmer's, while his men were to take a score of different paths from Coudray to Brilbault, taking care to cover the whole Saint-Chartier line.

Monsieur de Bois-Doré, meanwhile, was to ride to Montlevic, and thence start alone for the rendezvous, after scattering his escort in the same manner, in order to avoid all suspicion on the part of anyone who might be watching his movements.

When all these arrangements were made, they could count upon bringing into the field about a hundred stout and cautious men, upon whom they could rely. Bois-Doré alone supplied almost fifty, and still left half a score of trusty fellows to guard the château and his lovely guest Lauriane.

In order that the spies who were presumed to be watching him might not suspect him of any design upon Brilbault, the marquis took Mario with him to the château of Montlevic, to pay a visit to his youthful neighbors.

The D'Orsannes were grandsons of Antoine d'Orsanne, who was lieutenant-general of Berry and a Calvinist.

The marquis and Mario passed an hour there; after which Bois-Doré told Aristandre to take the child back to Briantes, while he remounted his horse to ride alone to Etalié, a hamlet on the road from La Châtre to Thevet, at the top of a hill called Le Terrier.

When Mario, who was puzzled by all these precautions, asked leave to accompany him, he replied that he was going to sup with Guillaume d'Ars, and that he would return early.

The child sighed as he mounted his little horse, for he had a feeling that something was about to happen, and, by dint of listening to the conversation of gentlemen, the pretty peasant of the Pyrenees had soon become a gentleman himself, in the romantic and chivalrous sense still attributed to that title by the excellent marquis.

Everyone knows how marvellously the child modifies and transforms himself to adjust himself to the environment to which he is transplanted. Mario was already dreaming of noble feats of arms, running giants through and rescuing captive damsels.

He tried to insist after his manner, obeying without a murmur, but fastening his loving and persuasive eyes upon the old man, who adored him.

"No, my dear count," replied Bois-Doré, who understood perfectly his silent prayer; "I cannot leave alone in my château at night the sweet girl who has been placed in my care. Remember that she is your sister and your lady, and that, when I am compelled to be absent, your place is beside her, to serve her, to divert her and, if need be, to defend her."

Mario was vanquished by this exaggerated flattery, and, spurring his horse, rode away toward Briantes at a gallop.

Aristandre followed him, and was to return to the marquis as soon as he had escorted the child back to the château.

The night, like the preceding one, was decidedly mild for the season. The sky, sometimes overcast, sometimes swept clear by gusts of warm air, was very dark when the young horseman and his attendant galloped into the ravine and rode under the venerable trees of the village.

As they rapidly ascended one of the narrow undulating roads, lined with hedges, which served the purposes of streets between the thirty or forty *firesides* of which the village consisted, Mario's horse, which was leading, shied and snorted with terror.

"What is that?" said the child, sitting like a rock in his saddle. "A drunken man asleep in the road? Pick him up, Aristandre, and take him to his family."

"Monsieur le comte," replied the coachman, who had instantly dismounted, "if he is drunk, you might say he is dead drunk, for he doesn't move any more than a stone."

"Shall I help you?" said the child, dismounting.

He went nearer and tried to distinguish the features of the man, who answered none of Aristandre's questions.

"He may belong hereabout," said the coachman with his accustomed stolidity; "I don't know him; but what I do know is that he is dead or the next thing to it."

"Dead!" cried the child; "right here, in the middle of the village! and no one thinks of helping him!"

He ran to the nearest house and found it empty; the fire was burning brightly, and the tea-kettle, abandoned to its fate, was sputtering in the ashes; the settle was upset across the room.

Mario called in vain, no one answered.

He was about to run to another house, for they were separated from one another by large enclosures thickly planted with trees, when the report of firearms and strange rumbling noises, drowning the clatter of his horse's hoofs on the stones, made him jump and abruptly draw rein.

"Do you hear, monsieur le comte?" cried Aristandre, who had carried the body to the side of the road, and had remounted to join his young master; "that comes from the château, and there's something strange going on there, for sure!"

"Let us hurry!" said Mario, urging his steed to a gallop. "If it's a fête, they are making a great noise over it!"

"Wait! wait!" cried the coachman, doubling his speed to stop Mario's horse; "that is no fête! There wouldn't be a fête at the château without you and monsieur le marquis. They are fighting! Do you hear how they are yelling and cursing? And see, there's another dead man, or a horribly wounded Christian, at the foot of the wall! Fly, monsieur; hide, for the love of God! I will go to see what the matter is, and come back and tell you."

"You are laughing at me!" cried Mario, tearing himself free; "hide, when they are attacking my father's château? What about my Lauriane? let us hasten to her defence!"

He galloped across the drawbridge, which was lowered, a most extraordinary circumstance after nightfall.

By the light of a stack of straw which was blazing merrily in front of the farm buildings, Mario obtained a confused view of a most incomprehensible scene.

The marquis's retainers were engaged in a hand-to-hand conflict with a numerous band of horned, hairy, shiny creatures, "in every respect more like devils than men." —Musket or pistol shots rang out from time to time, but it was not a battle according to rule; it was a mêlée, following a sudden and unfortunate surprise. They saw frantic groups writhe and struggle for an instant, then suddenly disappear, when the flame of the burning straw was obscured by dense clouds of smoke.

The coachman held Mario in his arms, so that he could not rush into the fray. He struggled in vain, and wept with rage.

At last he was forced to listen to reason.

"You see, monsieur," said honest Aristandre, "you prevent me from going and taking a hand yonder! And yet my fist is worth four of an ordinary man's. But the devil could not make me let go my hold of you, for I am responsible for you; so I won't do it until you swear that you will keep quiet."

"Go then," replied Mario, "I swear it."

"But if you stay here, some straggler may see you. Come, I'll hide you in the garden."

And, without awaiting the child's consent, the coachman lifted him from his horse and carried him into the garden, the gate of which was at the left, not far from the entrance tower. He locked him in there, and ran off to throw himself into the mêlée.

Dull and uninteresting as we know mere descriptions of locality to be, we are compelled, in order to enable the reader to understand what follows, to remind him of the general arrangement of the small estate of Briantes. The recollection of many venerable country houses, built upon the same plan, and still existing with slight changes, will assist him to form an idea of the one with which we are here concerned.

I will suppose that we enter by the drawbridge which spans the outer moat; let us pause a moment at that point.

The *sarrasine* is raised. Let us examine this system of defence.

The *orgue*, or *sarrasine*, or, as it was then called, the *sarracinesque*, was a sort of portcullis, less expensive and less heavy than the iron portcullis. It consisted of a series of movable stakes, independent of one another, and moving up and down, like the portcullis, in the archway of the gate-tower. More time was required to set in motion the mechanism of the *sarrasine* than that of the ordinary portcullis made in a single piece; but it had this advantage, that a single person, stationed in the *salle de manœuvre*, or room from which it was worked, could, if need were, raise one of the stakes and admit a fugitive, without making too large an opening of which the besiegers could avail themselves.

This room was a sort of corridor inside the gate-tower and above the arch, with openings which enabled those on guard there to look down upon whoever might attempt to go in or out. These openings also enabled them to fire or hurl projectiles on the besiegers, when they had succeeded in crossing the moat and destroying the *sarrasine*, and the battle was renewed under the archway.

This room communicated with the *moucharabi*, a low, crenellated, *mascherolé* gallery, which crowned the arch of the portcullis on the outer face of the tower. From that point bullets and stones could be rained upon the enemy to prevent their destroying the *sarrasine*.

The gate-tower of Briantes, which contained these defensive appliances, was a heavy oval mass, built on the edge of the moat. It was called the tower of the *huis*, to distinguish it from the *huisset*, of which we shall speak in a moment. The *huis*, or gate, opened into the immense enclosure which contained the farm buildings, the dove-cote, the heron-yard, the mall, etc., and which was invariably called the *basse-cour*, because it was always on a lower level than the courtyard.

On our left is the high garden wall, pierced at regular intervals with narrow loopholes, from which, in case of surprise, the enemy could be harassed after making themselves masters of the *basse-cour*.

A paved road ran all the way along this wall to the second line of defences, where the second moat, supplied with water by the little stream, extended to the pond at the end of the courtyard.

Over this moat, bordered by its turfed counterscarp, was thrown the stationary bridge, a bridge built of stone, and very old, as indicated by the sharp angle which it made with the tower at its inner end.

This was customary in the Middle Ages. Some antiquaries explain the custom by pointing out that the archers in the assaulting party, when they raised their arms to fire, laid their sides open to the fire of the besieged.

Others tell us that this angle broke the force of an assault very materially. It matters little.

The tower of the *huisset* stood between this stationary bridge and the courtyard. It contained a small iron portcullis and stout oaken gates studded with nails with enormous heads.

This tower formed, with the moat, the only defence of the manor, properly so-called.

When he gratified his own tastes by razing the donjon of his fathers and replacing it by the pavilion called the *grand'maison*, the marquis had said to himself, and justly, that, whether in the shape of a castle or a villa, his country house would not hold out an hour against an attack with cannon. But, against the paltry means of attack which bandits or hostile neighbors could command, the broad, deep moat filled with a swiftly-running stream, the little falconets placed on each side of the *huisset*, and the loopholes cut diagonally in the wall on the *basse-cour* or farmyard side, were capable of holding out a considerable time. As a matter of comfort and convenience rather than of prudence, the manor was always well supplied with provisions and forage.

Let us add that walls and moats, always kept in perfect repair, enclosed the whole domain—even the garden—and that, if Aristandre had taken time for reflection, he would have carried Mario out of the farmyard, into the village, and not into the garden, which was as likely to become a prison for him as a place of safety.

But one never thinks of everything, and Aristandre never dreamed that the enemy could not be repelled with a turn of the hand.

The honest fellow was not noted for vividness of imagination; it was fortunate for him that he did not allow himself to be excited by the fantastic and truly frightful figures which were presented to his astonished eyes. Being as credulous as other men, he took counsel with himself as he ran, but without slackening his headlong pace; and, when he had struck down one or two of them, he made the philosophical reflection that they were *canaille*, nothing more.

Mario, with his face pressed against the garden gate, throbbing with ardor and excitement soon lost sight of him.

The burning mill had fallen in; the fighting continued during the darkness; the child could follow only with his ears the confused sounds of the changing scenes of the action.

He judged that the arrival of the sturdy and intrepid Aristandre revived the courage of the defenders, but after a few moments of uncertainty, which seemed to him like centuries, he thought that the assailants must be gaining ground, for the shouts and scuffling receded to the second bridge, and, after a moment of ghastly silence, he heard a pistol shot and the splash of a body falling into the stream.

A few seconds later the portcullis of the *huisset* fell with a great crash, and a volley from the falconets forced the party that had rushed upon the bridge to fall back with horrible imprecations.

One act of this incomprehensible drama was finished; the besieged had been driven back and confined in the courtyard; the invaders were masters of the *basse-cour*.

Mario was alone; Aristandre was probably dead, since he abandoned him in the midst or at least within reach of enemies who might burst into the garden at any moment by breaking down the gate, and take him prisoner.

And there was no means of escape for him except to scale that gate at the risk of falling into the hands of those demons! There was no exit from the garden except into the *basse-cour*; it had no direct communication of any sort with the château.

Mario was afraid; and then, too, the thought of the death of Aristandre, and, perhaps, of other faithful servants equally dear to him, brought tears to his eyes. Even his poor little horse, whom he had left at the entrance to the *basse-cour*, with the reins on his neck, came into his mind and added to his distress.

Lauriane and Mercedes were safe, doubtless, and there were still many defenders about them, for the deathly silence in the direction of the village indicated that men and beasts had taken refuge within the enclosure at the outset, in order to receive the enemy under shelter of the walls. It was the custom of the period that, at the slightest alarm, vassals should repair to the seignioral château at once, to seek and offer aid. They always took their families and cattle with them.

"But if Lauriane and my good Moor have any idea that I am here," thought poor Mario, "how worried they will be about me! Let us hope that they don't suspect that I have returned! And dear old Adamas—I am sure he is like a madman! If only they haven't taken him prisoner!"

His tears flowed silently; crouching in a clump of trimmed yews, he dared not show himself at the gate, where he might be discovered by the enemy, nor go farther away and lose sight of what he could still see of the scene of confusion being enacted in the *basse-cour*.

He heard the howls of those besiegers who were wounded by the shot from the falconets. They had been taken to the farmhouse, and there were evidently wounded and dying men there belonging to the besieged force as well, for Mario could distinguish voices that seemed to be exchanging reproaches and threats. But it was all very vague; it was a considerable distance from the garden to the farm-house; moreover, the little stream, swollen by the winter rains, was making a deal of noise.

The besieged had opened the gates and sluices of the pond to increase the depth of water in the moat and make it flow more swiftly.

A reddish gleam appeared above the door of the château; doubtless a fire had been lighted in the courtyard, so that they could see one another, reckon up their fighting strength and prepare their defence. The besiegers' fire had ceased to cast more than a sort of ruddy reflection, by which Mario could see many indistinct shadows moving rapidly to and fro.

Suddenly he heard footsteps and voices approaching him, and thought that they were coming to explore the garden.

He kept perfectly still and saw two fantastically arrayed individuals pass the gate, on the outer side, and go toward the entrance tower.

He held his breath and succeeded in overhearing this fragment of dialogue:

"The infernal curs will not arrive before him!"

"So much the better I our share will be all the bigger!"

"Idiots, to think that you alone can capture— —"

CHAPTER XLIX

The voices died away, but Mario had recognized them. They were the voices of La Flèche and old Sancho.

His courage suddenly returned, although there was nothing encouraging in that discovery.

It had been impossible to keep Mario long in ignorance of the affair of La Rochaille, and he fully realized that his father's murderer, D'Alvimar's fidus Achates, was thenceforth the deadliest foe of the name of Bois-Doré; but La Flèche's complicity in this bold stroke led the child to hope that Sancho's auxiliaries were the band of gypsies who had been his companions in misery.

He reflected, justly enough, that those vagrants had in all probability joined forces with other more desperate rascals; but even so, an attack of that sort seemed to him much less to be dreaded than a regular raid organized by the provincial authorities, such as they had had reason to fear; and for a moment he had an idea of trying to win over La Flèche, if he could obtain an interview with him alone. But his distrust returned when he remembered the brutal and threatening air with which the gypsy had talked with him on that same spot months before.

Thereupon he began to reflect on the words he had just heard. He felt that he needed all his faculties in order to understand them and take advantage of them at need.

Doubtless the assailants expected reinforcements, whose arrival was delayed too long to suit Sancho. "They will not arrive before him!"— The *him* could be no other than the marquis, whose return they dreaded.— "So much the better, our share will be all the bigger!" indicated that La Flèche was impelled by the hope of pillage. "Idiots, to think that you alone can capture"—the château presumably—was a confession of the inability of the assailants to maintain a siege of the manor with any chance of success.

In short, Mario, who had seen the besmeared, masked, ghastly, grotesque faces,—disguises assumed by the gypsies in all probability to terrify the peasants of the village and the farm,—and who, despite his courage, had been himself terrified by them, was immensely relieved when he found that he had to do with villains of flesh and blood, rather than with supernatural creatures and mysterious dangers.

Being unable to do anything for the moment except remain in hiding, he waited until the voices and footsteps had died away, before leaving the gate himself to seek shelter from the cold night air in one of the little structures in the garden.

He thought, with good reason, that the labyrinth, with all the windings of which he was so familiar, would enable him to elude any possible pursuit for some time, and he entered it, bending his steps without hesitation toward the little cottage which was metaphorically called the *Palace of Astrée*.

He was no sooner inside than he fancied that he heard footsteps on the gravel of the circular path.

He listened.

"It is either the wind blowing the dry leaves about," he thought, "or some creature from the farm coming here for shelter. But, in that case, the garden gate must be open! If it is, I am lost! O God! have pity on me!"

The noise was so faint, however, that Mario made bold to look out through the curtain of ivy which covered the walls of his retreat, and he saw a tiny person who was looking all about, in apparent uncertainty, as if seeking refuge in the same place.

Mario had not had time to close the door of the cottage behind him; the small being entered, and said in a low voice:

"Are you here, Mario?"

"Why, is it you, Pilar?" said the child, with an involuntary thrill of pleasure, as he recognized his former little companion, whom he had believed to be dead.

But he added sadly:

"Are you looking for me, in order to betray me?"

"No, no, Mario!" she replied. "I want to run away from La Flèche. Save me, my Mario, for I am too unhappy with that accursed man!"

"But how can I save you, when I do not even know how to save myself?—Either go away from here, or else stay here without me, my poor Pilar; for those bandits, when they come to look for you, will find me too."

"No, no; La Flèche thinks that he left me over yonder with the dead man!"

"What dead man?"

"They called him D'Alvimar. He died the other night, and they buried him this morning."

"You are dreaming—or else I don't understand. No matter! You ran away?"

"Yes; I knew that they were coming here to take your château and your treasure; I climbed out of a little bit of a window, like a cat, and I followed them at a distance. I hoped they would kill La Flèche and those wicked villains, who have never had any pity on me."

"What villains?"

"The trick-playing gypsies whom you know, and many others whom you don't know, who have joined them. They made me suffer at Brilbault, I tell you!"

"Where is Brilbault? Isn't it an old ruin near——"

"I don't know. I never went out. They roamed about all day and left me with the wounded man, who was always dying, and his old servant, who hated me because he said I was the one who brought monsieur bad luck and prevented him from getting well. I would have liked to have him die sooner; for I hated them, too, the vile Spaniards! and I made lots of spells against them. At last the youngest one died, in the midst of those wild men, who drank and sang and yelled all night, and prevented me from sleeping. So I am sick. I am feverish all the time. Perhaps that's lucky for me, because it keeps me from being hungry."

"My poor girl, here is all the money I have about me. If you succeed in escaping, it will be of some use to you; but, although I don't in the least understand what you tell me, it seems to me that you were crazy to come here instead of going far away from La Flèche. It makes me afraid that you are acting in concert with him to——"

"No, no, Mario! keep your money! and, if you think that I mean to betray you, go and hide somewhere else; I won't follow you. I am not a wicked girl to you, Mario. You are the only person in the whole world that I love! I came here thinking that, while they were fighting, I might go into the château and stay with you. But your peasants were too frightened; some of them were killed, the others fled into your great courtyard. Your servants defended themselves bravely; but they weren't the strongest! I was hidden under some boards on the inside of the garden wall. I could see everything through a little crack. I saw you come into the courtyard on your horse: I saw a tall man lock you in here. I didn't recognize you right off, because of your fine clothes; but when you started to come to this little house and I saw you walk, I knew your gait, and I followed you."

"And now what are we going to do? Play at hide and seek, as well as we can, in this garden, where they will certainly come and search?"

"What do you suppose they will come into a garden for? They know very well that there's no fruit to steal in winter. Besides the villains have already found plenty to eat and drink in the big buildings yonder. That's the farm, isn't it? I know well enough what they do when they get into a house that isn't defended. I don't need to see them, I tell you! They kill the cattle and prepare the spit; they knock in the heads of wine casks; they burst open closets; they fill their pockets, their wallets and their bellies. In an hour, they will all be mad, they will fight among themselves and maim each other. Ah! if your stupid servant hadn't locked us in here, it wouldn't be hard to escape! But of course there must be a hole that we can crawl through somewhere in this garden wall! I am a bit of a creature and you are not stout. Sometimes you can reach the top of a wall by climbing a tree. Do you know how to climb and jump, Mario?"

"Yes, indeed; but I know that there isn't any hole or any tree that will help us. There's the pond at the end of the courtyard, but I don't know how to swim as yet. It has been so cold ever since I have been here that they couldn't teach me. There's a little boat that they could send us from the château if they knew we were here. But how are we to make them see us? it is too dark; and just listen! the water makes too much noise running over the dam! Ah! my poor Aristandre must be taken or dead, since——"

"No, my dear little count of the good Lord!" said a hoarse voice outside, trying to speak low; "Aristandre is here, looking for you and listening to you."

"Ah! my dear charioteer!" cried Mario, throwing his arms around the great head which was thrust through the low round window of the little cottage. "Is it really you! But how wet you are! *Mon Dieu!* is it blood?"

"No, it's water, thank God!" replied Aristandre, "cold water! But I didn't drink any of it, luckily for me! I was pushed, pushed, carried onto the stone bridge in spite of myself, by our devils of peasants as they fell back on the courtyard. I saw that I was going to be forced into the courtyard with them, and then I couldn't come out again to find you. So I fired my last pistol shot and jumped into the stream. Devilish stream! I thought I never should get out of it, especially as they fired on me from the château, taking me for an enemy. However, here I am! I have been looking for you for a quarter of an hour; I had an idea that you would be in the *affinoire*"—that was Aristandre's name for the labyrinth—"but, although I've known it ten years, I don't know how to find my way in it yet. Come! we must get away from here. Let us try! You must do just as I say. But who in the devil have you there?"

"Someone whom you must save with me, an unfortunate little girl."

"From the village? Faith! never mind, we will save her if we can. You first! I am going to see what is happening in the *basse-cour*; do you stay here and talk low."

Aristandre returned in a few moments. He seemed troubled.

"It is no easy matter to go away," he said to the children. "Ah! those villagers! how they must have bungled to let the farm be taken! And, now that the hounds are drinking themselves stupid, if they should make a sortie from the château, they could kill them like swine to the last man! They think that they have demons to deal with, but I say that they are human beings in disguise, pure *canaille*! Just hear them yell and sing!"

"Well, let us make the most of their carousing," said Mario; "let us cross yonder corner of the *basse-cour*, where there seems to be no one, and run to the tower of the *huis*."

"Oh! the deuce! to be sure! But the beggars have locked themselves in! They know well enough that monsieur le marquis may come during the night, and he will have to lay siege to his own tower."

"Yes," cried Mario, "that is why I saw Sancho go in that direction with La Flèche."

"Sancho? La Flèche? you recognized them? Ah! I have a mind to go by myself and fall upon those illustrious captains!"

"No, no!" said Pilar, "they are stronger and wickeder than you think!"

"But, if they have simply locked the gate, we can open it," said Mario, whose mind worked more quickly than the coachman's. "And if they have left anybody on guard there, why between us, Aristandre, we can try to kill them so that we can pass. Do you hesitate? We must do it, you see, my friend. We must hurry and warn my father. If we don't, our people here will allow the château to be taken, they are so terrified. When the villains have finished gorging themselves, they will try to set it on fire. Who knows what may happen? Come, come, coachman, my good fellow," added the child, drawing his little rapier, "take a stake, a club, a tree, no matter what, and let us go!"

"Stay, stay, my dear little master!" rejoined Aristandre, "there are some tools here; let me look. Good! I have a shovel; no! a spade! I like that better!

Now, I am not afraid of any man! But, listen to me; do you know where your papa is?"

"No! you must take me to him."

"If I come out all right, yes; if not, you will have to go all alone. Do you know where Etalié is?"

"Yes, I have been there. I know the way."

"Do you know the *Geault-Rouge* inn?"

"The *Coq-Rouge*? Yes, I have been there twice. It isn't hard to find, it's the only house in the place. Well?"

"Your papa will be there until ten o'clock. If you arrive too late, go to Brilbault; he will be there."

"Brilbault at the foot of Coudray hill?"

"Yes. He will be there with his people. It's a long way; you will never be able to do it on foot!"

"I will go straight to Brilbault," said Pilar. "I know the way; I have just come from there!"

"Yes," said the coachman; "go, little one; you can warn Monsieur Robin. Do you know him? You don't belong about here, do you?"

"No matter, I will find him."

"Or Monsieur d'Ars; will you remember?"

"I know him, I saw him once."

"Off we go, then! Ah! Monsieur Mario, if I could only lay my hand on your horse! you could go faster and not kill yourself running."

"I know how to run," said Mario; "don't think about the horse, it is out of the question."

"One minute more," continued Aristandre, "and pay attention. The drawbridge is raised; you know how to drop it, don't you? It doesn't weigh much."

"That's very easy!"

"But the *sarrasine* is down! But don't be alarmed; I will go up into the room where we work it. If there's anybody there, so much the worse for them; I'll strike and kill, and raise one of the stakes! Don't lose time by waiting for me. Pass through, steal away, fly! If the stake falls on the girl, so much the worse for her; you cannot help it, nor I. God guard you! Keep on running, I will overtake you."

"But, if you are——"

Mario stopped short; his heart sank.

"If I am laid out, you mean? Well, it will be of no use for you to grieve, it will not help matters. If you stop to pity me, you will lose your head and your legs! You must think of nothing but running."

"No, my friend, your risk is too great; let us remain concealed here."

"And suppose, while we are hiding, they burn up Madame Lauriane, your Mercedes, Adamas—and my poor carriage horses in the stable yonder! Besides—Look you, I am going alone. When the road is clear you can pass."

"Come on! come on!" said Mario. "Everything for Lauriane and Mercedes!"

He was about to rush out of the garden, when Pilar detained him.

"Remember that other villains are to come here—I know it. If you meet them, hide carefully, for your gold buttons gleam in the darkness like diamonds, and they will kill you just to get your clothes."

"I have an idea!" exclaimed Mario. "I will put on my gypsy rags, which are right here."

The reader will remember the rustic, sentimental and philosophic trophy, which had been suspended in the cottage with great pomp.

Mario hastily took it down, and in two minutes, having laid aside silk, velvet and lace, he was dressed in his former costume; whereupon they proceeded to the *huis*, walking noiselessly and without speaking.

They had only about fifty paces to walks along the wall outside the garden. They walked that distance, without hindrance at least, if not without danger, to the sound of loud laughter, shrieks, blasphemies and hoarse singing from the farm-house.

The tower of the *huis* was dark and silent. Aristandre placed the two children close to the *sarrasine*, Mario in front, almost touching the first stake at the left. Then he took his hand and placed it on the ring of the chain which held the drawbridge in the air. There was nothing for him to do but to take that ring from the hook set in the wall.

They did not venture to exchange another word. All about them, on the staircase, over their heads, there might be, there undoubtedly were, sentinels, sleeping or careless.

Mario could not press the coachman's hand in his own, for his were clinging to the detached ring and the dragging chain. He put his lips to that rough hand and hurriedly imprinted a silent kiss upon it; perhaps it was an eternal farewell.

Aristandre, deeply moved, abruptly withdrew his great paw, none the less, as if to say: "Nonsense! don't think of anything but yourself;" and, crossing himself fervently in the darkness, he resolutely ascended the short steep staircase to the *salle de manœuvre.*

"Who goes there?" cried a deep voice which Mario instantly recognized as Sancho's.

And as the coachman continued to ascend and approached the left side of the gallery, the voice added:

"Will you answer, blockhead? Are you drunk? Answer, or I fire on you!"

In an instant there was a report; but the stake was raised, Mario let go the chain, darted across the bridge, and fled without looking back. It seemed to him that the alarm was given on the *moucharabi,* and that a bullet whistled by his ears; he did not hear the report, the blood was making so much noise in his head.

When he was out of range, he paused and leaned against a tree, for his strength failed him at the thought of what was taking place between Aristandre and the enemy's sentinels.

He heard a great uproar in the tower, and something that sounded like the blows of a pickaxe on stone. It was Aristandre's spade, which he kept whirling about his head in the darkness; but he prudently kept silent, in order to be taken for a drunken gypsy, and Mario, straining his ears to hear his loud voice among the others, lost hope, and, with hope, courage to fly without him.

The poor boy was thinking so little of himself that he did not even start when he felt a hand on his arm.

It was Pilar, who had run faster than he, and was retracing her steps to find him.

"Well, well, what are you doing here?" she said. "Come, while they are killing him! When they have finished killing him, they will chase us!"

The little gypsy's ghastly sang-froid horrified Mario. Reared amid scenes of violence and bloodshed, she hardly knew what fear meant, and had not the faintest conception of pity.

But, by virtue of some swift sequence of ideas, Mario thought of Lauriane, and all the resolution of which a child is capable returned to his heart.

He ran on once more, and, motioning to Pilar to take the lower road, turned into the road leading to the plateau of Le Chaumois. A few steps farther on he stumbled over an object which lay across the road. It was the second dead body which Aristandre had pointed out to him, but which they had not had time to examine. Feeling the body under him, Mario was bathed in cold perspiration; perhaps it was Adamas! He mustered courage to touch it, and having satisfied himself that the clothes were those of a peasant, he hurried forward.

The sight of the pale sky over the bare fields made him breathe more freely; the darkness was stifling him. He took a bee-line across the fields, but a new terror awaited him there. A pale, indistinct form seemed to be flitting over the furrows. It came toward him. He tried to elude it, but it followed him. It was an animal of some sort chasing him. All the old women's tales about the white greyhound, and the imp that cries: "*Robert is dead!*" flashed through his mind.

But of a sudden the beast neighed and came near enough to be recognized. It was Mario's dear little horse, which had scented him from afar and came to offer him his help.

"Ah! my dear Coquet!" cried the child seizing his mane, "you come in the nick of time! and did you recognize me, poor fellow, in spite of these clothes, which you never saw? You were terribly frightened during that horrid battle, weren't you? You ran off at once, before they raised the bridge, and you were eating dry thistles here instead of your oats! Let us be off! we will both of us sup when we have time!"

As he chattered thus to his horse, Mario rearranged the stirrups, which had suffered somewhat in the bushes. Then, having mounted, he rode away like an arrow.

We will leave him for the moment and return to Briantes, where the plight of the besieged garrison causes us some anxiety.

CHAPTER L

When Mario and Aristandre arrived at Briantes, not a quarter of an hour had elapsed since the bandits had made their sudden appearance there.

Lauriane was about sitting down to supper when she heard confused outcries and the report of firearms in the direction of the village—we might say, according to the custom in the province, the *bourg*, since the little settlement was fortified in very ancient times; but the old Gallo-Roman stone wall was demolished to the level of the ground in many places, and it was a long time since the people had ceased to incur the expense of maintaining gates.

These noises, which the people in the château and those at the farm-house as well, supposed at first to be caused by villagers turning out to hunt some creature that had stolen into their enclosures, speedily assumed a more alarming character.

Everyone seized upon the first weapon that came to hand, and the farmers, brandishing their flails, hurried to the tower of the *huis*. But they were instantly forced back and their efforts paralyzed by the people from the village, who, rushing from all directions, came together at the approaches to the bridge, and in their terror overturned and trampled on the men who were running to their assistance.

And yet the attacking party consisted of only about fifty men, followed by a number of women and children; but it will be remembered that the marquis had ordered out and despatched to the attack on Brilbault all the stout and intrepid men in his little fief, so that the population surprised by the brigands consisted at that moment of women and children, crippled old men, or weak, half-grown boys.

The sight of the horrible masks worn by the bandits produced the effect they had anticipated. A general panic seized the peasants, and fear afforded them only so much strength as was necessary to prevent the loyal retainers from the château from going forth to meet the foe.

One of the dead bodies that Mario found on the road was that of a deformed young man who fell and was trampled under foot by the fugitives;

the other, a poor old fellow who alone tried to face the enemy and was struck down by Sancho with the butt of his gun.

They had barely time to cross the bridge, and could not raise it because of the stragglers who whined and cried and implored shelter for themselves and their cattle. The enemy took advantage of the confusion to overtake them.

Thereupon the battle began under the archway of the *huis*, where the defenders of the château, surrounded by crying children and animals that were either inert and stupid or wounded and frantic, were instantly forced to fall back.

They had no sooner retreated to the *basse-cour* than the peasants abandoned them and rushed madly to the stone bridge; so that the brave fellows, numbering no more than half a score, were surrounded by the brigands and forced to fall back to the *huisset*, heroically contesting every inch of the ground.

One of the bravest, Charasson the farmer, was killed; two others were wounded. They would all have fallen there, for the redoubtable Sancho fought with the frenzy of desperation, had it not been for the dastardly behavior of La Flèche and his consorts, "who were eager for pillage, and in nowise eager for hard knocks."

Reduced to seven, the gallant defenders were obliged to retreat into the courtyard; the which was no easy matter, because the courtyard was so crowded. They were so hotly pressed by Sancho that a great number of the beasts were left outside, or in their excitement plunged into the moat.

During this desperate struggle, which, however, had lasted barely ten minutes, Lauriane and Mercedes at first stood, silent and trembling, on the platform of the tower of the *huisset*.

When they saw their people give way, being simultaneously inspired by the courage which fear imparts to the weak when they are not idiots, they ran to the falconets, which were always ready to be discharged. They hurriedly lighted the matches, and held themselves in readiness to fire, encouraging each other, and trying to remember what they had seen Mario and the other young men of the household taught to do by way of practice. But it was not yet possible to fire on the enemy, they were so inextricably mingled with the defenders of the château.

But what was Adamas doing at that supreme moment? Adamas was in the bowels of the earth.

The reader will remember hearing of a secret passage, by means of which Lucilio's escape was to be effected, in case of need. This passage passed under the moat and led to a sunken road which had been filled with gravel by the freshets of the last few years. Adamas had imagined that to clear the opening would require only a few hours' labor on the part of his ditchers. But the damage was more extensive than he supposed, and in three days they had not succeeded in making the passage practicable.

He went every evening to see what had been done during the day, and he was buried there during the battle, making his daily inspection, taking measurements, without the slightest suspicion of the tumult that reigned out-of-doors.

When he emerged from his hole, the entrance to which was under the staircase in the turret, he was like a drunken man for some moments and believed that he was dreaming; but, being a man of expedients, he speedily recovered his presence of mind.

He arrived just at the moment when the besieged fell back into the courtyard and the enemy were on the point of forcing their way in as well, everyone having lost his head.

Active and always well shod, like the true *homme de chambre* that he was, he gave but one bound to the tower of the *huisset* and dropped the portcullis in the face of the assailants, and, in fact, on the backs of some of them, so that the base of that instrument of exclusion did not reach the ground. He discovered it in time.

"Clindor!" he shouted to the bewildered page, who was preparing to close the gates behind the portcullis, "stay, stay! What's the reason that the portcullis doesn't fall? I still have a foot of it above the groove."

Clindor, who was not very brave, although he did his utmost to be, looked and recoiled in horror.

"I should think so," he said, "there are three men under it!"

"*Numes célestes*! our men! Look, I say, you triple sucking calf!"

"No, no, theirs."

"So much the better, by Mercury! Come here, quickly, some of you! Get on top of the portcullis! Bear down! bear down! Don't you see that those dead bodies will enable the living to crawl under the iron teeth, and that, when they are once under the archway, they will set fire to our gates! Down, down, you fellows! Break the heads of anyone who tries to pass, with hammers or feet or musket-butts. Mow them down with your scythe, living and dead, good Andoche! And you, Châtaignier, have you another charge?

Have at that red-nose protruding there! So! bravo! by the god Teutates, that is well! right in the mouth! That makes one less of them!"

Mingling thus eloquent appeals with colloquial phrases whereby he deigned to descend to the level of the common herd, Adamas had the satisfaction of seeing the portcullis flatten the bodies beneath it, and the assailants fall back to the end of the bridge.

"Now to the falconets!" he cried. "Move quicker than that, my Cupids! Come, come, ten thousand devils! Aim! aim! Make me a fricassee of these birds of darkness!"

The miniature artillery of the château disheartened the bandits, who had nothing with which to reply to it; so they carried away their wounded and decided, in default of anything better, to go and sack the abandoned farmhouse and banquet there.

They tossed live calves and sheep into the embers of the burned mill, whence there soon arose an acrid odor of burning wool. They pushed back with pitchforks the unfortunate creatures which sought to escape from that torture. They devoured them half raw, half charred. The casks in the farmhouse cellar were burst in. One and all became more or less intoxicated, even the children and the wounded. They threw the body of the ill-fated farmer into the fire, and they would have dealt out the same treatment to the two servants who were prisoners in their hands, except for the hope of ransom; and even so they spared them against the wishes of Sancho, who was unwilling to give quarter to anyone.

The old Spaniard did not think of eating or drinking or stealing. It was against his will that the Brilbault band had gone before the more useful auxiliaries whose arrival he awaited with impatience in order to consummate his vengeance. He was anxious, not lest he should lose his own life, for he had made up his mind beforehand to sacrifice that, but lest his undertaking should fail by reason of the haste and greed of the wretched creatures whom he had enlisted in it.

Being unable to hold them back until the hour at which it was arranged that his real allies should open the march and lead the expedition, he had accompanied them in order that no other than himself should have the privilege of torturing the *beaux messieurs de Bois-Doré*, if they should have the ill-luck to fall into the hands of those marauders.

In the heat of the battle, he, the only fanatically brave man in the party, had naturally taken his place at their head. But, when the battle was won, he ceased to be of any consequence to them; and soon, as we have seen, he took upon himself the duty of guarding the tower of the *huis*, where a surprise was to be feared, and whence he watched anxiously for the arrival of those who were to effect the capture and sacking of the château, and, as a result, the destruction of all those who had been concerned in D'Alvimar's death, either as cause or instrument.

If the people in the château were more prudent than those in the *basse-cour*, they were no more tranquil, and they hastily took all the measures necessary to defend themselves against a fresh attack.

They saw and heard the carousing of the bandits, and if they had chosen to sacrifice the farm-house, it would have been easy enough to dislodge them with their long muskets.

But not only did they hope for the arrival of reinforcements during the night, before the wretches should think of setting fire to the buildings in the *basse-cour*, but they were afraid to fire, because of the prisoners, the number of whom they did not know, and of the cattle, which were too large to be taken whole into the stomachs of those starved creatures.

They counted heads, and the absence of the unfortunate fellows who had fallen or been taken was discovered.

Adamas ordered all the useless people of the village into the stables. They gave the poor creatures plenty of fresh straw, bidding them keep perfectly quiet and lament in whispers, which it was not easy to induce them to do.

Lauriane and Mercedes busied themselves nursing the wounded and feeding the children.

Meanwhile Adamas posted his force at all the places exposed to the fire of the assailants, in such manner that they could neutralize it by their fire; and to prevent anyone from sleeping on his post, he passed his time going from one to another, distributing words of praise and encouragement, exhibiting hope, fear, or absolute confidence in the result of the siege, according to the temperament of each person he addressed. The shrewd Adamas, who had never handled any other weapon than the comb and the curling-iron, manifestly played the rôle of the fly on the coach, a rôle which he was able to make very useful, and which those who are familiar with Berrichon moderation and apathy know to be very necessary.

When everything was arranged, Adamas, worn out with fatigue and excitement, threw himself on a chair in the kitchen to take breath, were it for no more than five minutes, and to collect his wits.

His heart was very heavy, and he dared not confide his distress to anyone. He alone knew that Mario was not to accompany his father to

Brilbault, and that, if he were not already taken, he might arrive at any moment and fall into the hands of the enemy.

Neither Lauriane nor Mercedes shared his suffering; to avoid worrying them, the marquis had concealed his plans from them. So far as they knew, he had simply taken his people out for a *battue*. They had felt that something more serious was in the air, from his preoccupied manner and the frequent conferences he had held with his friends and servants throughout the day; but they were too well aware of his paternal affection to fear that he would expose Mario to any danger, and they both imagined that he would pass the night at the château of Ars or of Coudray.

Adamas was beset by innumerable perplexities, debating within himself whether he ought not to set everybody at work clearing the secret passage, in order to go out that way to meet Mario and send word to the marquis, at the same time enabling the women to escape. But he had measured the ground so many times that he knew that many hours' work would still be required, and during that time the château, being no longer guarded, might well be invaded. Then what would become of them, confined in that issueless underground passage, the entrance to which would not be likely to escape the notice of the plunderers?

He was interrupted in his agitated reflections by Clindor, who approached him on tiptoe.

"What are you doing here, you worthless page?" he demanded angrily.

And, forgetting that he was resting himself, he added:

"Is this a night to rest?"

"No, I know it isn't," replied the page; "but I am looking for——"

"For whom? Tell me quickly!"

"The coachman! haven't you seen him?"

"Aristandre? Have you seen him about here I ask, that you are looking for him? Answer me!"

"I haven't seen him in the château; but, as sure as you are sitting there, I saw him on the stone bridge, while they were fighting there."

"Death of my life! he isn't in the château, I will swear to that! But Mario! he was to bring Mario home! Did you see Mario?"

"No; I thought of him and I looked all about; Mario wasn't there."

"God be praised! If Mario had come with him, you wouldn't have seen one without the other. He wouldn't have gone a foot away from him. He wouldn't have taken part in the battle. Doubtless monsieur kept the child with him and sent the coachman back to tell us. But the poor coachman! You say that he was fighting?"

"Like thirty devils!"

"I am sure of it! and then what?"

"Then, then—the portcullis fell and I ran to shut the gates."

"Hell fire! perhaps it fell on—Here, take this torch, and come!"

"No, no! I saw the men that were crushed. He wasn't one of them."

"You didn't see clearly, you were frightened!"

"I, frightened! Upon my word!"

"No matter, come, I tell you!"

And Adamas ran and opened the gates and looked in fear and trembling at the bodies flattened under the iron teeth. They were so crushed and mutilated, that the ghastly spectacle caused the torch to fall from the page's hands.

Adamas rose with an oath; but, by the light of the smoking torch, sputtering and dying in the blood, he saw Aristandre standing beside him.

"Ah! my friend!" he cried, throwing his arms around his neck. "Mario! where is Mario?"

"Saved!" said the coachman, "and I too, but not without difficulty! A glass of gin or brandy, quick! my teeth are chattering and I don't want to die, *sacrebleu*! I may still be good for something inside here!"

"What a state you are in, my poor friend!" said Adamas, dragging him away to the kitchen, where Clindor gave him something to drink; "where the devil have you come from?"

"*Parbleu*! from the pond," replied the coachman, who was covered with mud; "how else could I have got in? For a quarter of an hour I have been stamping about in the grass and the mud."

He tore his clothes into strips and planted himself in front of the fire, saying:

"Look, Adamas, and see if I am not losing too much blood, and stop it for me, old fellow, for I feel very weak!"

Adamas examined him; he had something like ten wounds and as many bruises.

"*Numes célestes*!" cried Adamas; "I don't see a single sound spot on your poor corpse!"

"Corpse yourself!" cried the coachman, tossing off another bumper. "Do you take me for a ghost? To be sure I have come back from a long distance; but I'm better now; my hide's as thick as my horses', thank God! Don't let me bleed, that's all I ask. It's a bad thing for a man to lose all the blood in his body."

Adamas washed him and dressed his wounds with marvellous skill.

Thanks to the thickness of his skin and the herculean strength of his muscles, the wounded man had escaped serious injury.

"And the child?" said Adamas, as he dressed him in dry clothes which Clindor had brought; "was the child in danger?"

Aristandre told everything that had happened down to the time that he raised the stake of the *sarrasine*.

"The child got through," he said; "the beggars on the *moucharabi* fired at him but didn't hit him. I had that hound of a Sancho by the throat at that moment. I might have strangled him, but I let him go and ran out on the *moucharabi*, and I saw Mario running like the wind; then I fell on the other two curs. I had only a spade, but I routed them in fine shape, I tell you! Sancho came at me again with his broken rapier, and tried to scratch me with the hilt, I think, for he struck at my head and face when he couldn't reach my stomach. Ah! the old madman, how hard he strikes! And then, you see, I was already wounded and had not my strength! But it warmed me up a little all the same, because I had already swam across the pond once to join dear little Mario in the garden, and I was shivering. However, I couldn't make an end of the old devil, and that is all I regret. When I heard others coming to his assistance, I slipped down the staircase, and as his legs aren't so active as his arm is heavy, I succeeded in returning to the garden without his knowing where I had gone. And from there faith, I had no other choice than to come back here by way of the pond, and here I am!"

"Coachman!" cried Adamas, who, unlike many men, felt a sincere admiration for exploits of which he knew that he was incapable, "you are as great as Monsieur d'Urfé's greatest heroes! and if monsieur takes my advice, he will have you represented in tapestry in his salon, to perpetuate the memory of your courage and your stout heart."

"If it's only a question of being great," replied the artless Aristandre, "I can safely say that I have the size. But I am going to see my horses; after that, we will think about making a little sortie to clear the *basse-cour* of these vermin. What do you say about it, old fellow?"

The prudent Adamas was not heartily in favor of the plan.

While they are discussing projects of attack and defence, we will join Mario, who has just arrived in sight of the great tree by which the hill of Etalié is crowned to this day.

The child looked up at the stars which he had learned to know during his life among the shepherds: it was about half-past nine.

At that period there was a single house in that solitude; it was an inn and at the same time a sort of hunting rendezvous.

The hill, situated amid plains of vast extent and teeming with game, was often honored by the sojourn of noblemen of the province, who assembled to hunt the hare and to dine or sup at the sign of the *Geault-Rouge*.

This will explain the fact that an inn so small, situated so near a large town that it could not hope to entertain wealthy travellers, possessed in the person of Master Pignoux, landlord of the *Geault-Rouge*, a cook of the rarest excellence.

When the gentlemen of the neighborhood indulged in the sport of fishing in the ponds of Thevet, they always sent in haste for Master Pignoux, who would come with his wife, set up his canteen on the water's edge, and serve them, under some lovely arbor, those marvellous *matelotes* [6] —they were then called *étuvées*—which had made his reputation. He also went about to the towns and châteaux near by, for wedding and other festivals, and, it was said, could have taught Monsieur le Prince's master cooks a thing or two.

The *Geault-Rouge* was a solidly built structure, of two high stories, covered with tiles of a brilliant red which could be seen a league away. Through the influence of the noblemen of the neighborhood, Master Pignoux had obtained permission to put a vane on his roof, a privilege of the nobility to which he declared that he was entitled, as he so often had occasion to entertain the nobility. The incessant shrill shrieking of that vane, which seemed to be the objective point of all the winds of the plain, blended with the perpetual creaking of the great iron sign representing the *Geault-Rouge* in its glory, which swung haughtily at the end of a staff projecting from a window on the second floor.

Opposite the house, on the other side of the road, was a very large thatch-covered stable, and long sheds for the accommodation of the retinues by whom the noble sportsmen were commonly attended. The inn itself was specially reserved for the nobles themselves.

Everyone knows that in those days inns were distinguished as *hostelleries, gîtes* and *repues*. The *gîtes* gave special attention to providing lodging for the night, the *repues* to furnishing dinner for travellers; the latter were wretched taverns where well-to-do people stopped only in default of some better place, and where they were sometimes fed upon crow, ass's meat, and *Sancerre eels*, that is to say, snakes. The *gîtes*, on the contrary, were often very sumptuous.

Inns were also divided into those for people on foot and those for people on horseback. One could take two meals there. On the sign of the *Geault-Rouge* were these words, in huge letters:

HOSTELRY LICENSED BY THE KING

and below:

DINNER FOR MOUNTED TRAVELLERS, 12 SOLS;

LODGING FOR THE SAME, 20 SOLS

The inn-keeper's privilege was confirmed by letters-patent from the king. Pedestrians could not be entertained at an inn for the accommodation of mounted travellers, and *vice versa*.

"The French laws prevent the former from spending too much, the latter from spending too little." [7]

Mario, seeing that the inn was brilliantly lighted, was not surprised to hear his little horse neigh with pleasure when he was within two hundred yards. He supposed that he recognized his surroundings.

But he was surprised when he suddenly turned to the left and seemed unwilling to resume the straight road.

The child, who was on the alert, pricked up his ears. It seemed to him that he could hear the sound of horses's feet in the direction of the inn, which the night mist still prevented him from seeing distinctly. He was overjoyed.

"My father must be here," he said to himself, "with all his people; perhaps with Monsieur d'Ars and his suite. I will hurry on."

But Coquet required so much urging to go forward, that his young rider thought that he ought to try to fathom the intelligent creature's idea. He drew rein, and heard, much nearer at hand than the inn stable, the familiar neigh of Rosidor, the marquis's faithful palfrey.

"So my father is over there, is he?" he said to himself. "I must be careful not to pass him on the road."

And as he could distinguish nothing at his left except what seemed to be dense underbrush, he dropped the reins on Coquet's neck, feeling certain that he would find a way to join his stable companion.

Coquet entered the underbrush and halted in front of a dilapidated, tumble-down hovel.

It was the original *Geault-Rouge* inn, abandoned to its own destruction twenty years before; Bois-Doré, Guillaume and Monsieur Robin having cooperated to build the new one and present it to Master Pignoux as a token of their esteem for his probity and his culinary skill.

[6] A dish compounded of several sorts of fish, with an elaborate sauce.

[7] Monteil, *History of Frenchmen of Various Ranks*.

CHAPTER LI

Mario entered without difficulty, there being no door.

He put his hand upon Rosidor, whom he recognized by his accoutrements and his fine coat, as well as by his caressing voice; and the finding of his father's horse concealed in a ruin caused him to reflect.

He looked about, called his father cautiously, and, having satisfied himself that he was alone, conceived it to be his duty to imitate the example which seemed to be given him, by fastening Coquet beside Rosidor, and proceeding on foot, and as noiselessly as possible, toward the new inn.

He crept along the bushes and suddenly came upon a party of mounted men, who seemed to be pitching their camp in that place, some busied about their horses, which they were taking to the great stable opposite; others, who had already attended to that duty, stood in the road, exchanging in undertones and with a mysterious air words which Mario could not understand.

He glided among them unobserved; but when he stood in the doorway of the great kitchen of the inn, illuminated by the bright fire on the hearth which shone through the door, he felt a rough hand seize him by the collar, and a gruff voice said to him in French, but with a very pronounced German accent:

"No admittance!"

At the same time he saw two tall dark-skinned men, armed to the teeth, standing guard on each side of the door.

Thereupon Sancho's words recurred to his memory, and what Pilar had said of the reinforcement expected by the bandits.

"I have tumbled into a wasp's-nest," he thought; "but I am disguised and they will take me for a little beggar. I must find out if my father is here."

So he put out his hand and began to beg, in the piteous tone that he had heard the gypsies adopt and had sometimes adopted himself, laughing in his sleeve, during his travels with that honorable company.

They released him at once, but ordered him to go away, and, when he pretended not to understand, they threatened him by going through the motions of taking aim at him.

He was about to go, being fully determined to return, when another voice, coming from the inn, issued an order in German; whereupon, instead of turning him out-of-doors, they seized him by the collar again and pushed him into the kitchen.

There, before he had time to collect his thoughts, he found himself confronted by a tall, thin, dark individual, in military costume, who said to him with an Italian accent:

"Come here, boy, and if you have a letter, give it to me."

"I haven't any letter," replied Mario, looking the stranger in the face with perfect self-possession.

"A verbal message then, eh? Speak!"

"Before I speak," said the boy, with great presence of mind, "I must know to whom I am speaking."

"*Diable!*" said the stranger with a scornful smile, "we are a very wary youth; that is well enough! This is the countersign: *Saccage* and *Macabre*. What name has been given you?"

"La Flèche," replied Mario, at random.

"What? what is that?" said the Italian frowning. "There's no rhyme there."

"Wait!" cried Mario, inspired by that reply, "that isn't all. Isn't there a *pillage* in your countersign?"

"That rhymes better," said the other, smiling dismally; "but that isn't all yet, you little monkey! Your memory is failing you!"

"Perhaps so," said the child; "there's another word, I know. Isn't it Sancho?"

"There we are! Now then, stand in this corner and don't stir. I am Lieutenant Saccage; Captain Macabre will be here in a quarter of an hour. He's the one to whom you must give your message, which I care very little about, for my part. I say, you fellows, hold your tongues!" he shouted to the horsemen, who were going to and fro around the house, talking a little louder than seemed to be necessary.

Profound silence ensued, and he who styled himself Lieutenant Saccage said to Mario, who was meditating upon the means of gaining admittance to another room, to find his father or someone who could give him some news of him:

"My good friend, it is well that you should know the countersign, for your protection. We send away or arrest everyone who tries to enter this house; we fire on everyone who tries to go out. Do you understand that?"

"But I have no reason for trying to go out," replied Mario, cautiously; "I am looking round to see if there's anything to eat; I am hungry."

"That makes no difference to me, my boy. We are hungry too, and we're waiting for the captain to give us orders to eat."

Mario was not hungry. He was very anxious. In the room at the rear, which was a sort of pantry and serving-room, he saw Mistress Pignoux and her servant bustling about. It seemed to him that the former saw him and recognized him, and that she even spoke to the servant, as if to warn her not to mention the discovery.

But all this might well be a delusion, and Mario waited for a moment when Saccage's back should be turned, to try to exchange a word or a glance with the hostess. He knew that everybody in the house worshipped his father and himself.

He adopted the plan of pretending to fall asleep, and Saccage soon went out to give some order.

Thereupon the child rushed up to Madame Pignoux, saying:

"It is I! not a word! where is my father?"

"Upstairs!" replied Madame Pignoux hastily; although advanced in years, she was still a robust woman, with a firm foot and a keen eye.

She pointed to the wooden staircase leading to the dining-room, called the *salle d'honneur* at the *Geault-Rouge*.

But, as the child was already climbing the stairs, she detained him.

"No!" she said, "they don't know that he is here! Don't stir, my young master. They would kill him!"

"Who are these men?"

"A wicked lot! Do you know what *arêtes* are?"

"No! Wait a moment! Perhaps you mean *reitres*?"

"Yes, that's the word. My servant Jacques, who has served in the army, recognized them. They are brigands who burn and kill wherever they go."

"But they haven't done you any harm, have they?"

"No; they want food and drink; afterwards God only knows whether they won't burn the house and us with it! That's the way they pay their reckoning."

"Madame Pignoux, my father must escape from here! How can he do it?"

"Impossible at present! They are guarding all the doors, and your papa is too old to jump out of a window. Indeed, what would be the use? The house is surrounded, and they won't even let us go to the hen-coop and the cellar without following at our heels."

"But you must at least hide my father! Ah! I am very sure now that it's he they are after! Where is he?"

"In my man's room, who luckily isn't at home! He has gone to cook a wedding banquet at La Châtre and won't return till to-morrow. They called for him by name."

"Who? my father?"

"No, my man! I would like to know how it happens that they know him! I told them he was sick, and I said it very loud so that your papa could hear it upstairs. I hope that it will occur to him to get into bed."

"But didn't they suggest going upstairs?"

"Yes, indeed; they looked into the *salle d'honneur*, and they said——"

"But they are coming back; we must stop talking," said Mario.

And he hurried back to his corner in the kitchen and resumed his drowsy attitude.

"Come, old witch, make haste!" cried Saccage, returning with two of his followers; "lay the table and give us the best you have. Captain Macabre is here. Do you fellows see that the men observe the order: *Silence and patience!*" he said to his soldiers. "No one must think of eating before the captain is at the table. The captain halts here to obtain a good supper, and doesn't propose to have the pantry ransacked and nothing but bones left for him and his officers. Remember the fellows who were hanged at Linières for laying hands on the provisions! Go!—I spoke for your ears, madame she-ape," he added, addressing the hostess as soon as the soldiers had gone, "so that you might know that this is no time for snivelling and heaving sighs. Look alive and put on the spit. To work, I say! and if the joint is burned by your fault, look out for your old carcass!"

"How do you expect me to hurry, when I have to do everything almost alone?" said Madame Pignoux, unmoved by his insults. "There are only us two old women here. Let them give me back my servant so that he can lay the table. I can't be upstairs and down at the same time, can I?"

"Your servant is under suspicion, old woman. He acted as if he meant to run away when he saw us, and then he tried to hide the oats. He has had a good thrashing and is now working for us."

"Well, how about this urchin?" rejoined the hostess, talking away as she spitted her chickens; "is he one of your band? couldn't he help me?"

"Help her, good-for-naught," said Saccage to Mario, "and do your work neatly!"

Mario rose with affected indifference, and asked what he should do.

"What's that? go upstairs with the maid," cried Madame Pignoux, "and lay the cloth in a hurry."

Mario went up, and said to the servant:

"My father? which room is he in? Tell me quickly!"

She led him up to the second floor and the child scratched gently at the door, which was locked and bolted inside.

The marquis instantly recognized that little hand, which scratched so every morning at his bedroom door.

"O God!" he cried, hurriedly opening the door, "you here? But what does this costume mean? Whom did you come with? how? why?"

"I haven't any time to explain," replied Mario. "I am alone; I want you to escape from here. Do as I have done, father; disguise yourself."

"Yes, to be sure," said the servant; "here are master's clothes; put them on, monsieur le mar— —"

"No marquises!" said Mario; "leave us, my good girl; and you, father, shall be Master Pignoux."

"But why show myself?" observed the marquis, as he mechanically unbuttoned his vest; "I shall not be able to act a part as you do, my child."

"Yes, you will, yes, you will, my father! But, tell me, don't you know a *reitre* named Macabre? It seems to me I have heard you mention that name."

"Macabre? Yes, to be sure, I know that name and the man too, if it's the same one who— —"

"Is it a long time since he saw you?"

"The devil! yes! something like twenty or thirty years—perhaps more!"

"Well, that is all right! Show yourself without fear; play the inn-keeper, and we will find a way to escape."

"That will not be possible, my child," said the marquis, continuing to undress. "We have crafty rascals to deal with. Just fancy that they came up with no more noise than if it had been a troop of mules going at a footpace under the charge of a single man. I had no suspicion; the hostess was asleep in the chimney corner. I was in the living-room, reading *Astrée*, while waiting until it was time to start."

"Let us hide *Astrée*! Cooks do not read books bound in silk," said Mario, seizing the volume, which the marquis had instinctively placed beside his hat when he took possession of the inn-keeper's chamber.

And, as the marquis removed each piece of his clothing, the child concealed it also under the firewood in a small loft adjoining.

"But did they not recognize you as a gentleman, my poor child?" continued the marquis, intensely excited as we may believe. "*Mon Dieu*! have they done you no harm?"

"No, no; let us talk about you, father. Didn't you try to leave the house before they had stationed their sentinels?"

"No, certainly not. I had no suspicion! They made so little noise that I thought that some muleteer had stopped here; and not until they had surrounded the house did they raise their voices slightly, and then I saw through the window that I was caught in a trap by the worst sort of cutthroats and villains within my knowledge. I kept perfectly still, thinking that they would soon go away; but I heard some Italian words, which I partly understood. They intend, I believe, to stay here until daybreak. Thereupon I said to myself that my people, finding that I did not arrive at Brilbault, where I am expected at ten o'clock, would be anxious about me, and would come during the night to look for me here, where they know that I was to stop. It would be better to wait for them. There are only about a dozen of these *reitres*; I was able to count them pretty accurately, and when our people arrive I shall have no difficulty in cutting our way to them through these knaves with my sword."

"Father," said Mario, who was looking out of the window, "there are at least twenty-five of them! for here is another numerous party just riding up. Our people are not thinking as yet of coming to look for you, and at any moment these fellows may search the house from top to bottom for plunder."

"Well, my child, here I am disguised from top to toe. Stay with me, as if you were nursing the sick landlord. If they come up here, they will not disturb us. They maltreat and hold to ransom only well-dressed and well-mounted people. Ah! by the way, my horse will betray me. They must have seen him."

"Your horse is hidden, and so is mine."

"Really? Then it must have been that worthy ostler who found a way to put him out of sight. But what is the matter with the brigands that they are shouting so? Do you hear them?"

"They are calling me. Stay here, father; don't lock yourself in: that would arouse suspicion. Hark! they are going into the room below. I must go! Listen to everything; the partitions are very thin. Try to understand, and be all ready to come if I call you."

CHAPTER LII

Mario ran like a cat down the narrow staircase leading from the inn-keeper's chamber to the *salle d'honneur*, and found himself in the presence of Captain Macabre, who, at the same instant, entered the room with heavy tread by the staircase leading from the kitchen.

Lieutenant Saccage was also there with two or three other men of no less hang-dog aspect.

The appearance of the individual who bore the sinister name of Macabre was less repellent at first glance than his lieutenant's. The latter was treacherous and cold, with a fiendish laugh. Macabre's face indicated nothing worse than brutalized roughness, which strove to appear imposing.

There was no place for a smile upon that face stupefied by fatigue and dissipation. The muscles seemed to have grown stiff—to have become ossified; the light eyes had a fixed stare like eyes made of enamel. The strongly marked features resembled Mr. Punch's, minus the animated, sly expression. A great scar across the jaw had paralyzed one corner of the mouth and separated in a curious way the gray and red beard, which seemed to grow in different directions, and, as to part of it, against the grain. A great hairy mole emphasized the hump on his protuberant nose. His fingers bristled with gray hair to the roots of the nails.

He was short and thin, but broad-shouldered, and as compactly built as a wild-boar, with tawny coat and head set close to the shoulders, like that beast. He seemed quite old, but his appearance still indicated herculean strength. His rasping voice, still maintained at the high pitch of the military officer in the mouth of a fool, sounded like a peal of thunder with the influenza, and made the glasses on the table rattle.

He was dressed after the fashion of the *reitres*, in doublet and tassets of buffalo hide, with a helmet and breastplate of burnished iron. A wretched stripped black feather adorned that black and gleaming helmet. He carried the stout, broad German sword, against which the glistening lances of the French gendarmerie were easily shattered; flint-lock pistols, to which our soldiers foolishly preferred the old match-lock weapons; a short musket, and a bandoleer with little black leather compartments containing charges of powder and ball, completed this individual's campaign equipment.

His private escort, or, as was still said at this time, his *lance*, consisted of two carbineers for scouting purposes, and two *coutilliers*, who performed the twofold functions of pages and farriers.

He had also seven soldiers, well-armed and mounted as light-horse, who never left him, and who were the cream of his *cornette*, or troop of picked men. We may translate, in this way, by equivalent terms to those in use at this time, the titles and different grades of this tribe of foreign adventurers, whose organization, equipment and staff each leader modified, according to his whim or his power.

Mario had not erred in estimating at twenty-five men the band accompanying the captain, added to that already at the inn under his lieutenant's command.

"Here's a filthy tavern!" cried the captain in a disdainful tone, scraping the heavy soles of his great muddy boots on the clean and glistening rungs of a walnut chair. "What sort of a fire is that for travellers by night? Are you short of wood in this barrack?"

"Alas! monsieur," said the servant, tossing an armful of wood on the fire, which was already burning brightly, "we can do no better; this is a flat country and wood is scarce."

MACABRE AND HIS BAND AT THE INN.

*"Look you, my toothless beauty; this is the way
we warm ourselves when wood is dear!"*

*And he tossed the chair on which he had
just wiped his feet into the fire.*

"There's a stupid girl, and uglier, if possible, than her mistress!" rejoined the courteous Macabre. "Look you, my toothless beauty; this is the way we warm ourselves when wood is dear!"

And he tossed the chair on which he had just wiped his feet into the fire.

"And now, lieutenant," he continued coolly, turning to Saccage, "you say there's a little ragamuffin here, sent by those — — "

"Here you are at last!" replied Saccage, raising his foot to impel Mario more rapidly toward the venerable captain.

Mario eluded the outrage by darting nimbly under the *reitre's* foot, and, standing in front of the other brute, said to him coolly:

"I am here, and this is my message; for I gave your lieutenant the countersign. You cannot stay in this inn, because a large body of armed men is coming here to-night. You cannot attack the château, which is well guarded. You must go back where you came from, or you will get into trouble; Sancho sends this message to you."

"Your Sancho is truly an old ass," retorted the captain.

And he added, accompanying each word with an oath which it is hardly worth while to repeat in order to convey an idea of the charm of his conversation:

"I haven't travelled a hundred leagues through a hostile country to go back empty-handed. Go and tell the man who sent you that Captain Macabre knows the country better than he does and cares devilish little about a well-guarded château! Tell him that I have forty horsemen, for there are fifteen more behind me, who are coming on in charge of *my wife*, and that forty *reitres* are as good as an army. Come, off with you, and go to the devil, gypsy!"

"Don't send him away, captain," said Saccage, who seemed the more judicious member of the council; "it's of no use for us to have anything more to do with that Spanish lunatic and that gypsy scum. It is quite unnecessary to send this sharp young messenger to say that you are going on. They would follow us and would simply embarrass us and burn and rob all around us. Do what your wife told you. Stay here till midnight, and then you will arrive long before daybreak, for it's only two leagues from here to Briantes. So don't let this little fellow go. I'll throw him out of the window, if you choose; that will prevent his running."

"No! no unnecessary severity," bleated the captain in falsetto. "I have become a humane and gentle man since I have had a tender-hearted spouse. Is the house properly guarded?"

"A fly could not get in without my permission."

"Then let us sup in peace, as soon as my Proserpine arrives. Have you given orders?"

"Yes; but in spite of Madame Proserpine's fine promises about the comforts of this inn, we shall sup but poorly here, I am afraid. The wonderful cook of whom she said so much is in bed, at the point of death, and the woman is losing her wits. The servant is a traitor whom we have to watch, and the maid is a frightened old fool who breaks everything she touches and doesn't forward matters."

"That's because you speak harshly to them, my friend! You always have insults and threats on your lips! Ten thousand devils! as my wife has often told you, you lack tact. Where is this damned hostess? summon her, and let me restore courage to her belly with a cuff or two!"

Walking heavily to the stairs, he called Madame Pignoux, heaping the coarsest epithets upon her, apparently to set his lieutenant an example of mildness and courtesy.

This whole conversation was carried on in French.

Macabre, who was of German descent, was born at Bourges and had passed his early youth in Berry. Except for a somewhat extended vocabulary for use in his military capacity, he spoke the language of his fathers with difficulty and without pleasure. The Italian Saccage murdered French with more facility than German. Thus they had difficulty in understanding each other when they spoke the latter tongue, and moreover they considered themselves so entirely masters of the situation that they scorned to take any precautions before Mario and the people of the house. Mario, who had taken a great risk when he tried to make the *reitres* retrace their steps, and who was likely to be contradicted at any moment by some genuine messenger from Sancho or La Flèche, realized that it would be too audacious for him to insist for the moment. He feigned indifference and preoccupation as he laid the table, but did not lose a word of what the two adventurers said to each other.

It was quite true that Sancho had promised to send a messenger to Etalié, which he had designated as the last halting-place of the *reitres*. But that messenger, who was a gypsy like the rest, and who hoped that the château of Briantes might be taken and pillaged without the aid of the Germans, had no idea of doing the errand, but went in search of plunder in the deserted village, pending the time fixed for the assault upon the manor by his companions.

The hostess, in obedience to Macabre's polite summons, came upstairs and faced him bravely.

"What is the use of big words, Captain Macabre?" said she, putting her arms akimbo. "We know each other of old, and I know very well that you will pay your reckoning and that of your devils of *lansquenets* [8] with oaths and destruction of property. I don't receive you for my own pleasure, and I know very well that it is more likely to be for my ruin. But I am a reasonable woman and no more foolish than another. So I face ill fortune with a stout heart and serve you to the best of my ability, in order to escape bad treatment and be rid of your faces the sooner. If you are at all reasonable yourself, captain, you will say to yourself that you had better not injure me to no purpose, but let me alone, and remember that I know how to fry and roast as well as another."

"In God's name, who are you, old chatterbox?" said the captain, trying to turn his stiff neck in its iron gorget, in order to look at Madame Pignoux.

"My maiden name was Marie Mouton, and I was your cantinière during the siege of Sancerre; and one day I fricasseed a stale crust for you and you smacked your lips over it."

"That may be; I remember the crust, which was good, but not you, who are ugly. But if you have served the good cause, I forgive your chatter."

"And what do you call the good cause now? For you and your like have changed so many times!"

"Hold your tongue, my dear Bonbec. I don't talk religion with people of your sort."

"Understand, too," interposed Saccage with a sneer, "that the good cause is always the one we serve!"

"Is this the time for jabbering," continued Macabre, "when my Proserpine approaches and I order you to make haste?"

"I cannot work any faster," replied La Pignoux; "why did you call me upstairs?"

"Because I propose that your husband, who is supposed to be a decent sort of cook, shall get up, dead or alive, and put his hand to the dough."

"That is impossible; my man is all twisted up with pain, and hasn't cooked for a long time."

"You lie, my dear; your man is a tool of old—Enough! I know about you; my wife has told me——"

"Old who? what do you mean?"

"Methinks you question me, strumpet!" said the captain, with a burlesque dignity which he assumed in perfect good faith.

"Why not?" retorted the hostess. "And your wife, as you call her,—who is she, to have kept you so well informed?"

"Hold your tongue, and when my goddess arrives, serve her on your knees," said Macabre with a fatuous smile in which his crooked mouth extended to his left eye.

Then, recurring to his fixed idea, which was to feast bountifully and regale his goddess handsomely, he insisted that the inn-keeper should be made to get up.

"By hell!" exclaimed Saccage, drawing his sword, "there is no difficulty about that; I have always heard that you must grease stiff joints to make them work, and I will find a way to unearth this pretended dying man whatever hole he may be hiding in! Come with me, scouts! and run your swords everywhere, whether it's into flesh or marrow."

"That is unnecessary," said Mario, jumping in front of the unsheathed sword; "I will go and bring him; I know where Master Pignoux is! I know him, and when I tell him that he has the honor of receiving Captain Macabre in person, he will come at once."

"That is a pretty boy!" said Macabre, looking after Mario as he left the room. "I must give him to my wife to wait on her. She asks me every day for a trim little page."

"You will make nothing of a gypsy," said Saccage. "This imp has an impudent, sneering air."

"You are mistaken! I consider him very pretty myself!" rejoined the captain, who did not enjoy being contradicted too much, and with whom the lieutenant had been a little too outspoken for several days past, for reasons which we shall soon learn, and which Macabre was beginning to suspect.

The marquis, being anxious about Mario, was standing in a small passageway near the *salle d'honneur* and doing his utmost to hear everything; but his ear grasped only snatches of the conversation, and Mario, hurrying out in search of him, hastily told him what had taken place, in as few words as possible.

He had not time, nor indeed had he the inclination, to tell what was happening at Briantes; he felt that the marquis already had enough upon his mind to extricate himself from his present plight, and that he ought not to disturb him by giving him other motives for apprehension.

The *reitres* being as ignorant as he of the attack precipitated by the gypsies, there was no risk that the marquis would learn it from another mouth than his when the proper moment should arrive.

But would that moment arrive? The present situation would have seemed desperate to an experienced person, and the marquis, who knew only a part of it, deemed it very serious. But Mario had the happy faith of childhood: he saw only half of the danger.

"If we escape from here, as I hope," he thought, "my father and I will have a hearty laugh at the figure we cut at this moment!"

[8] The *reitres* were still called *lansquenets* in France, although they no longer carried lances.

CHAPTER LIII

In truth, the poor marquis, disguised as a cook, was very laughable.

He had done the work conscientiously. He had taken off his wig and concealed his bare skull beneath an oilcloth cap shaped like a cake-mould.

His face, thus bereft of its ebon curls, and smeared with soot, was not recognizable; nor were his great white hands, which were stained to correspond with his face.

He had succeeded in hiding his fine white shirt under a countryman's smock, and was shod in shabby felt slippers; a coarse apron, thrown over the whole, covered his broadcloth breeches, which were not very magnificent, for he had attired himself very simply for the projected nocturnal expedition to Brilbault, which circumstance proved to be very fortunate in this emergency.

Being informed by Mario that Macabre seemed to be a stupid, vainglorious clown, he realized that it was his cue to inspire confidence in him, and at the outset he saw that no flattery would be too rank for him to swallow.

"Illustrious and gallant captain," he said, bowing to the ground, "I beg you to excuse my poor fool of a wife, who did not know what a great warrior and scholar we had under our roof. It is quite true that I am ill with the gout, but your affable and martial air would bring the dead to life, and I remember too well my service under your banner not to be determined, though I must leave my life in my fires, to serve you to the extent of such small talents as heaven has given me."

"Good! good!" said Saccage to the captain, "there is nothing like threatening! They are all claiming to have served under you."

"That's all right," rejoined Macabre, "provided he serves me well now. And after all, monsieur le lieutenant, it's not impossible that the old fellow may have known me long ago, during the war in the province. I had enough share in it for everybody to remember me. Scullion! you may tell me of your campaigns at dessert, for I see from your manner and your gait that the gout hasn't spoiled the carriage of a soldier. You have a curious odor about you," he added, referring to the perfumes with which the marquis, despite his disguise, was thoroughly impregnated; "it smells like confectionery! No matter! I will bet that you have been a lansquenet in your day, eh?"

"I was one for a whole year," replied Bois-Doré, who knew by heart the whole of Master Pignoux's checkered existence and Macabre's villainous youth. "Why, I saw you worry the Huguenots of Bourges during the massacre in the prisons, in company with that terrible vine-dresser who was called *Le Grand Vinaigrier*."

"Oho!" cried the Italian, glancing at his captain with a mocking air, "didn't I tell you that you were a great Papist, my captain?"

"Everything in its season!" retorted Macabre, with philosophical tranquillity; "my father, who was the captain of the great tower of Bourges with the late Monsieur de Pisseloup, protected the poor heretics in the province as well as he could. For my part, I fired crooked when I couldn't do anything better. But I got back into the straight road, and I am more sincere than you, Monsieur l'Italien, with your relics hidden under your German breastplate."

The Italian made a sharp retort, and Macabre, angry with him for raising his voice in presence of his pages and his men-at-arms, although they understood very little French, bade him be silent, and asked the marquis what he could give him to eat.

Bois-Doré, who had referred to the incident of the Catholic massacres only to see in what waters young Macabre was sailing since he had grown old, felt more at ease.

This leader of partizans could not be acting under the patronage of the Prince de Condé. The marquis's knowledge was sufficiently extensive to enable him to talk of culinary matters like a man who knows his ground, and as, during his stay of two hours at the inn, he had discussed this momentous question with Madame Pignoux, to pass the time away, he was quite familiar with the contents of the pantry and the resources of the cellar.

"We shall have the honor to offer you," he said, "a quarter of wild-boar seasoned with spices, which will commend itself to you; a fine mess of Issoudun crabs cooked in beer— —"

"And well peppered, I hope," said the captain. "My wife loves highly-seasoned dishes."

"We will put in a taste of Spanish pimento."

And, having enumerated all the dishes, the marquis added:

"But would not your illustrious lady like some sweet dishes after the joint?"

"The devil! yes. I had nearly forgotten that she recommended a certain *omelette au musc*."

"Perhaps your lordship means *aux pistaches*? That is a dish of my own invention."

"The deuce you say! She told me that it was invented by the old man."

"The old man? Who dares, boast of having discovered before me the *omelette au riz* and *aux pistaches*?"

"Faith, old Bois-Doré, if I must mention that idiot of idiots in good company!"

Bois-Doré bit his lips.

"Who, pray, does the marquis the honor to repeat his absurd boasts?" he said. "Does madame your wife deign to know him?"

"It would seem so!" retorted Macabre, "and I know, also, my old rascal, that you are that triple hound of a false marquis's humble servant, and that he taught you how to cook; but I don't care a straw! You are watched and your ears will answer to me for your ragouts."

The marquis saw that he had no other resource than to speak ill of himself, and he did not spare himself, ridiculing his own rank and character in most amusing terms; but he could not decide to couple with his accursed and calumniated name the epithet *old*, which his contemporary Macabre insolently used to decry him.

The captain persisted in a most offensive way.

"That old dyspeptic must be pretty well broken up," he said, "for when I saw him last he was like a long lath, with no beard on his chin, and I nearly broke him in two by mistake."

"Indeed?" said Bois-Doré, recalling the youthful adventure which he had recently related to Adamas; "did you do him the honor of measuring swords with him?"

"No, my good man, I didn't stoop to that. He was on horseback, carrying munitions of war to our enemies. I took him by one leg and, stretching him at my feet, I left him for dead and seized his convoy."

"Which consisted of powder and ball?" queried Bois-Doré, unable to refrain from laughing inwardly at the absurd boasting of the man whom he had overturned with a kick, and at the remembrance of that famous stock of munitions of war, consisting of children's toys.

"It was a good capture!" replied the captain. "But we have talked enough, old jabberer! Go downstairs and have an eye to everything."

Bois-Doré, relegated to his ovens, was compelled to leave Mario, whom the captain detained.

As he left the room he cast a glance at his son: a glance of intense apprehension, which the child returned with one of the utmost confidence. He felt that Macabre was not ill-disposed toward him.

"Now, my boy," said the captain, "come here and tell me, if you can, who you are!"

"Faith, I don't know anything about it; captain," replied Mario, who had not had time as yet to forget the gypsy mode of speech; "I was stolen or picked up on the road somewhere by the dark-skinned devils called Egyptians."

"What can you do?"

"Three fine things," replied Mario, opportunely remembering La Flèche's lofty maxims: "fast, watch, and run; with that we can go a long way and get out of any scrape."

"He's a sharp boy," said Macabre, glancing at his lieutenant, who, to display his ill-humor, had turned his back on him, sitting astride his chair, his head and hands resting on the back, and his side to the fire. Macabre considered his position disrespectful, and told him so in cynical terms. Saccage rose without speaking and left the room.

Mario observed everything, and the discord between the two leaders seemed to him a good omen. He determined to take advantage of it, if possible, and if opportunity offered.

Macabre resumed the conversation with him.

"How does it happen," he said, "that I didn't see you at Brilbault last night?"

Mario was not long embarrassed by that question.

"I wasn't there," he said; "I was collecting chickens in the neighborhood, just to save them from the foxes and the pip."

"Do you know how to steal chickens? Well, that is a natural accomplishment which may be very useful. But tell me if the Spaniard finished his dying?"

"Monsieur d'Alvimar?" said Mario, beginning to understand Pilar's story, and no longer to look upon it as a dream.

"Yes, yes," said Macabre, "that dog of a Papist who turned my stomach with his prayers!"

"He died this morning."

"He did well, the lunatic! And what about Sancho? He's much more of a man; bigoted as he is, he understands matters. Where is he now?"

"He is hiding."

"Why doesn't he join me here?"

"As I told you, you are in danger here, and he knows it."

"What danger? Will old Pignoux betray us?"

"No, the poor man doesn't know anything at all about it; what could he do against you?"

"But from whom are we in danger?"

"A party of gentlemen who are looking for you at Brilbault at this moment, and who will soon pass here, with a big escort, on their way to sleep at Briantes."

"Did you see them?"

"Yes."

"How many of them are there?"

"Perhaps two hundred mounted men!" said Mario trying to frighten his man.

"So the plan is discovered, is it?" said Macabre, evidently shaken.

"It seems so!"

The captain seemed to reflect, in so far as his stony or, more accurately, his horny face could be said to denote any mental preoccupation.

Mario's heart beat fast under his rags. For a moment he thought that his stratagem would be successful and that Macabre would decide to retrace his steps. But the captain began to talk German with his scouts, who left the room at once, and Macabre resumed his graceful attitude, one leg thrown over the andiron, the other across the chair the lieutenant had left.

Mario ventured to question him.

"Well, captain," he said, "are you going to turn back?"

"To Linières? No, indeed, my little monkey! My horses are tired and my men too. For my own part I slept so tittle at Brilbault last night that I propose to make it up here. Woe to the man who disturbs me!"

These plans for slumber aroused hope anew in Mario's heart.

"If these people are very tired," he thought, "a moment will come when we shall be able to escape."

He did not, as the marquis did, rely upon the arrival of his friends and servants. Pilar, by advising them of the capture of the *basse-cour* at Briantes, would lead them to hurry thither instantly, expecting that the marquis would take the same direction; for the little gypsy, whose intellect was shrewd beyond her years, would not fail to tell them that Mario had started off to warn his father.

As he was making these reflections, Lieutenant Saccage re-entered the room, and, addressing Macabre, who was dozing before the fire, said in a half-humble, half-insolent tone:

"Allow me to inform you, captain, that, thanks to your plan of dividing us up into small parties, we lose much time; your wife and her party have not arrived, and if you sit a long while at table, as you usually do, our whole plan may fail. The proper course would be not to have a feast, but to eat quietly, sleep a couple of hours, and go forward before the passers-by have time to speed the news of our coming."

"Detain the passers-by!" rejoined Macabre, calmly. "Didn't we agree on that? You will have no great task, for we didn't meet a cat from Linières here, and this country's as empty as a church in '62. But these are useless words. I hear my Proserpine's voice. She comes! Let us go to meet her!"

As he spoke, Macabre rose with an effort and went down to the kitchen.

"The captain's growing old!" said Saccage, in Italian, to one of the farriers who stood like statues in front of the door.

"No," was the reply, "he has taken a wife, and that is worse! He thinks of nothing but carousing, and he doesn't know when it's time to march."

Mario, who was studying Latin with Lucilio, understood the substance of this colloquy, and followed the lieutenant and the two troopers to the kitchen.

As soon as he arrived there, paying no heed to the new arrivals who were crowding through the door, he glided to Bois-Doré's side, who was cooking for dear life with Madame Pignoux, saying to himself that the sooner the enemy was at table, the sooner there might be some opportunity to escape.

"Ah! here you are, my child," said the marquis in an undertone; "have they maltreated you?"

"No, no," said Mario, "the captain and I are on the best of terms. Let me help you, father. We can talk while they are not thinking about us."

"Very well, but we must not look at each other; watch me when I speak to the hostess.—Madame Pignoux, give me the butter!" he called aloud; then added in an undertone: "What is going on by the door, my good woman?"

"A lady dismounting from her horse. Don't turn round, she may happen to know you."

"Mustard, boy!" said the marquis, tapping Mario on the shoulder.— "Don't you turn either," he whispered in his ear.—"Madame Pignoux," leaning toward the hostess, "try to see her face."

"I don't recognize her," said La Pignoux; "she has a mass of hair and feathers. She's a powerful woman!"

CHAPTER LIV

Our three friends were standing at the end of the kitchen by the oven, with their backs to the door and their faces turned toward a window, through which they could see the figures of the sentinels walking to and fro outside, carbine in hand.

There were two on each side of the house; an unnecessarily large supply, for the house had only two doors, one opening on the road, the other of the pantry, opening on a small garden enclosed by a hedge.

All the windows on the ground-floor and first floor were provided with stout bars. It was hopeless to think of forcing their way out.

And yet the marquis sighed with impatience.

"Ah! my son, why are you here?" he said to Mario. "With this stout kitchen knife I could soon get rid of the two sentinels walking back and forth in front of the pantry door. But with you—I should not dare; I am a coward."

"And if my man was here," rejoined Madame Pignoux, "old as he is, he and Jacques would take care of the others. But I am very much afraid they have killed my poor servant! Good God! there he is! Just see how those devils have treated him! He's all covered with blood!"

Jacques le Bréchaud, so-called because he was gap-toothed, [9] was ugly, crafty and bad-tempered, but brave and devoted.

"Don't pay any attention to me," he said, "but give me a dish-clout to wipe my face."

"Why, they have split your head open, my poor fellow!" said the marquis, passing him his lace handkerchief, which he found in his breeches, pocket.

Mario seized the handkerchief, which might have betrayed their identity, and tossed it into the hot fire, where it disappeared like a match.

Jacques wiped away the blood and bandaged his wound with a napkin.

"Don't be alarmed," he said to Madame Pignoux; "they let me come here to wait on them. Give me the larding-knife, and the night shall not pass without my ripping up one or two of them."

"You will get yourself killed," said the hostess. "That's of no consequence," replied Jacques.

"But you will get us killed too!"

"Jacques," said the marquis, "look at this child, and don't say a word. Help him to leave this house, if you can, but be prudent if you love us."

Jacques glanced stealthily at Mario, and, without making any reply, went several times to the pantry, as if to attend to his duties, but in reality to examine the men who were pacing back and forth with the regularity of machines.

"Those German curs!" he said to the marquis, "they don't eat nor drink nor sleep until they have killed off everybody."

"And they know what discipline means too!" rejoined the marquis, with a sigh. "Ah! it can't be denied that the *reitres* are stout soldiers! If our good Henri had had ten thousand of them, he would have been king ten years earlier!"

"Cook, father, cook!" said Mario, "the lieutenant is looking at you!"

"He may look at me all he chooses, my son; I know how to handle a saucepan as well as Master Pignoux himself."

"That's the truth," said the hostess; "anyone would swear that you had studied cooking!"

"I studied it in the field, Madame Pignoux; I have made a fricassee for my Henri with my sword at my side and my helmet on my head. Who would have dreamed that I would ever do the same for a Macabre and his better half? She is some prostitute, I fancy!"

At that moment Madame Proserpine's voice rose above the others, which had drowned it thus far.

"Pah! how it smells of burned fat!" she exclaimed; "it is enough to make one sick! Let's go up; let's go up at once! Come, lieutenant, give me your hand, *sacrebleu!*"

Monsieur de Bois-Doré and his son glanced at each other then looked down into their saucepans.

This amazon, who, after conversing confidentially with the captain and lieutenant at the door of the inn, now strode slowly across the kitchen, resplendent in her warlike costume, and tossing beneath the multicolored plumes of her headgear her abundant bright red mane, this Madame Proserpine, the more or less lawful spouse of Captain Macabre, was the marquis's former housekeeper, Mario's personal enemy, Guillette Carcat of La Châtre, Bellinde of Briantes.

"We are lost," thought the marquis; "she will surely recognize us!"

"We are saved," thought Mario; "she does not recognize us!"

And, to make his disguise more complete, he too enveloped himself in an enormous apron which came to his chin, and passed his little soot-begrimed hands over his red cheeks.

Bellinde passed on without turning. But it was impossible to think of flight. *Madame* desired to be served instantly.

The ex-housekeeper, formerly a prudish and demure damsel, had undergone a sudden metamorphosis. On becoming the companion of an old swash-buckler, she had adopted the military manners and the imperious and shrewish tone which were the natural expression of her real nature, long held in restraint and glossed over at Briantes. Her person had developed with corresponding luxuriance. Being no longer obliged to indulge secretly in stolen liquors and delicacies, she had abandoned herself greedily to her gluttonous instincts. Being abundantly supplied with money, provisions and spirits by the forethought of Macabre, who always appropriated the lion's share of all booty, she drowned each day, in the fumes of debauchery, the remorse and disgust born of her subjection to a species of monster.

The pleasure of doing nothing but ride about the country and issue orders was also some compensation to her. The vicissitudes and excesses of her new life as an adventuress had speedily altered her features and almost doubled her size. Her face, naturally high-colored, had already taken on the blotched, purplish appearance of dissipation and over-indulgence. Proud of her luxuriant red mane, she allowed it to fall over her shoulders with absurd ostentation, and bedizened herself, without a trace of discernment, with all sorts of objects which Master Macabre had collected, more frequently by treachery than in honorable warfare.

Madame therefore was in haste to eat and drink, after a long journey in the saddle, and was overjoyed to think that she was to taste at last the fine cooking of Master Pignoux, which she had so often heard extolled at Briantes.

It mattered little to her that five-and-twenty stout troopers—they were miserable rascals by the way, we must not forget that—were waiting at the door with empty stomachs. The dissatisfaction which her conduct caused them did not disturb her in the slightest degree; she had no suspicion of it, her idiot of a husband having given her the rank of lieutenant and the command of a portion of his band, with whom she shared her booty when she was in good humor, and who were devoted to her from interested motives.

The fifteen brigands whom she had brought, and who took possession of the kitchen, while the others were relegated to the stables or ordered to mount guard, displayed at first the greatest eagerness in the preparation of her supper; they counted upon her leavings, and while some laid the table, hustling and abusing the inn servants, others spurred on Bois-Doré the *chef*, his supposed wife and Mario, the improvised turnspit, to satisfy the lieutenantess's appetite as speedily as possible.

For this reason they could not think of exchanging a word or looking toward the door. There was nothing to be done but cook, and cook they did with might and main.

This was one of the crises in the marquis's life, when he rose to the occasion.

He made ragouts worthy of a better fate, seasoned and dressed the dishes, greased the spider and turned the omelet with the graceful ease of a science which at last imposed respect on those cutthroats, despite their impatience.

As he was about to serve the soup, the marquis saw Jacques le Bréchaud put out his hand as if to put in more salt. He instinctively declined that uncalled-for assistance; but he was surprised to find that Jacques persisted, and, on taking hold of his hand he saw that the salt had a peculiar look.

"Let me do it," said Jacques, "they like their soup well-salted."

And his face wore a strange smile which impressed the marquis.

"No poison, Jacques!" he whispered; "that is cowardly, and cowardice brings bad luck! God alone can save us! Let us not anger God!"

Jacques dropped the rat poison with which he had proposed to season the soup for the charming guests of the *Geault-Rouge*. The marquis's generous and sentimental outburst was inexplicable to him; but he submitted to his ascendancy with a sort of superstitious awe.

Bois-Doré handed the soup and the whole first course to Madame Proserpine's bearded pages; he breathed a little more freely; they seemed disposed to give him somewhat more liberty.

Mario went to the door from time to time, indeed he might have made his escape at that moment by pretending to go out to the shed to fetch wood; but he was careful not to mention the fact to his father. He would have insisted upon his taking advantage of it, and not for anything in the world would the child have parted from him.

"If my father is to be killed," he thought, "I will die with him; but I shall not abandon the hope of saving him until the last moment."

Madame Pignoux also began to hope. Madame Proserpine's men seemed more insolent but somewhat less forbidding than those who had been in the kitchen before.

They were almost all Frenchmen and young. They issued their orders as cynically as the others; but there was a sort of boisterous gayety in their manner which might mean that they were good fellows at bottom, or, at least, that they might forget themselves for a moment.

But an order from the top of the stairs fell like a thunderbolt on the captives: Madame Proserpine summoned Master Pignoux and his wife to her presence.

"I will come, I am coming, as fast as I can!" cried the hostess, hurrying upstairs.

And she appeared before the lieutenantess and respectfully requested to know her wishes, taking care not to seem to recognize her, or else to humble herself before her as a personage of vastly greater consequence than the servant who used to take the marquis's little dogs out to walk.

"My orders were for your husband to appear also," observed La Bellinde, flattered by Madame Pignoux's submission. "Go and call him, my good woman."

"Excuse me," said La Pignoux, "my husband is in a terrible heat, and too much smoked up to appear in a dirty cap and apron before a lady like you."

"Do you think that you are more enticing, you old gallows-bird?" cried the captain. "Bah! you can't fool me. I want to see the face of your donkey of a husband, and no excuse will go down. Look you, rascals," he said to La Proserpine's attendants, "how happens it that when your lieutenant gives an order, you make her repeat it? Death of my life! Must I go myself and fetch that double-dyed traitor?"

At that moment, Bois-Doré, who had been compelled by force to ascend the staircase, was pushed into the room, and so roughly that he well-nigh fell on his knees at La Proserpine's feet.

Poor Mario followed, trembling with fear for him and with wrath against the villainous troopers. If his old father had fallen, the child would have lost patience and have defended him at the risk of being cut in pieces.

Luckily for them both, the marquis did not lose his head and determined to risk everything, staking his fate on the success of his disguise.

As luck would have it, Proserpine paid no heed to his features. She knew the genuine Pignoux very well; she did not deign to raise her eyes to his face at once, engrossed as she was by the exceedingly familiar homage paid to her by Lieutenant Saccage, who, being seated by her side, made the most of every moment when Macabre was not watching them closely.

Thus the marquis was able to take his stand behind Proserpine, in the attitude of a humble retainer awaiting orders; and, with a clever manœuvre he caused Mario to stand behind him.

"Ah! there you are at last, gallows-bird!" cried the captain, bringing his fist down on the table. "Your fear betrays your treachery, and I see through your vile schemes!"

Bois-Doré, believing that he was detected, was on the point of casting his disguise to the winds and making such use of the carving-knife as to be sure of dying without ignominy; but Mario was there and paralyzed his courage. In his uncertainty as to the meaning of the words addressed to him, he refrained from replying and thus allowing La Proserpine to hear his voice.

He contented himself by staring at Macabre with a self-possessed air. That was, although he did not know it, the wisest attitude he could assume.

"Zounds! will you speak?" roared the captain, who had seemed somewhat disturbed and was evidently reassured by his innocent air. "You play the simpleton, you miserable rascal! but you must know that by failing to come here yourself so that we could pull your ears to bring you to your senses, you disregarded all the rules and all the proprieties of your beastly trade."

Bois-Doré, being determined not to speak, made a gesture equivalent to an interrogation point, with a shake of the head which seemed to say: "What is all this about?"

"Have you lost your tongue, with which you chattered so fast a little while ago?" continued Macabre; "or have you never learned, you triple idiot, that a landlord ought always to be the first to taste the food and drink he provides? Do you think that I am so sure of you that I am willing to take the risk of poison? Come, be quick about it, you infernal beast, swallow what you see on this plate and in this goblet, or *mordieu!* I'll make you swallow my sword!"

As he spoke he pointed to a plate on which he had placed a portion of all the dishes on the table and a goblet filled with wine from all the jars.

The marquis was greatly relieved when he learned why he was wanted, especially as La Proserpine did not glance at him when he stooped over the table to take the plate and the glass.

The custom of requiring an inn-keeper to taste his dishes had fallen into disuse since the close of the great civil wars, in the central provinces at least; travellers had ceased to exercise that privilege, as inn-keepers had ceased to require travellers to disarm before entering their houses.

But Macabre acted as if he were in a conquered province, and it was useless to argue with the stronger party. So the marquis performed his task courageously, with a smile of disdain for the affront put upon his honor. He swallowed the contents of the plate and glass in silence, bestowing upon Jacques le Bréchaud an eloquent glance, which said:

"Generosity brings good luck, you see, Jacques!" And Jacques, who adored the marquis, crossed himself and returned to the kitchen.

[9] *Brèche-dents.*

CHAPTER LV

Everything went well.

Macabre and his subordinates, crushed by the haughty glance and haughty silence of the majestic cook, were delighted to be able to do honor to his toothsome dishes, and perhaps he would not have been required to appear again; but an unfortunate moment of distraction on his part spoiled everything.

La Proserpine dropped the feather fan which she carried in her belt, with a dagger and two pistols; and with the fatal instinct of courtesy which never failed him, even with respect to his housekeeper, the marquis stooped to pick up the trinket, which he handed to her with suppressed excitement, realizing his blunder too late.

There was an expression of surprise and uncertainty in La Proserpine's eyes for a moment, a moment that seemed as long as a century; at last the lady cried, putting her hand to her pistols:

"May I die in torment if this is Master Pignoux!"

"What? what does this mean?" cried Macabre in his turn. "Come here, old turnspit, and show your dirty snout to the company. By the death of the devil! if there's any trickery, and some scurvy spoil-sauce has usurped the duties of chief cook, I'll make a skimmer of his hide!"

The marquis did not listen to the brigand's threats; he felt that the crisis had come, and pushed Mario out of the room, saying:

"Go down stairs, my wife is calling you!"

Then he turned resolutely and faced La Proserpine, and looked her in the eye with that lofty dignity which only the brave man can summon to his aid against cowardly adversaries.

Despite her master's burlesque attire, Bellinde could not escape a sensation of respect and remorse. She held in her hands the life of the man whom she desired to humble and rob, but not to torture and murder. She hesitated another moment, then said:

"Faith, Master Pignoux, I do recognize you now! but *mordi*! you are much changed! Have you been very sick, pray?"

"Yes, madame," replied Bois-Doré, touched by her kindly impulse; "I have had a fatiguing time in my house since I was compelled to part with a person who served me well."

"I know whom you mean," rejoined Bellinde. "She was a treasure whom you didn't appreciate and turned out-of-doors like a dog. Yes, yes, I know how it happened. You were entirely in the wrong, and now you regret it! But it's too late, you see! she will never serve you again!"

"She will do well never to serve anyone, if she can do without it; but I flatter myself that, wherever she may be, she has not forgotten my generosity to her. I dismissed her without a word of reproach and did not treat her stingily; she may have told you so."

"Enough; we will speak of this later. Serve us with your best, and now go back to your work, old man. Go!"

As he went out, he saw her whisper to one of her men.

"We are saved!" he said to Mario in the hall. "She did not betray me, and she has given orders to let us go."

And the marquis, in his innocence, walked with Mario toward the kitchen door; but he was much mistaken: La Proserpine had, on the contrary, issued even stricter orders for the blockade.

So they had no choice but to continue to busy themselves with the composition of the famous *omelette aux pistaches*.

About an hour passed without any perceptible change in this absurd yet tragical situation.

There was a great uproar in the dining-room. Macabre was shouting and swearing and singing. There were alternations of brutal merriment and brutal rage.

This is what was taking place:

Lieutenant Saccage was as outspoken and concise as his name. It seemed ridiculous to him to prepare for a sharp and decisive blow, which demanded a swift and silent march, by a supper which he well knew would degenerate into a carouse.

Macabre was a desperado addicted to all the excesses which were the real motive of his expeditions. He had not, like his lieutenant, the qualities of the shrewd speculator, and, if I were not afraid of profaning words, I would say that, in his adventurous life, he wallowed in a sort of drunkenness, which was the poetry, a sombre and brutish sort of poetry, of that life. He was as much gypsy as thief, squandering all he acquired, and rich only by fits and starts.

The other amassed wealth in cold blood and put it aside. He understood business, spent nothing in dissipation, and was hoarding a fortune. In our day he would have been a sharper in higher station; he would have cheated in a black coat and lived in good society, instead of scouring the high roads and stripping wayfarers.

Each century has its own peculiar methods of traffic, and during the civil wars of the sixteenth and seventeenth centuries, brigandage was a regular branch of industry, conducted on business principles.

Saccage hoped to get rid of Macabre. He would not have dared to attack him in front; but he did as monsieur le prince did with the King of France: he urged his master into danger, calculating that a volley of musketry would carry him off and leave his place empty for him.

Guided by this idea, he strove to make himself agreeable to La Proserpine, who had charge of the cash-box and the jewel-case; and the lady, while handling her chance husband with care, did not discourage the embryo husband whom the chances of war might make useful to her at any moment.

This system of coquetry was beginning to be manifest to Macabre, and he was torn between his natural inclination to allow himself to be led by the nose, and his desire to discipline his goddess in vigorous fashion.

He was sorely tempted too, every moment in the day, to break the pitcher over his rival's head, but he realized how essential the lieutenant's activity and never-failing soundness of judgment were to him, who could never resign himself to the necessity of remaining sober and living on the alert.

So that, fatigued by this alternation of angry outbreaks and reconciliations, which was repeated at every halting-place, the captain adopted the plan of drowning his cares in the vintage of the hills of La Châtre, and, after talking much nonsense, began to feel an unconquerable longing to take a nap, with his nose amid the remains of a pie on his plate.

Not until then could Saccage talk seriously with Proserpine.

"You see, my Bradamante," he said, "that this old sot is good for nothing, and if you follow my advice we shall leave him here to sleep off his wine and go on and pillage the château. To-morrow, when we return, we will pick up our noble commander, who would simply serve to embarrass our expedition now."

Proserpine was nourishing a newly conceived idea, a bold and extraordinary idea, which she was careful not to impart to the lieutenant. She pretended to accede to his wish to make all necessary preparations for departure.

"Go and see that the whole party have something to eat," she said; "I will watch this sleeping man, and if he wakes I will give him more drink so that he will go to sleep again."

Saccage went down to the pantry, demanded that the whole stock of salt pork and dried meats should be delivered to him, and then went to the stable where his men and the captain's were quartered.

The provisions and the wine were distributed under his eyes with careful parsimony; he assured himself that the sentries were at their stations. Proserpine's men were at table in the kitchen, regaling themselves with the abundant broken meats from the officers' supper.

Meanwhile the amazon summoned the chief cook, who found her warming her stout, booted legs, in a masculine attitude. They were alone, for the captain was snoring in his pie.

"Sit you down, marquis, and let us talk," she said with a laughable air of condescension. "It is necessary that you should understand your situation and mine, and I will tell you much in a few words, for time presses."

The marquis seated himself without speaking.

"I must tell you," continued the lady-brigand, "that when you discharged me so discourteously from your château, I entered the service of Madame de Gartempe, who was going away to the Messin country in Lorraine, where she has large estates."

"I know it," said the marquis, "you were employed by a lady of rank, and you did not lower yourself. How does it happen— —"

"That I left her so soon? I had taken it into my head to be pious when I was with you, because one likes to do the opposite of what one's masters do; and that is why, finding my great lady too exacting for my conscience, I turned to the Reformers, which served to make her dismiss me, much more harshly than you did, I admit!

"About that time there came to the Messin country a band of adventurers of all nations, who had served under the gallant captain who is known thereabout as the Bastard of Mansfeld; they had been beaten by the

Emperor's Catholic troops on the other side of the Rhine and were seeking their fortune in Alsace and Lorraine.

"Everybody was terribly afraid of those people, I myself with the rest; but chance brought me in contact with one of them, whom you see here, who, having saved a tidy sum, had just dismissed his men and was thinking about returning to Bourges to settle down and end his days in peace. He remembered Berry so well that we soon became acquainted, and he offered me his heart and his hand.

"I don't know why I hesitated to bind myself to him; but one thing that is very certain, my dear marquis, is that your château will be taken to-night and burned to-morrow morning."

"So that is really the object of your expedition?" said the marquis, affecting perfect tranquillity. "Was it you who suggested that idea to Captain Macabre? I cannot believe that you are such a wicked and revengeful person as that."

"The idea did not come from me; but I unintentionally suggested it to this rapacious beast, by imprudently mentioning your treasure. He no sooner found out that you had such a thing than he overwhelmed me with questions, and I, having no idea what he was coming at, gave him enough details to satisfy him that it would be easy to seize it. The effect of my imprudent words was increased by some letters which I was imprudent enough to show him. One came from Monsieur Poulain, the other from Sancho. Both of them gave news of Monsieur d'Alvimar; both believed me to be still devoted to what they call good principles; and as it is a good thing to have friends everywhere, I took care not to let them know what company I was in. And so, my dear marquis, Macabre went off to Alsace one day and hunted up several of his old *reitres*; he enlisted some others who asked nothing better than to take the field again, and took for his second in command Lieutenant Saccage, who is a clever and intelligent man; and, when all that was done, he came to Linières, and went from there last night, with some of his men, to Brilbault, having arranged to meet the others to-night at this isolated inn."

Bois-Doré listened with close attention, but succeeded in concealing the surprise and anxiety which all these disclosures caused him.

Recalling the ghosts at Brilbault, he mechanically looked at the wall of the room in which he then was, and saw reproduced there the face with the huge hooked nose and long moustaches, together with the plumed helmet of Captain Macabre. It was the same profile that he had seen at Brilbault, and doubtless Poulain the rector, whom he had thought that he recognized, was also of the party. Moreover had he not heard from Proserpine's lips that D'Alvimar had survived the duel at La Rochaille?

He abstained from any reflection and confined himself to questioning the lady, who confirmed all his apprehensions.

D'Alvimar had been horrified beyond measure to find the Huguenot Macabre by his deathbed. But Sancho had sworn to join the *reitres*, with as many of the gypsies as would consent to accompany him, as soon as D'Alvimar had breathed his last.

"Macabre returned to Thevet this morning," added Proserpine, "where Saccage and I were waiting for him, with our people camped outside the town, where we were careful not to frighten or injure anybody. In that way, thanks to the caution and good discipline of our troopers, we have been able to ride more than a hundred leagues through France without once having to fight. We passed ourselves off as mercenaries sold to the king, and exhibited false commissions. By that means, you see, those of our men who may want to go and seek their fortune in the Huguenot camp or elsewhere will be able to get to Poitou. Macabre expects to give them a free rein, reserving the right to decamp with your booty if he sees that they are getting into any too unsavory business. And so, my dear marquis, we are in a fair way to ruin you, and, unluckily for you, you have thrown yourself into the hands of people who are fully determined to take your life."

"That is to say that my fate is in your hands," replied the marquis, "and you tell me so to make sure that I understand how grateful I ought to be to you. Rest assured, Bellinde, that my gratitude will not be confined to words, and that, if you will abandon the plan of leading these men to Briantes, it will be more profitable to you than to share my property with this band of thieves!"

"So far as that goes, I have told you, marquis, that I am not the leader; but I can assist you to get rid of the captain and make the lieutenant listen to reason, for he loves money better than fighting."

"So you want a ransom for me and the château, do you? In the first place, fix the amount for my person, which is, I confess, defenceless and in your power. As for the château — —"

"As for the château, you are thinking that, when you are once free, you will defend it! So you won't be free until we have got through with it, unless — —"

"Unless I pay?"

"Unless you sign, monsieur le marquis! for your signature is sacred to anyone who knows, as your faithful Bellinde does, what the honor of a gentleman like you is worth."

"What do you want me to sign?" said the marquis, readily resigned to his fate whenever money was in question.

Proserpine kept silence for an instant. Her face assumed an expression of diabolical malice, mingled nevertheless with a strange perturbation, as if she were somewhat inclined to blush for her temerity.

"Come, come," said the marquis, "speak, and let us have done with it at once, before your companion wakes."

"My companion is not my husband, as you must know, monsieur le marquis," replied the amazon in a mincing tone. "He is very ugly and very stupid—and, although you are no younger than he, you still have attractions—to which I have not always been so insensible as I seemed."

"What nonsense are you talking, my poor Bellinde? Come, a truce to jesting. Let us have done!"

"I am not jesting, marquis! I have always had an intense longing to be a woman of quality, and, if I must conclude, this is my last and only word: Be free! no ransom! Go, hurry home and defend your château, if I cannot prevent them from attacking it; and whatever the result of the affair may be, you will keep the promise you are going to put in writing, to make me your lawful wife and sole legatee."

"My wife, you!" cried the marquis, recoiling in utter stupefaction; "can you dream of such a thing? My legatee? when Mario——"

"Ah! there we are! the pretty boy is the stumbling-block. But never fear, I will treat him well if he behaves to me as he ought, and at my death your property can go back to him, provided that I am satisfied with him."

"You are mad, Bellinde!" cried the marquis, rising, "unless this is all a game——"

"It is not a game; and if you don't write at once what I demand," she said, rising in her turn, "why, death of my life! I will wake the captain and call my people upstairs!"

"Have me murdered, if you think best," replied Bois-Doré; "I will never give my consent to your mad whim! But understand that I will not allow my throat to be cut like a sheep, and that——"

The marquis, unsheathing his knife, had rushed toward the door to receive the assassins, whom Bellinde, suffocated with anger, was trying in vain to call, when Macabre suddenly staggered to his feet and threw at his *wife's* head a jug which would certainly have killed her if his hand had been steadier.

"Miserable slut!" he cried, chasing her about the room. "Ah! so you propose to marry your old marquis, do you? Perhaps you think I am deaf, and you don't know that Captain Macabre sleeps with one eye and one ear open! Stay here, marquis! I have nothing against you, for you refused the offers of this damned Potiphar. Stay here, I say! Help me catch this she-devil! I propose to wring her neck in proper form and make a drum-head of her skin!"

Despite these alluring invitations, the marquis, leaving the lovers at odds, had rushed into the hall, and Mario, terrified at the noise in the dining-room, had started to go to him. But they could neither go up nor down. On the one hand, Proserpine, pursued by Macabre, who was belaboring her with the rung of a chair, tumbled upon them on the stairs; on the other hand, the amazon's *reitres* rushed to the spot to adjust the conjugal dispute.

It was soon done.

La Proserpine, all dishevelled, rose and threw herself into the midst of them, and they, with no respect for the captain, seized him roughly, carried him back into the dining-room and locked him in there, laughing at his outcries and his threats.

Proserpine, accustomed to these tempests, was not long in recovering herself. She had no sooner swallowed a glass of gin, which one of her pages handed her, than she looked about with the eye of a bird of prey for her victim, who had taken refuge in a corner.

"The cook, the cook!" she cried. "Bring the cook before me."

CHAPTER LVI

They dragged forward the marquis and Mario, who clung desperately to him.

Bellinde recognized the child at the first glance, and her face, blanched by fear, flushed purple with savage joy.

"My friends," she cried, "we have the wild boar and the shote, and there's a chance for a handsome ransom for us, for us alone, you understand! no sharing with the Germans,"—she designated thus the captain's *reitres*,— "nor with Monsieur Saccage and his Italians! The Bois-Doré and the young one belong to us alone, and *vive la France, tudieu*! Pen, paper and ink—and quickly! The marquis must sign his ransom! I know all about his property, and I warrant you that he'll not conceal any of it from me! A thousand gold crowns for each of these fine fellows, do you hear, marquis? and for myself the promise that I asked of you."

"I will give you my whole fortune, wicked woman, if my son's life is spared. Give me the pen—give it to me!"

"No," replied Proserpine. "It is not your property alone that I want, but your name, and you must sign the promise of marriage."

The marquis would not have believed that the termagant would dare to announce her aspirations before witnesses. But the *reitres*, far from being scandalized, applauded, as if it were a most excellent trick, and the blood mounted to Bois-Doré's face in his intense abhorrence of the abject and absurd rôle assigned to him.

"You ask too much of me, madame," he said, shrugging his shoulders; "take my gold and my estates, but my honor——"

"Is that your last word, old idiot? Come hither, comrades! a rope, and string up this brat!"

As she spoke, the degraded creature pointed to a great iron hook suspended from the ceiling in the kitchen, which was used to support the weights of the huge spit.

In a twinkling they seized Mario, who exclaimed:

"Refuse! refuse, father! I will endure anything!"

But the marquis could not endure for a second the thought of seeing his child tortured.

"Give me the pen," he cried; "I consent! I will sign whatever you choose!"

"Let us give him a jerk or two all the same," said one of the brigands, beginning to attach the rope to Mario; "it will make the old fellow's handwriting freer."

"Yes, do so," said Proserpine. "That wicked child well deserves it."

The marquis became frantic; but he soon calmed down when he looked at his poor child, whose cheeks were white with terror despite his courage. It was useless to resist. Mario was in their power.

Bois-Doré fell at Proserpine's feet.

"Do not torture my child!" he cried; "I yield, I submit, I will marry you; what more do you want than my word?"

"I want your hand and seal," was the reply.

The marquis took the pen in his trembling hand, and wrote at the dictation of that fury:

"I, Sylvain-Jean-Pierre-Louis Bouron du Noyer, Marquis de Bois-Doré, do promise and swear to Demoiselle Guillette Carcat, *alias* Bellinde, *alias* Proserpine — —"

At that point a terrible uproar was heard outside, and Proserpine's men rushed to the door.

The tumult was caused by the captain's Germans, who, being summoned by him from the window, hastened to set him free. The guards at the door were Italians of Saccage's command, and their orders were not to allow any person to go in or out.

The three troops were constantly quarrelling among themselves, like their leaders, who upheld their own men while striving to keep them apart. But this time it was impossible; Saccage, who had also been attracted by Macabre's outcries, and thought that Proserpine was in the act of doing away with her tyrant, exerted himself to prevent the Germans from going to his assistance. As for the lieutenantess's Frenchmen, they had no love for either of the other factions; and they all began to attack one another, without resorting to their weapons as yet, but abusing one another savagely, and fighting with hands and feet.

This uproar was accompanied by the crashing of furniture in the room above, where Macabre was fighting like a demon to set himself free, and by the piercing shrieks of La Proserpine encouraging her partizans, for she was beginning to fear for her own life if they should be worsted.

We may imagine that the marquis did not await the result of the combat before thinking of flight. In one bound he was at his son's side, trying to unbind him, but the knot was so artistically tied that, in his excitement, he was unable to untie it.

"Cut it! cut it!" said Madame Pignoux.

But the old man's hand trembled convulsively. He was afraid of wounding the child with the knife.

"Let me do it!" said Mario, pushing them both away.

And with perfect self-possession he skilfully untied the knot.

The marquis took him in his arms and followed the landlady and her maid-servant, whom he saw running toward the pantry.

As he left the house he nearly fell at the threshold. A body lay across the doorway; it was Jacques le Bréchaud's. He was dead; but beside him lay the bodies of two *reitres*, one run through with a spit, the other half beheaded with the larding-knife, Jacques had had his revenge, and had cleared the path. His ugly but powerful face wore a terrifying expression; it seemed to be contracted by a triumphant laugh, and the teeth were parted as if they would bite.

The marquis saw at a glance that there was nothing to be done for the poor fellow. He held Mario close to his breast and ran as fast as he could.

"Put me down," said the child, "we can run better. Please put me down!"

But the marquis fancied that he could hear the clicking of the terrible flint-lock pistols behind him, and he wished to make his body a rampart for his son.

When he found that he was out of range, he decided to let him run too, and they hurried toward the thicket where the half-ruined roof of the former hostelry lay hidden.

As they ran they saw Madame Pignoux and her servant also making their escape. Those two old women made their hearts ache. But to call them would be to destroy them and themselves with them. They were running across the fields, apparently heading for some hiding place known to them as a place of safety.

The Beaux Messieurs de Bois-Doré leaped upon their horses. They were very careful not to descend the Terrier by the road, but took one of the narrow paths, bordered by tall blackthorns, which wind about between the fields.

The battle of the *reitres* might end abruptly at any moment. They were well mounted and able to follow close upon their prey; but the light gallop of Rosidor and Coquet made little noise on the wet earth, and as the path they were following was constantly intersected by others, the pursuers would have to separate to overtake them.

The first and most essential thing was to gain ground; so the Bois-Dorés thought of nothing at first but throwing the enemy off the scent by plunging at random into that labyrinth of muddy paths, which became blinder and blinder as they approached the valley.

After about ten minutes of hard riding, the marquis drew rein and bade Mario do likewise.

"Halt!" he said, "and open your sharp ears. Are we pursued?"

Mario listened, but the hard breathing of his breathless horse prevented him from hearing well.

He dismounted, walked away a few steps and returned.

"I can hear nothing," he said.

"So much the worse!" said the marquis; "they have finished fighting and they must be thinking of us. Mount again quickly, my boy, and let us ride on. We must succeed in reaching Brilbault, where our friends and servants are."

"No, father, no," said Mario, who was already in the saddle. "There is no one left at Brilbault now. We must ride to Briantes by the cross-road. Oh! please don't hesitate, father, and be sure that I am right. I am perfectly certain of what I say."

Bois-Doré yielded without understanding. It was no time for discussion.

They rode in a straight line toward the hamlet of Lacs, through the great grain-growing tract which, as it all belonged to the seignioral estate of Montlevy, was not, at that time, cut up into many smaller parcels enclosed by hedges.

Our fugitives rode half the distance without seeing any bands of mounted men on the road, which they followed on a parallel line at a distance of two or three gun-shots.

To the marquis's mind this was a bad sign. The quarrel among the *reitres* could not have been prolonged until then. As soon as the Germans discovered that Macabre was not being assassinated, but was simply locked into the room because of drunkenness, the whole trouble would subside, and La Proserpine was not the woman to forget the prisoners, for whom she hoped to obtain a substantial ransom, if nothing more.

"If they don't come down upon us by the travelled road," thought the marquis, "it must be because they have seen us crossing the flat, and are waiting for us by the wood of Veille, in the sunken roads with which Bellinde is probably familiar. Perhaps the knaves are nearer to us than we think; for the mist is becoming dense, and I am beginning to be doubtful whether those figures I see yonder are young oaks or mounted men waiting for us."

He stopped Mario again to tell him of his apprehensions.

Mario looked at the trees and said:

"Let us go on! there are no mounted men there."

They rode forward. But as they skirted the copse which, at that time, extended to the farm of Aubiers, they suddenly found themselves at close quarters with a party of horsemen who were approaching at their right, and who shouted "Halt!" in resounding tones.

They were French voices, but Bellinde's adventurers were Frenchmen.

The marquis hesitated an instant. It was no easy matter to recognize those men, who were still in the shadow of the trees, while the Bois-Dorés were far enough in the open to be fully exposed to them.

"Let us ride straight on!" said Mario. "If they are not enemies, we shall soon find it out."

"*Vive Dieu!*" replied the marquis, "they must be the *reitres*, for they are following us! Ride hard, my dear child."

And he thought:

"May God give my poor horses strength of leg!"

But the horses had travelled too far over the heavy ploughed land not to have lost their first freshness, and the men behind them pressed them so close that the marquis expected every moment to hear bullets whistling about his ears. He lost ground by trying, in spite of Mario's remonstrances, to keep behind him so that he might receive the first discharge.

One horseman, better mounted than the rest, almost overtook him and shouted:

"Will you stop, you knave, or must I kill you?"

"God be praised, it is Guillaume!" cried Mario; "I know his voice!"

They turned about and were not a little surprised when Guillaume charged upon them and threatened to pull the marquis from his horse.

"How now, cousin!" said Bois-Doré; "don't you recognize me?"

"Ah! who in the devil would recognize you in that rig?" replied Guillaume. "What is that white thing you have on your head, cousin, and what sort of a petticoat are you wearing floating about your hips? I was most anxious for news of you; then, when we approached, I thought that I recognized your horse and Mario's. But I concluded that you were robbers who had stolen the horses, perhaps after murdering you! Can that be Mario? Upon my word, you are both arrayed in strange fashion!"

"True," said the marquis, remembering his kitchen apron and his oilcloth cap, which he had not thought, nor indeed had leisure to remove; "I am not equipped as a warrior, and you will oblige me, cousin, by supplying me with a hat and arms, for I have nothing but a kitchen knife at my side, and we may have a fight on our hands at any moment."

"Here, here," said Guillaume, handing him his own hat, and the weapons of his most trusty servant; "put them on quickly and let us not delay; for it seems that your château is in danger."

Bois-Doré thought that Guillaume was ill-informed.

"No," he said, "the *reitres* were still at Etalié half an hour ago."

"The *reitres* at Etalié?" exclaimed Guillaume. "In that case we have nothing to lose by hurrying, unless we want to be caught between two fires!"

There was no time for explanations; they galloped at full speed toward Briantes.

On the way Guillaume's troop was increased by Bois-Doré's servants, who, after a vain search at Brilbault, had received the little gypsy's warning, and were returning to the château at all risks, not placing much faith in her message, but believing it to be some ruse on the part of her comrades to throw them off the scent.

They had decided to return only because Pilar had told them that their master was warned and was himself returning; having failed to meet him at the general rendezvous at Brilbault, they had concluded that the warning, whether true or false, had been conveyed to him, and that it would be useless to go to Etalié in search of him.

CHAPTER LVII

Monsieur Robin had not believed a word of Pilar's story. He had started none the less with his escort, but had made no great haste, and it was to be feared that he had fallen in with the *reitres*, for when the others came in sight of Briantes he had not overtaken them.

They were anxious too concerning Master Jovelin, who had started first for Brilbault with five or six of the Briantes men, and whom they were surprised not to pick up on the road, for they had ridden very fast; so fast that they had no time to communicate these reflections to one another.

In many novels I have read of long conversations carried on between the characters while their horses were cleaving the air and devouring space; but I have never been able to understand how such a thing could be possible in real life.

Although it was about one o'clock in the morning, it was as light as at noon-day when they rode through the village. The farm-buildings were in flames.

At that sight all doubt was at an end, and they rushed forward to attack the tower of the *huis*, which was closed and defended by Sancho and a few gypsies hastily collected by him when he first heard the gallop of the new-comers.

"What are we doing here, cousin?" said Guillaume to the marquis. "Our people are too much carried away by their ardor and do not wait for orders from anyone. We shall lose our best men, and probably gain nothing! Let us take measures to work in a useful way."

"Yes, to be sure," replied Bois-Doré, "try to keep them back. A moment more or less will not prevent my barn from burning; I care more for the lives of those good Christians than for all my crops. Call them back and calm them! I must attend first of all to this child, who causes me much anxiety."

As he spoke the marquis led Mario aside.

"My son," he said, "give me your word as a gentleman not to stir until I call you."

"Why, father!" cried Mario in dismay, "you talk to me just as Aristandre did a little while ago, and treat me like a baby in arms! Are these the lessons in honor and gallantry you give me to-day, when you — —"

"Silence, monsieur, and obey!" said the marquis, speaking to his beloved son for the first time in an imperious tone. "You are not old enough yet to fight, and I forbid it!"

Great tears came to the child's eyes. The marquis looked away to avoid seeing them, and leaving Mario in charge of a small reserve force of his faithful servants, he hastened to join Guillaume d'Ars, who had succeeded in reducing his forces to order and submission.

"It is quite useless," said the marquis, "to try to force the *huis*; two men can hold it for an hour unless we choose to sacrifice a score of our own men. Ah! cousin, it is all very well to fortify the *entrances* to the château, but it is extremely inconvenient when you want to get in yourself. The moat is fifteen feet deep at this point, and the bank is so steep, you see, that swimmers cannot land without being shot down from the *moucharabi*. Do you know what we must do? Look! The barn has fallen in. Well, it must have fallen into the moat and partly filled it. That is where we must force our way in. I will go there with my people. Do you stay here as if you were looking for boards and timbers to replace the drawbridge, which is hoisted, to mislead the enemy, whom you will prevent from escaping when we fall upon him. We, my friends," he said to his servants, "will steal quietly along behind the wall; its shadow will conceal us, notwithstanding the bright fire that is consuming our crops."

The marquis's plan was very judicious, and what he foresaw had actually taken place. The moat was partly filled up and the wall crushed by the fall of the barn. But it was necessary to pass over blazing débris and through billows of flame and smoke. The horses recoiled in fright.

"Dismount, my friends, dismount!" cried the marquis, riding forward at a gallop into that hell.

Rosidor alone plunged fearlessly into it, leaped all the obstacles with marvellous agility, and, heedless of the risk of scorching his beautiful mane and the ribbons with which it was tressed, gallantly bore his master into the centre of the enclosure.

The marquis's luxuriant hair was in no danger. It was still reposing under the firewood at the *Geault-Rouge*.

His servants, already intensely wrought up by the desire to rejoin and rescue or else to avenge, their families, were electrified by their master's courage, and several of them followed him closely enough to prevent his falling into the hands of the enemy. But just as the bulk of the party were passing over the red-hot ruins, a shout of alarm uttered by one of the peasants of whom the party consisted, caused all the rest to halt and rush back in deadly terror.

The high gable end of the barn, which was still standing, began to crack under the action of the intense heat, and swayed outward, threatening to crush anyone who should attempt to pass. If they waited a second it would fall; then they would pass, however difficult the undertaking. That is what everyone thought, and they all waited. But seconds and minutes succeeded one another and the wall did not fall. And those seconds and minutes were centuries in the plight in which the marquis was at that instant. With about half a score of his men, he was face to face with the whole troop of gypsies, still numbering about thirty combatants.

Four hours had passed since Mario had escaped under the *sarrasine*; and in those four hours the bandits had not once thought of gorging themselves again. The first intoxication of their victory and the first gluttony of their appetite had soon given place to the persistent hope of obtaining possession of the château. They had tried all methods to make their way in by surprise. Several of them had fallen, thanks to the vigilance of Adamas and Aristandre, seconded by the presence of mind, sound advice and incessant activity of Lauriane and the Moor. Finding all their efforts unavailing, they had set fire to the barn, hoping to induce the besieged to make a sortie in order to save the buildings and crops. Not without expending vast treasures of eloquence did the sage Adamas succeed in restraining Aristandre, who would have thrown himself head foremost into the trap. Indeed it was necessary for Lauriane to exert her authority, and to point out to him that, if he should fall in his undertaking, all the poor creatures shut up in the château, beginning with herself, were irrevocably lost.

During the hour that the barn had been burning, Aristandre, in a frenzy of exasperation, had exhausted all the oaths and imprecations in his vocabulary. Condemned to inaction, he was fuming and fretting, and even cursing Adamas and Lauriane, Mercedes and young Clindor, who also preached patience—in a word all those who prevented him from acting—when Adamas, who had climbed to the top of the tower-staircase, shouted to him from the cupola:

"Monsieur is there! monsieur is there! I can't see him, but he is there. I will swear to it! for they are fighting, and I am sure that I recognized his voice above all the rest."

"Yes, yes!" cried Mercedes from one of the windows on the courtyard; "Mario must be there, for little Fleurial is like a mad creature; he has smelt him. Look! I cannot hold him!"

"Aristandre!" cried Lauriane, "go out! Let us all go out; it is time!"

Aristandre had already gone. Heedless whether anybody followed him or not, he darted to the marquis's side and delivered him from La Flèche, who, supple as a snake, had leaped to the saddle behind him, and was suffocating him in his wiry, muscular arms, but could not succeed in unhorsing him.

Aristandre seized the gypsy by one leg, at the risk of dragging the marquis with him. He hurled him to the ground and trampled upon him, taking care to crush his ribs; then, leaving him there, dead or unconscious, he threw himself upon the others.

The servants of the château had gone out also, even Clindor, and even poor little Fleurial, who slipped through the legs of the excited Moor, ran between the legs of the marquis, who was too much engrossed to notice him, and at last disappeared in the hurly-burly, to go in search of Mario.

Lauriane, intensely excited, armed herself and attempted to go out.

"In heaven's name," said Adamas, placing himself in front of her, "do not do that! If monsieur sees that his dear daughter is in danger, he will lose his wits, and you will be responsible for his being killed. And then you see, madame, there is nobody left here to help me close the gate, which may be the salvation of our friends. Who knows what may happen? Stay here to help me in case of need."

"But the Moor has gone!" cried Lauriane. "Look, Adamas, look! the dear creature is looking for Mario! She is following the little dog! Great heaven! great heaven! Mercedes, come back! you will be killed!"

Mercedes could not hear amid the din of the battle. Indeed, she did not choose to hear: she was thinking of her child and nothing else. She was literally passing through fire and steel; she would have passed through granite.

The marquis and Aristandre, being gallantly supported, were soon masters of the field, and began to force the gypsies back; a part toward the ruins of the barn, a part toward the tower of the *huis*. Those who passed the high wall of the barn, heedless of its impending fall, were greeted with pikes and clubs by the vassals of Bois-Doré, who had begun to cross that dreaded strip of territory.

They killed and captured several of them. The others turned back, and the whole band, now numbering no more than a score, retreated along the wall and entered the archway of the *huis*.

"Put out the fire!" cried Bois-Doré, seeing that it was spreading to the other farm buildings, "and leave us to complete the rout of these curs!"

He addressed the peasants and the women and children who had ventured forth from the château; then hurried away with his servants to the vaulted archway, where a strange battle was in progress between the fleeing bandits and Sancho, the sole guardian of the exit.

Sancho was guided by a single implacable idea. He had seen the marquis place Mario, with an escort, out of range behind a house in the village. The child was well sheltered and well guarded. But it was impossible that he would not, sooner or later, leave that shelter and come within range of an arquebus.

Sancho was standing there on the watch, his gun-barrel resting on one of the crenellations of the *moucharabi*, his body well hidden, his eye fixed on the corner of the wall at which his prey would appear sooner or later. The dark-browed Spaniard had the incalculable advantage that no anxiety concerning his own life could turn him aside from his purpose. He had no thought of the morrow in his mind, nor even of the passing moment, pregnant with perils. He asked of heaven but a single moment to gloat over and accomplish his revenge.

And so, when the routed gypsies came and threw themselves, howling with fear, against the heavy stakes of the *sarrasine*, Sancho moved no more than the stones of the arch. In vain did frantic, desperate voices shout to him:

"The bridge! the portcullis! the bridge!"

He was deaf; of what consequence were his confederates in his eyes?

The gypsies were compelled to rush to the *chambre de manœuvre*, in order to set themselves free. Their wives and children uttered piteous cries.

It was a counterpart of the scene of terror and confusion that had taken place on that same spot a few hours earlier, among the bewildered vassals of the estate.

Bois-Doré, still mounted and surrounded by his men, had all that was left of that horde of thieves and murderers in a cage. Their women, who had become veritable furies in defence of their children, turned upon him in the frenzy of desperation.

"Surrender! surrender all of you!" cried the marquis, seized with compassion; "I will spare you for the sake of the children!"

But no one surrendered: the miserable wretches did not believe in the generosity of the victor. They did not understand kindness—a rare quality among the noblemen of that period, we must agree.

The marquis was compelled to restrain his men, in order, as he said afterward, to prevent a *massacre of the innocents*, if, indeed, there were any innocents among those little savages, already trained to all the wickedness of which they were capable.

At last the *sarrasine* was raised and the bridge lowered.

Guillaume, who was as generous as the marquis, would have spared the weak; but, to the great surprise of Bois-Doré, the fugitives passed unhindered. Guillaume and his force were not there.

"Ten thousand devils!" cried Aristandre, "those demons will escape. Forward! forward! after them! Ah! monsieur, we ought to have chopped them up into small pieces while we had them here!"

He hurried away in pursuit, leaving the marquis alone under the archway, now open and unobstructed. He was very anxious concerning Mario, but dared not ride across the bridge for fear of riding down his own men, who were on foot and crowding across that narrow thoroughfare to overtake the fugitives.

At last the bridge was clear. Victors and vanquished had passed out of sight. The marquis was able to cross, and saw Mario coming toward him on his right. The child thought that he might safely leave his place of shelter now that the affray seemed to be at an end.

So far as the bandits were concerned, there was apparently no further danger; the fugitives had no thought but to escape as best they could in any direction; some concealed themselves here and there with much art, while the pursuers passed on.

A single one of the defeated assailants had not stirred, and no one gave a thought to him: that one was Sancho, who was still on his knees, completely hidden, in a corner of the *moucharabi*. From that little machicolated gallery he could have hurled stones down upon the men of Briantes, for there was always a supply of them in the *chambre de manœuvre*, of convenient size in respect to the openings. But Sancho did not desire to betray his presence. He wished to live a few moments longer; he was watching Mario approach, and taking aim at his leisure, when he saw the marquis at the other end of the bridge, much nearer, almost within reach.

Thereupon a violent conflict took place in his mind. Which victim should he select? In those days there were no double-barreled guns. The distance between the father and the child was too short to allow him to reload.

In his struggle with Aristandre, Sancho had broken one of his pistols, while the other was snatched from him by that powerful antagonist.

By a refinement of vindictive hatred, Sancho decided to kill Mario. To see him die would surely be more agonizing to the marquis than to die himself.

But that moment of hesitation had disturbed the equanimity of that cold-blooded ferocity. He fired, and the bullet struck a foot below Mario's breast, who was mounted on his little horse, and pierced the body of the Moor, who had joined him and was walking by his side.

Mercedes fell without a sound.

MERCEDES WOUNDED BEFORE THE CHÂTEAU.

"Help, help, my friends!" cried Bois-Doré,
finding that he was alone with his son, and
exposed to the assaults of invisible foes.

"Help, help, my friends!" cried Bois-Doré, finding that he was alone with his son, and exposed to the assaults of invisible foes.

His call was answered only by Lauriane and Adamas, who, when they saw the bandits put to flight, had abandoned the tower of the huisset and had come out to join the others.

While they with the help of the distracted Mario raised the poor Moorish woman from the ground, the marquis looked up toward the *moucharabi* and saw the tall figure of Sancho, who, recognizing the Moor, the original cause of his master's death, was somewhat consoled for having missed his aim. With no thought of escaping, he was hurriedly reloading his weapon.

Bois-Doré recognized him at once, although that side of the tower was only faintly lighted by the conflagration. But he had no loaded weapon, so he jumped down from his horse and returned to the archway to go up to the moucharabi, considering with good reason that D'Alvimar's avenger was the most formidable of all the enemies with whom he had ever had to deal.

Sancho saw him coming, divined his purpose, and without pausing to hurl projectiles which might miss him, he darted to the stairs leading to the *chambre de manœuvre*, determined to stab him, his knife being the only one of his weapons which was not at that moment useless.

Bois-Doré was about to ascend the stairs, holding his sword over his head, when he seemed to have a presentiment of the course so treacherous an adversary was likely to pursue.

He lowered the point of his sword and with it felt each stair in the darkness, divining that Sancho was crouching somewhere there, on the alert to pounce upon him and hurl him backward. He clung with one hand to the rail therefore, but did not protect his body sufficiently.

Sancho, warned by the ringing of the steel on the stairs, sprang to his feet, leaped down several steps, and fell violently upon Bois-Doré, whom he threw backward and seized by the throat; then, kneeling upon his chest, he cried:

"I have you now, accursed Huguenot! expect no mercy, as you had none for— —"

Before concluding his sentence, he felt for the marquis's heart; then, raising the knife in the other hand, added:

"*For my son's soul!*"

The marquis, stunned by his fall, defended himself but feebly, and it was apparently all over with him, when Sancho felt upon his face two tiny, faltering hands, which suddenly tore his flesh savagely, so that he had to make a movement to rid himself of them.

Instantly a sudden thought led him to relax his hold of the marquis.

"The child first!" he cried.

But the words were forced back into his throat, and the thought interrupted in his brain by a terrible explosion.

Mario had followed the marquis. He had heard him fall. He had felt in the darkness Sancho's face. He had known from the feeling that it was not Bois-Doré's. He had placed against that rough, hairy skull the muzzle of a pistol snatched from Clindor as he passed, and had fired point-blank.

He had avenged his fathers death and saved his uncle's life.

CHAPTER LVIII

The marquis did not know at once what rescuing angel had come to his assistance.

He freed himself from the body of Sancho, whose bent knees were still pressing upon him. He threw out his arms at random, thinking that he was attacked by a new enemy, who had missed him.

His arms came in contact with Mario, who was struggling to lift him, exclaiming in a heart-broken tone:

"Father, my poor father, are you dead?—No, you embrace me. Are you wounded?"

"No, it is nothing! just a little suffocated, that is all," replied the marquis. "But what has happened? Where is that infamous knave?"

"I think that I must have killed him," said Mario, "for he doesn't move."

"Do not trust him, do not trust him!" cried Bois-Doré, rising with an effort, and dragging his beloved child to the foot of the stairs. "So long as the serpent breathes, he tries to bite!"

At that moment Clindor arrived with a torch, and they saw Sancho lying inert and disfigured. He was still breathing, and one of his great fierce eyes, glaring confusedly through the blood, seemed to say: "I die twice over since you survive me!"

"What! my poor David, did you kill this Goliath!" cried the marquis, as soon as he began to collect his thoughts.

"Ah! father, I killed him two minutes too late," replied Mario, who was like one intoxicated, and whose grief returned with his memory; "I think that my Mercedes is dead!"

"Poor girl! Let us hope not!" said the marquis with a sigh.

They recrossed the bridge to go to her, while Clindor, who was terribly afraid that Sancho, contrary to all appearances, would rise again, pierced the wretched creature's throat with a halberd.

The Moor had risen to her feet. She insisted that they should pay no heed to her, although she could hardly stand. She was grievously wounded;

the bullet had passed through her right arm, which was about Mario's waist when the shot was fired; but she was thinking only of Mario, who was no longer at her side; and when she found him there again she smiled and lost consciousness.

They carried her to the château, whither Mario and Lauriane accompanied her, holding her hand and weeping bitterly, for they believed that she was lost.

The marquis remained outside.

Guillaume's absence seemed to him of evil augury, and he rode forward, fancying that he heard, on the higher ground, sounds of more serious import than were likely to be caused simply by the capture or resistance of a few fugitives.

As he advanced, the sounds became more alarming, and when he emerged from the ravine he saw a number of men, vassals of Ars and Briantes, retreating toward him in disorder.

"Halt, my friends!" he cried. "What is going on here, and how happens it that brave fellows like you seem to be showing your heels?"

"Ah! is it you, monsieur le marquis!" replied one of the demoralized men. "We must return to the château and fight behind the walls; for the *reitres* are coming. Monsieur d'Ars being warned of their approach by Monsieur Mario, rode back to meet them, and he is engaged with them. But what can we expect to do against those fellows? They say a *reitre* is stronger and crueller than the Christians, and they have cannon too; they would have used them against us already if they had not been afraid of hitting their own men, in the confusion into which Monsieur d'Ars has thrown them."

"Monsieur d'Ars has borne himself gallantly and prudently, my children!" said the marquis; "and if fear of the *reitres* made you retreat, you are not worthy to be in his service or mine. Go and hide behind the walls; but I warn you that, if I am forced to fall back and shut myself up in the château, I will turn you out as fellows who eat too much and do not fight enough."

These reproaches brought several of them to their senses; the rest took flight; almost all of these were in Guillaume's service. They were not cowards by any means; but the *reitres* had left such terrible memories in the province, and legend had added thereto such appalling and prodigious details, that one needed to be doubly brave to face them.

The marquis, attended by the stoutest-hearted of them, who already blushed for their demoralization, soon joined Guillaume, who was leading a gallant charge upon Captain Macabre.

The darkness, which, however, had become much less dense, enabled Guillaume to lie in ambush, in order to fall suddenly upon them and prevent them from going forward to cannonade the château; for they actually had a small field-piece, of which Bois-Doré, when a prisoner at Etalié, had not suspected the existence.

Everybody knows that a single paltry cannon would suffice to batter down those little fortresses, which were skilfully disposed to repel the assaults of besiegers in the Middle Ages, but utterly helpless in face of modern siege guns. The most formidable castles of the feudal period, in Berry, crumbled like card-houses under Richelieu and Louis XIV., when the royal power undertook to put down the armed nobility; and it is surprising to find how few soldiers and cannon-balls sufficed for such great execution.

It was most essential therefore for the marquis to prevent them, at any cost, from approaching the château, and he dashed forward to support Guillaume, who bore himself most gallantly despite the desertion of the greater part of his force.

But he soon had to fall back before the onset of the *reitres*, who had the advantage of position as well as of numbers, and the battle seemed lost when they heard the sounds of fighting at the enemy's rear, as if they were caught between two fires.

Monsieur Robin de Coulogne had come up with his men at the critical moment. His moderation was providential. If he had followed the *reitres* more closely, he would have overtaken them sooner, and probably would not have found them an easy prey.

Thus hemmed in, the *reitres* fought desperately, especially Macabre's stout Germans, and La Proserpine's hot-headed Frenchmen. Saccage's Italians gave way first, for they detested both Macabre and Proserpine, and had not the slightest desire to die for them.

They tried to steal away and reach the château by a détour; but they were met on the road by Aristandre, who, having gone in pursuit of the gypsies, knew nothing of the attack of the *reitres*, and fell upon them without any idea as to who or what they were.

As he had quite a numerous party, and as he laid the lieutenant low at the outset, the others were speedily routed, and, fearing a fresh display of generosity by Bois-Doré, the coachman lost no time in despatching those who were taken, Lieutenant Saccage at their head.

The latter's belt proved to be a valuable capture; but Aristandre did not choose to appropriate it, but reserved it for general distribution.

A moment later, as he was hurrying to join the marquis, he fell in with one of the men who had accompanied Lucilio to Brilbault.

"Ho! Denison!" he shouted to him, "what have you done with our bagpiper?"

"Ask me rather," replied Denison, "what those brigands of *reitres* have done with him. God knows! We started for Etalié with him to find monsieur le marquis, but at the foot of the hill we were surrounded by those devils, who pulled us from our horses and made us prisoners. At first, they proposed to shoot Master Jovelin on the spot. They were frantic because he did not reply to them, and they took his silence for contempt. But there was a lady there who recognized him and said that monsieur le marquis would pay a very big ransom for him. So they bound him like the rest of us, and at this moment he and the other four of us must either be free like me, or have been killed in the battle. As for the lady, who was dressed like an officer, I don't know who she is; but may the devil take me if you wouldn't say she was our Demoiselle Bellinde!"

"Well, Denison, let us go and see," replied Aristandre, "and let us save all our friends if it can be done!"

The honest coachman, as he ran, collected as many men as he could, and attacked the flank of the *reitres* skilfully and most opportunely.

Assailed thus on three sides, and reduced to half their original number, for Bois-Doré, Guillaume and Monsieur Robin had killed as many as Saccage had taken away by his defection, the compact little battalion of *reitres* devoted their energies to effecting their retreat in good order. But so small a force was too easily surrounded; their cannon, which was with the rear-guard, had already fallen into Monsieur Robin's hands. They could not even disperse. They were forced to surrender at discretion, with the exception of a few who were blinded with rage and whom it was necessary to kill, but not until they had inflicted some damage upon their unmounted adversaries.

Some time, was lost in disarming and binding the prisoners; for they could hardly trust the promises of *reitres*; and day was breaking when they all assembled, victors and vanquished, in the courtyard of the château.

The fire among the farm buildings was extinguished. The damage was great, doubtless; but the marquis paid little heed to it; he wiped away the perspiration and the powder which obscured his sight, and looked about with much emotion in search of the objects of his affection: first of all, Mario, who was not thereto congratulate him, which fact made him fear that the Moor was in a bad way; then Lauriane, who made haste to encourage him concerning Mercedes's condition; then Adamas, who was kissing his feet in a frenzy of joy; then Jovelin and Aristandre, who had not yet appeared, and his worthy farmer, whose death they concealed from him; and lastly all his loyal retainers and vassals, whose number had diminished during that fatal night.

But, while he was asking for them all in turn, he interrupted himself to inquire anew for Mario with sudden anxiety.

Two or three times during his desperate combat with the *reitres*, he had fancied that he saw his child's face hovering about him in the twilight.

"Ah! at last, Aristandre!" he exclaimed, as he spied the coachman on horseback by his side; "have you seen my son? Answer me quickly!"

Aristandre stammered some incoherent words. His great face was drawn by fatigue and confused by inexplicable embarrassment.

The marquis turned as pale as death.

Adamas, who was gazing at him ecstatically, soon perceived his suffering.

"No, no, monsieur!" he said, as Mario jumped into his arms from Squilindre's back, where he had been hiding behind the coachman's bulky figure. "Here he is as fresh and sound as a rose from the Lignon!"

"What were you doing there behind the coachman, monsieur le comte?" said the marquis after embracing his heir.

"Alas! my kind master, forgive me," said Aristandre, who also had dismounted. "When I went to the stable to get Squilindre to carry me against those devils of German horses, I just locked Coquet up so that monsieur le comte could not ride him; for I had seen your demon—forgive me! your darling son prowling around there, and I suspected that he meant to run into danger. But, just as I was in the thick of the fight, I felt something against my side! I didn't pay much attention to it at first, it was so light! But lo and behold, I found I had four arms: two long ones and two short ones. With the two long ones I managed my horse and struck down the enemy; with the two short ones, I reloaded my pistols, and handled my pike so quickly that I did the work of two men. What would you have had me do? I was in a scrimmage where it wouldn't have been a good thing for my little double to put him down on the ground, so I kept on and came out of it whole, thank God! after thrashing the enemy soundly, and riding down more than one villain who wanted your life, which God preserve, monsieur le marquis! with this brave old coach horse, who is an excellent war-horse at need, monsieur! If I did wrong, punish me; but don't blame monsieur le comte; for, by the name of—, he's a fine little—, who pounded those— Germans like a—, and who will soon be a—, like you, master!"

"Enough, enough flattery, my good fellow," rejoined Bois-Doré, pressing the coachman's hand. "If you must teach your young master to disobey, at all events do not teach him to swear like a heathen."

"Did I disobey you, father?" said Mario; "you forbade me to attack the gypsies, but you didn't say anything about the *reitres.*"

The marquis took his child in his arms, and could not resist the temptation to exhibit him proudly to his friends, telling them how he had rescued his uncle from the hands of the terrible Sancho.

"Well, my young hero," he added, embracing him again, "it is useless for me to try to keep you in leash; you are your own master. At eleven years of age, you have avenged your father's death with your own hand, and won your spurs of knighthood. Go and kneel at your lady's feet; for you have earned the right to hope to win her heart some day."

Lauriane kissed Mario fraternally without hesitation, and Mario returned her caress without blushing. The moment had not arrived when their holy friendship was to be changed into a holy love.

They returned together to Mercedes, after relieving the marquis's mind concerning Lucilio, who was an excellent surgeon and was already in attendance upon her. Mario had not chosen to boast of having contributed to the rescue of his friend, who had thereafter fought stoutly at his side.

The Moor was so overjoyed by Mario's return and by the tutor's nursing, that she felt no pain from her wound.

After it was dressed, Lucilio turned his attention to the wounded men, even among the prisoners, whom they were making preparations to send, under a strong escort, to the prison at La Châtre.

The *reitres* were sitting in the *basse-cour*, around the dying embers of the fire, in dire discomfiture; Captain Macabre, who was drunk during the battle and was severely wounded, did nothing but beg for brandy to enable him to forget his misery; Bellinde was so terribly frightened while the battle was in progress, that she was fairly dazed; which fact saved her from feeling the humiliation of being exposed to the contempt and reproaches of the servants and vassals whom she had so long despised and disciplined.

She was the object of some consideration on the part of the village women because of her gorgeous costume, by which they were involuntarily dazzled.

But when Adamas learned of the preposterous attempt she had made to force the marquis to marry her, and her manifest purpose to torture Mario, he was so vehement in commending her to general execration, that the marquis had to hasten her departure for the prison. He even had the generosity, in spite of Adamas's remonstrances, to allow her to retain her jewels, her purse and a horse to carry her.

All the other horses belonging to the *reitres*, excellent beasts and well equipped, as well as the weapons and the officers' money, were distributed among the brave fellows who had taken them; nor would the marquis keep any part of the booty for himself. He turned his attention at once to the needs of his unfortunate vassals, who had been robbed and maltreated by the gypsies.

CHAPTER LIX

They separated as soon as the prisoners had departed, in charge of Monsieur Robin and a large escort of men of the neighborhood, who had been attracted by the uproar of the battle, a little tardily perhaps, but in time at all events to allow the combatants to procure the rest which they sadly needed.

Jean le Clope, who arrived among the last and was already half tipsy, was overjoyed and highly honored to join the escort. He had an old grudge against Captain Macabre, and had lost his leg in an engagement with *reitres*.

So he entered the town of La Châtre, with his nose in the air, assuming the airs of Captain Fracasse, and telling everybody who chose to listen that, *with his bright sword, he slew fourteen of them.*

He pointed out the most important prisoners, saying of each one:

"I captured that fellow."

When the *basse-cour* was restored to order, there was still much confusion in the courtyard of the château.

The ground-floor apartments were transformed into a hospital for men and animals. The kitchen and dining-room were open to all who wished to warm themselves, and the marquis refused to sit down until he had attended to everybody's needs. Lucilio and Lauriane devoted themselves to the care of the wounded.

There were many varied incidents in this animated scene.

Here, lay a man shrieking and groaning while a bullet was being extracted; there, men were laughing and drinking together as they recalled the exploits of the night; and farther on, were others weeping for the dead.

Ugly, withered old hags made a terrible outcry about goats that could not be found; others had lost their children, and rushed hither and thither, wild-eyed, so choked with grief that they could not call them.

Mario, active and sympathetic, would go in search of them, while Adamas, always provident, caused a large trench to be dug, in a neighboring field, for the interment of those of the enemy who were killed. Their own dead were treated with more honor, and they went in search of Monsieur Poulain to recite prayers for them pending their burial.

They made much of the bravest. Almost everybody had been brave at the last moment; and yet, throughout the day they constantly found poor dazed creatures, still cowering behind wood-piles or in the dark corners of sheds, where they would have allowed themselves to be burned or suffocated without a word, they were so completely paralyzed by fear.

Amid all these scenes, tragic and grotesque, Bois-Doré and Guillaume were untiring inf their activity. Although ghastly and heart-rending sights met their eyes at every step, they were urged on by that somewhat feverish enthusiasm which always follows the happy ending of a great crisis.

What they had to deplore and regret was a mere trifle compared with what might have happened.

The marquis had remounted his horse in order to perform his charitable duties more quickly; his costume was incomprehensible to most of those who saw him pass. He still wore his cook's apron, now a mere rag, it is true, and stained with blood; so that many of his vassals thought that he had tied a strip of a banner about his waist as a symbol of victory. His long moustaches had been scorched in the fire, and Master Pignoux's oilskin cap, crushed under the hat that Bois-Doré had hurriedly donned, came down to his eyes; they thought that he was wounded in the head, and he was constantly met with anxious inquiries whether he was in much pain.

As the first spadefuls of earth were thrown on the dead bodies, one of them remonstrated. It was La Flèche, who declared that he was not quite dead.

The amateur grave-diggers were not much inclined to listen to him; but Mario happened to pass not far off and overheard the discussion. He ran to the spot and ordered them to disinter, the poor wretch. The order was obeyed with reluctance, but, despite all his seignioral authority, he could not induce anyone to take him to the hospital.

They all disappeared on various pretexts, and Mario was obliged to go in search of Aristandre, who obeyed without a murmur, and returned with him to the place where the dying gypsy lay on the moist, blood-stained ground.

But it was too late. La Flèche was lost beyond recall. He was hardly breathing; his haggard, staring eye indicated that his last moment was at hand.

"It is too late, monsieur," said Aristandre to his young master. "What would you have! It was I who crushed him, and I was not gentle about it; but it wasn't I who stuffed his mouth with dirt and stones to stifle him. I should never have thought of that."

"Dirt and stones?" repeated Mario, looking with horror and amazement at the gypsy, who was actually suffocating. "He spoke just now! he must have gnawed at the ground in his struggle against death!"

As he leaned over the wretched creature to try to relieve him, La Flèche, whose face already wore the pallor of a corpse, moved his arms as if to say: "It is useless; let me die in peace."

Then his arm fell with the forefinger extended, as if he were pointing to his murderer, and so remained, stiffened by death, which had already quenched the light of his eyes.

Mario's eyes instinctively turned in the direction indicated by that horrible gesture, and saw no one. Doubtless the gypsy, as he breathed his last, had seen a vision bearing some relation to his melancholy and evil life.

But Aristandre's attention was attracted by the fresh prints of tiny feet on the clayey soil. Those footprints were on all sides of the body, and seemed to indicate a trampling or stamping around the head; then they led away from the spot in the direction in which the gypsy's finger still pointed.

"There are some terrible children, eh?" said the honest coachman, calling Mario's attention to the marks. "I know that these gypsies are viler than dogs, and perhaps it was poor Charasson's boy, who, seeing that you were trying to save this beast, determined to finish him this way in order to avenge his father! It's a devilish invention all the same, and it is quite right to say that evil leads to evil."

"Yes, yes, my good friend," said the horrified Mario; "you understand that a dying man is no longer an enemy. But look in the bushes over there; isn't that little Pilar hiding?"

"I don't know who little Pilar is," Aristandre replied, "but I know that that little hussy is the one whose life I saved last night. See, there she goes again. She runs like a genuine cat. Do you recognize her now?"

"Yes," said Mario, "I know her too well, and it is clear that the evil one is in her. Let her go, coachman, and may she go far away from here!"

"Come, monsieur, don't stay in this horrible place," rejoined Aristandre. "I will put this villain's body underground, for the dogs and the crows scent him already, and monsieur le marquis would not like to have it lying around on his land."

Mario, being utterly exhausted, went to take a little rest.

When he had slept an hour in a chair, beside his dear Moor, who pretended to sleep in order to set his mind at rest, he began anew to go about the château and through the village, bearing assistance and consolation, accompanied by the lovable and unselfish Lauriane.

The marquis, having hastily repaired his toilet, received the lieutenant of the provost, and, with the assistance of Messieurs d'Ars and Coulogne, set forth the facts to the magistrates whose duty it was to do prompt and signal justice.

CHAPTER LX

The day was advancing.

The tranquillity of fatigue reigned in the village and the château. Mario and Lauriane, on returning from their round, craved a breath of fresh air, and went into the garden, the only part of the enclosure which had not been profaned by acts of violence and devastation.

As he told his friend in detail his own adventures, which she had not previously had time to comprehend, they arrived at the *Palace of Astrée*, in the labyrinth, where he had passed such an agitated hour during the preceding night.

The weather was mild. The two children sat down on the steps of the little cottage.

Mario, although he was not ill, had a touch of fever in his blood. Such a succession of violent emotions had matured him suddenly, as it were, and Lauriane, on booking at him, was struck by the expression of melancholy resolution which had so changed his sweet and transparent glance.

"My Mario," she said, "I fear that you are ill. You have been afraid and courageous, tired and untiring, happy and unhappy, all at once, during this last horrible night; but it is all passed. Master Jovelin assures us that Mercedes is safe, and she declares that she hardly, suffers at all. You saved our dear papa Sylvain's life and avenged your poor father's death. All this has transformed you into a noble, gallant youth; but you must not keep those folds on your brow, but think rather about thanking God for the assistance He gave you in this affair."

"I do think about it, my Lauriane," Mario replied, "but I am thinking also of something my father said to me this morning, after which you kissed me and said: 'Yes, yes.' I did not understand it, and you must explain it to me. My father said that I had *earned the right to hope to please you*. Does that mean that I have not pleased you hitherto?"

"No, indeed, Mario; you please me immensely, for I love you dearly."

"Good! But, when my father says sometimes laughingly that I shall be your husband, do you think that that might happen?

"Really, I do not know, Mario, but I hardly think so. I am two or three years older than you, and when you are a young man I shall be what might be called an old maid."

"And yet, Lauriane, Adamas told me that you married your cousin Hélyon, who was three or four years older than you. Did he ever blame you for being too young for him?"

"Why, yes, sometimes, before our marriage, when we played at quarrelling."

"Well, I think that he was wrong; I think that you are neither young nor old, and I shall always think that you are just right, because I shall always love you the way I love you now."

"You don't know anything about it, Mario; it is said that one's heart changes with one's age."

"That is not true with me. I still think my Mercedes young and lovable, and I have always loved her ever since I have been in the world. My father is old, so people say, but I enjoy myself more with him than with Clindor; and I don't see that age makes any difference between Master Lucilio and us. Do you get tired of me because I am younger?"

"No, Mario; you are much more sensible and attractive than other boys of your age, and you already know more than I do, in the studies we have together."

"Tell me, Lauriane, do you think me nicer than your other husband?"

"I must not say that, Mario. He was my husband, and you are not."

"Did you love him because he was your husband?"

"I cannot say; I did not love him much when he was only my cousin; I thought him too wild and too fond of making a disturbance. But when they took us to the Reformed Church together and said to us: 'Now you are married; you will not see each other again for seven or eight years, but it is your duty to love each other;' I answered: 'Very well;' and I prayed for my husband every day, asking God to do me the favor to make me love him when I should see him again."

"And you never saw him again! Were you grieved when he died?"

"Yes, Mario. He was my cousin, and I wept for him."

"And so if I should die, who am neither your cousin nor your husband, you wouldn't weep for me?"

"You must not talk about dying, Mario," said Lauriane; "they say that it brings bad luck when one is young. I don't want you to die, and I say again that I love you dearly."

"But you won't promise me when I shall be your husband?"

"Why, Mario, what good would it do you to have me for your wife? You do not even know whether you will want to marry when you are old enough."

"Yes, I do, Lauriane! I want nobody else for a wife but you, because you are good, and because you love everybody that I love. And as you say that a woman must love her husband, I know that you will always love me if we are married; but, if you marry someone else, you will never think about loving me. Then I shall be very unhappy, and it makes me want to cry just to think of it."

"And now you are really crying!" said Lauriane, wiping his eyes with her handkerchief. "Come, come, Mario, I tell you that you are ill to-night, and that you must have a good supper and a good night's sleep; for you are worrying about troubles that are still to come, instead of rejoicing over those that you conquered last night."

"What is past is past," said Mario; "what is to come—I don't know why I think so much about it to-day; but I do, and I cannot help it."

"You have been too much wrought up!"

"Perhaps so; but I do not feel tired; and I do not know why I thought of you all through the night, whenever my father and I were in great danger.— 'If we should both die,' I said to myself, 'who will save my Lauriane?'— Really, I thought of you as much, perhaps more than of my Mercedes and all the others. And I thought of you more when I met Pilar than at any other time."

"Why did that bad girl make you think of your Lauriane?"

Mario reflected a moment, then replied:

"You see, when I was travelling with the gypsies, I used often to play and talk with that child, who knows Spanish and a little Arabic, and who made me feel sorry for her, because she always seemed sick and unhappy. Mercedes and I were always as kind to her as we could be, and she was fond of us. She called Mercedes *mother* and me my *little husband*. And when I said: 'No, I don't want to be,' she would cry and sulk, so that I had to say to comfort her: 'Yes, yes, it is all right!' She did us a service last night, I agree; she went very promptly to give warning to Monsieur Robin and Monsieur Guillaume, as I told her to; but I had a horror of her all the same, because I knew that she was cruel and had no religion. And then that name of husband, which she had often given me against my will, made me sick, and I remembered that you and I had promised in sport to marry each other, and I saw the devil on one side of me, with her features, and my guardian angel on the other side, with yours."

As Mario concluded, a stone from the little cottage fell so near Lauriane that she had a narrow escape from being wounded.

The two children hastily departed, thinking that the cottage was falling to pieces; and they joined the marquis, who was awaiting them for dinner.

CHAPTER LXI

Meanwhile, Monsieur Poulain had been sought in vain to administer the sacrament to his dying parishioners; he could not be found.

His house had been pillaged by the gypsies before any others. His servant had been roughly used and was in bed, praying to heaven for the return of the rector, concerning whom she was unable to give any information. He had disappeared two days before.

At last, during the evening, just as Monsieur Robin and Guillaume d'Ars were about to retire with their men, leaving their wounded to the hospitable care of the marquis, Jean Faraudet, the farmer of Brilbault, appeared, and requested permission to make an important communication to his master.

This is what he had to tell; and we will describe at the same time the events of the previous evening at Brilbault, whither we have not as yet had leisure to follow the numerous persons who had assembled there by agreement, to surround and storm the old manor.

The arrangements had been so carefully made that no one failed to appear at the rendezvous except Monsieur de Bois-Doré, whose absence was not noticed at first, all the confederates being divided into small groups, which held communication with each other in total darkness when they approached the mysterious ruin.

The said ruin, being explored from roof to cellar, was found to be silent and empty. But they found traces of recent occupancy in that portion of the ground floor which the marquis had not dared to enter alone: hot embers in the fireplaces; rags and broken food on the floor.

They had also discovered an underground passage, with an exit at a considerable distance from the house, outside the enclosure. Such passages existed in all feudal châteaux. They were almost all filled up at the time of our narrative; but the gypsies had cleared this one and masked the opening cleverly enough.

They had carried their investigations no farther, not only because they deemed it useless, the enemy having already vanished, but because they were beginning to be alarmed about Monsieur de Bois-Doré and to scour the neighborhood for him. They were seriously alarmed when the little gypsy arrived and told her story.

More time was wasted in serious perplexity. Monsieur Robin thought that the marquis had fallen into some ambuscade, and he persisted in searching for him; whereas Monsieur d'Ars, to whom the child's statements seemed not improbable, decided to start for Briantes with his following. An hour later, Monsieur Robin concluded to do likewise.

When they had all ridden away, the farmer of Brilbault, who had received orders to continue the exploration of the château, had postponed the task to the following day, yielding to fatigue, as he said, and probably even more to a remnant of terror.

"When the day broke I was there"—it is Jean Faraudet who is speaking,—"and after turning and pulling over all the old wood and rubbish from one end of the place to the other, I spied a little hole that I hadn't seen, and there I found a man bound faster than any sheaf of grain; for his hands and feet were tied, and his mouth gagged with a bunch of straw which was very cunningly twisted around his neck like a rope. So the man seemed to be dead from head to foot. I picked him up and carried him to my house, where a little brandy brought him to after I had untied him and rubbed him."

"Who was the man?" inquired the marquis, thinking that it was D'Alvimar "you did not know him, did you?"

"Yes, indeed, Monsieur Sylvain," replied the farmer; "I had seen him many a time. It was Monsieur Poulain, the rector of your parish. It was more than four hours before he could speak a word, because he had strained himself so in trying to struggle in his bonds. At last he said to us:

"'I will not tell the authorities anything. I am not to blame for anything that may have happened; I swear by the holy oil and my baptism!'

"He had the fever all day and talked at random. This evening he felt better and wanted to go home, so I brought him behind me on my brood mare, saving your presence."

"Let us go and question him," said Guillaume, rising.

"No," said the marquis, "we will let him sleep. He needs it as much as we do ourselves. And what could he disclose that we do not know too well now? And of what could we accuse him? He went there to administer the sacrament to Monsieur d'Alvimar; that was his duty. When he learned what they were plotting there against me, if he did not threaten to betray it, he at least refused to take part in it. And that is why the gypsies bound and gagged him."

Guillaume observed that Monsieur Poulain was a dangerous rector for the parish of Briantes, and that he ought at the very least to be threatened with a charge of complicity in the affair of the *reitres*, as a means of keeping him quiet or driving him away.

The marquis absolutely refused to harass a man who seemed to him sufficiently punished already by the brutal treatment he had endured and the risk he had run of perishing in oblivion and silence in a prison.

"What!" said he, "by the grace of God, we got the better of forty *reitres*, well equipped and provided with a cannon; of a band of active and adroit thieves; of a terrible conflagration, and an execrable ambush; and we can think of such a thing as wreaking vengeance on a poor priest who can no longer injure us!"

The marquis forgot that he was not yet entirely out of danger.

Monsieur le Prince, who had set off in hot haste for the court, might not be well received there, and might suddenly return and vent his ill-humor on the nobles of his province.

It was most essential therefore that the marquis should at all events not allow a dangerous advocate of D'Alvimar's cause to intervene between the prince and himself. This consideration was suggested to the marquis on the following day by Lucilio; whereupon Bois-Doré hastened to call upon Monsieur Poulain as if to inquire for his health.

The rector, who was unable as yet to leave his easy-chair, he had suffered so intensely with cold, discomfort and fright, attempted to tell him that a fall from his horse had caused his injuries and had detained him twenty-four hours at the house of one of his confrères.

But Bois-Doré went straight to the fact, and talked to him with a mild and generous firmness; nor did he fail to show him D'Alvimar's notes and call his attention to the manner in which his deceased friend referred to himself and the prince.

Monsieur Poulain did not attempt to combat these revelations. His pride was much humbled by the atrocious perplexities in which he had suddenly become involved.

"Monsieur de Bois-Doré," he said with a sigh, wiping away the cold perspiration which stood out upon his brow at the recollection of his sufferings, "I have seen death at very close quarters. I did not think that I feared it, but it appeared to me in such hideous and cruel guise that I made a vow to retire to a convent if I ever came forth from that icy tomb in which I was buried alive. I have come forth, and it is my earnest purpose never again to take part for or against any person or any interest in this world. Henceforth I shall devote my life, in profound seclusion, to my salvation and to that alone; and if it be your pleasure to allot me a cell in the Abbey of Varennes, of which you are the fiduciary possessor, I should ask nothing more."

"So be it," replied Bois-Doré, "on condition that you inform me frankly and fully what took place at Brilbault. I will not fatigue you with useless questions; I know three-fourths of all that you know. I wish to know but one thing: whether Monsieur d'Alvimar confessed to you the assassination of my brother."

"You ask me to betray the secret of the confessional," replied Monsieur Poulain, "and I should refuse, as it is my duty to do, were it not that Monsieur d'Alvimar, who was sincerely penitent at the last, instructed me to reveal everything after his death and Sancho's, which latter he did not suppose to be so near at hand as it proved to be. I will tell you, therefore, that Monsieur d'Alvimar, descended through his mother from a noble family, and authorized, by the mystery surrounding his birth, to bear the name of his mother's husband, was, in reality, the issue of a guilty intrigue with Sancho, an ex-leader of brigands turned farmer."

"Really!" exclaimed the marquis. "That explains Sancho's last words, monsieur le recteur. He declared that he sacrificed me to the memory of *his son*! But how did this fact enter into Monsieur d'Alvimar's confession, unless he felt obliged to confess the sins of others as well?"

"Monsieur d'Alvimar had to confess his connection with Sancho in order to induce me not to deliver to the secular authorities the man whom he with shame and sorrow called the author of his days. He called him also the author of his crime and his misfortunes.

"It was that heartless and wicked man who had made him an accessory to the death of your brother, to whom the idea first occurred, and who stabbed him to the heart, while D'Alvimar consented to assist him and to profit by the crime. It is only too true that the sole object of that crime, the victim of which was unknown to its perpetrators, was to obtain possession of a sum of money and a casket of jewels which your brother had imprudently allowed them to see the night before, at an inn. At that period Monsieur d'Alvimar was very young, and so poor that he doubted whether he could pay the expenses of his journey to Paris, where he hoped to find patrons. He was ambitious; that is a great sin, I know, monsieur le marquis. It is the most dangerous bait that Satan holds forth. Sancho inspired and nourished that infernal ambition in his son. He had to overcome his repugnance, but he triumphed by pointing out to him that this murder was a sure opportunity which would never be repeated, and which would place him above the need of debasing himself by imploring the compassion of others.

"When D'Alvimar made this confession, Sancho was present; he hung his head and did not seek to excuse himself. On the contrary, when I hesitated to give absolution for a sin which did not seem to me to have been sufficiently expiated, Sancho vehemently accused himself, and I must confess that there was something grand in the passionate desire of that fierce soul for his son's salvation. I believed then that I was dealing with two Christians, both guilty and both repentant; but Sancho filled me with horror and dismay as soon as his son had breathed his last.

"It was a ghastly scene, monsieur, which I shall never forget while I live! The lower room in which we were, in that ruined château, had but one fireplace; and, although it was an enormous apartment, we were much cramped in the small space where we were sheltered from the cold air that rushed down from above. Monsieur d'Alvimar had nothing but straw for his bed, and only his cloak and Sancho's for covering. He was so exhausted by two months of agony that he resembled a spectre. However, Sancho had prepared him as best he could to receive the last consolations of religion; and the spectacle presented by that gentleman of distinguished bravery, resigned to his fate, amid a horde of gypsies, heretics and villains, saddened the heart and the eyes.

"Those miscreants, displeased at having to look on at a Christian ceremony, howled and swore and shouted derisively to avoid hearing the prayers of the Holy Church, which are detestable to them. It seems that it was always so during Monsieur d'Alvimar's last days in that place. Every night Sancho tried to take advantage of their slumber to repeat to his son the prayers that he desired; but, as soon as one of the gypsies detected him, the whole band, men, women and children, joined in a frightful uproar to drown his voice and not allow their own ears to be offended by any of the blessed words of our service.

"It was therefore in the midst of this horrible tumult, in which Sancho's authority—based upon the fact that he had some money hidden, which he doled out to them little by little—sometimes succeeded in restoring silence for a moment, that I administered the sacrament to that unhappy young man.

"He died reconciled with God, I trust; for he expressed much regret for his crime and begged me to inform Monsieur le Prince of the truth, if he, being deceived as I myself had been concerning the causes and circumstances of your duel, should molest you because of it."

"And have you resolved to do it, monsieur le recteur?" asked Bois-Doré, scrutinizing Monsieur Poulain's altered face.

"Yes, monsieur," was the reply, "on condition that you return seriously and sincerely to the path of duty."

"That is to say, that now you are bargaining with me for your testimony to the truth, in the name of the supreme truth?"

"No, monsieur; for what happened after D'Alvimar's death deprived me of the hope of converting you by the example of the repentance of your enemies. Sancho leaned over his son's pallid face and remained so for an instant, without speaking or shedding a tear; then he rose, swore aloud the execrable oath to avenge him by any and every means, and placed his hand in that of a vile and brutal Huguenot who was present."

"Captain Macabre?"

"Yes, monsieur, that was the ill-omened name they gave him.

"'I have sent for you,' said Sancho, 'to deliver the treasures of Bois-Doré into your hands; I will join you, and I promise you the aid of this band of volunteer scouts and skirmishers whom you see about you. I promised you through Bellinde a chance for an excellent *coup de main*, and the rector here, who hates Bois-Doré and who stands well with Monsieur le Prince, will assure you impunity.'

"Then it was, monsieur, that I objected."

"Doubtless!" rejoined Bois-Doré with a smile. "You were well aware that Monsieur le Prince desired my alleged treasure for himself alone, and that he was not the man to allow it to pass through the hands of such trustees."

Monsieur Poulain accepted the rebuke and hung his head with an expression, sincere or feigned, of repentance and humiliation.

Being urged to continue his narrative, he told how Captain Macabre had suggested blowing out his brains without ceremony to prevent his speaking, and how the gypsies had thrown themselves upon him to secure his clothes before they were ruined by blood.

"That discussion," continued Monsieur Poulain, "saved my life; for Sancho had time to suggest another plan. It was he who bound me and then imprisoned me as you have heard. But what a rescue! It seemed to me worse than a sudden and violent death, when the infamous villain, without assisting me or giving me a word of hope, left Brilbault with his gypsies, to attack your château."

"And what was done with D'Alvimar's body, I pray to know?" asked the marquis.

"I understand," replied the rector with a faint smile, wherein could be detected a trace of the old aversion, "that you are interested in finding it, in case proceedings should be instituted against you. But consider that that would not be evidence that could be used against you. If people chose to lie, they would be free to say that you buried your victim there with the help of your friend, Monsieur Robin. And so, monsieur le marquis, you must depend for your future security upon my loyalty alone, and I hereby offer you its guaranty."

"On what conditions, monsieur le recteur?"

"Conditions? I make no more conditions, my brother! From this day I am a recluse, withdrawn from the world. I have implored from your kindness the Abbey of Varennes."

"Oho!" said Bois-Doré, "the abbey? A simple cell was all that you wanted a moment ago."

"Will you allow so venerable an abbey to go to ruin, and entrust to boors the management of a community which is expected to set a noble example to the world?"

"Very good, I understand. We will see, monsieur le recteur, how you conduct yourself with respect to me, and you shall be abundantly gratified if I have reason to be. Meanwhile, I presume that you will not tell me where my brother's murderer is buried?"

"Pardon me, monsieur," replied the rector, who was too clever to appear to haggle, and who, moreover, was really striving to extricate himself from the tempests and passions of the age, provided that the penalty was not too severe; "I will tell you what I saw. Sancho seemed extremely anxious to rescue the body from any profanation on the part of the gypsies. He raised a flagstone in the centre of the floor of the room where we were, and he certainly interred his son there. For my part I saw nothing more;

they dragged me to my horrible dungeon, where I languished for eighteen mortal hours, alternating between unconsciousness and despair."

The marquis and the rector parted on excellent terms, and the latter made an effort to rise and officiate at the burial of his parishioners. But after the ceremony he was so ill that he sent for Master Jovelin, whose balsams and elixirs were much extolled as miraculous in their operation.

At first he had a great dread of placing his life in the hands of one whom he looked upon as a natural enemy. But the Italian's remedies relieved him so effectually that he was conscious of a sort of gratitude, especially when Lucilio obstinately refused all compensation.

The rector was compelled to offer his sincere thanks to the Beaux Messieurs de Bois-Doré, who, during his illness, ministered to his comfort personally and through others, with a solicitude equal to that which they displayed for their dearest friends.

CHAPTER LXII

Lauriane fell asleep, on the evening of her *matrimonial* interview with Mario, slightly disturbed concerning the undue agitation of that lovable child's heart, and his absorbing interest in the future. Inexperienced as she was, she had a somewhat clearer idea of life, and she foresaw that when Mario was old enough to distinguish between love and friendship, he would still be too young, as compared with her, to inspire her with any other sentiment than sisterly affection. She smiled sadly at the thought of a possible combination of circumstances which should require her to marry a child, after having been married when she was herself a child, and she said to herself that in that case her destiny would be a strange problem, perhaps a painful and fatal one.

She was depressed therefore, and summoned all her resolution to resist the influences which threatened to coerce her; for the marquis took his plan very seriously, and Monsieur de Beuvre in his letters evidently concealed beneath a jesting tone an earnest desire for the realization of that plan.

Lauriane did not resolutely demand love in her dreams of marriage and of happiness; but she felt vaguely that it would be too hard to marry twice without knowing love. It seemed to her therefore that a cloud, still very light, but disquieting none the less, hovered over her present tranquillity and her delightful relations with the Beaux Messieurs de Bois-Doré.

She was reassured however on the following day.

Mario had slept soundly; the roses of childhood bloomed anew on his soft cheeks; his lovely eyes had recovered their angelic limpidity, and a smile of trustful happiness played about his lips. He had become a child once more.

As soon as he found that his father had recovered from his fatigue, that his Mercedes was comfortable, and everybody stirring, he ran to the stable to greet his little horse, to the village to inquire for everybody's health, then to the garden to spin his top, and to the farmyard to clamber over the charred ruins.

Then he returned to wait affectionately upon his dear Moor, and he was devoted in his attention to her so long as she was obliged to keep her chamber. But as soon as all anxiety on her account was dispelled, he became once more the happy and light-hearted Mario, by turns assiduous in his studies and eager in his play, whom Lauriane could love and caress chastely as before, without fear of the morrow.

This change was most fortunate for the exceptional temperament of that sweet child. If he had been subjected much longer to the violent shocks which had succeeded each other so rapidly during that critical night, he must inevitably have been driven mad or completely broken down.

It should be said, however, that in those days rougher manners tended to make men's natures more pliant, and consequently more capable of resistance. The nervous excitement to which so many precocious natures succumb to-day, was more violent, but less general and less lasting than as we know it.

Sensibility, more frequently aroused by the emotions of external life, grew dull more quickly, and the keen emotions gave place to that intense desire to live, no matter how, which is man's salvation in times of disturbance and unhappiness.

Thus the winter passed pleasantly and cheerfully at the château of Briantes.

They worked at the frames of the new farm buildings, awaiting the time when the weather would allow the masons to work. The moat was cleared and the wall repaired provisionally with stones laid without mortar; Adamas had finally succeeded in reëstablishing subterranean communication with the open country, and the marquis had purchased his future peace with the provincial courtiers and churchmen by restoring divers precious objects to certain chapels in the province, in the shape of voluntary gifts. He had begged Madame la Princesse de Condé to accept a number of jewels for herself, and Adamas had artfully concealed those which in his mind were destined to adorn Mario's future bride.

The greater part of the gold and silver coin which the marquis had in reserve was expended in rebuilding, and in renewing his stock of grain for his household and his poor vassals. He had also to replace the cattle they had lost; for the Beaux Messieurs de Bois-Doré could not endure poverty in their neighborhood.

Lastly, the famous *treasure*, the value of which had been so exaggerated, and which had been the moving cause of such great calamities and such odious persecution, ceased to cause scandal by ceasing to be kept in hiding. The doors of the mysterious apartment were opened and remained open, in the sight and knowledge of all the world.

They tried to make sure of Monsieur Poulain by offering him a part of the booty; but he was shrewd enough to refuse; indeed, it was not material wealth that he coveted, but power and influence. He desired, he said, not *to possess*, but *to be*. That is why he insisted upon having the Abbey of Varennes, a far from wealthy institution, situated in a veritable hollow of verdure, on the small river Gourdon.

He desired no more land than was required to support himself and two or three brethren of the order. What he coveted was the title of abbot, and an apparent withdrawal from the world, which would relieve him from the daily duties of the rectorship.

Within a month he was fully cured of his desire to renounce the world, and it was his most cherished dream to make sure of his title and his daily bread, so that he might have leisure to insinuate himself into the confidence of those in high station and bear a part in diplomatic affairs, as so many other men, less capable and less patient than he, had done.

Bois-Doré understood his variety of ambition, and gratified it with a good grace. He felt sure that monsieur le prince, who was a great secularizer of abbeys to his own profit, would sooner or later force the surrender of this one on ungenerous terms, and he could not hope for a better opportunity to set the prince's autocratic disposition and Monsieur Poulain's personal interests against each other.

So the rector was invested with the abbey in consideration of an exceedingly modest tribute, and he departed to obtain his bishop's permission to give up his living.

Thus Monsieur Poulain saw the first phase of his dream of the future realized. What he had predicted to D'Alvimar was beginning to come to pass. He made his way by artfully exploiting the question of dissent in religious matters in his neighborhood. D'Alvimar, starving for money and revenge, had fallen without profit and without honor; Monsieur Poulain, on the watch for discontent and for means of acquiring influence, exempt from other passions and quick to sacrifice his hatreds to his interests, entered the road by what he called the right gate. It was, at all events, the surest.

The non-appearance of little Pilar caused surprise. The marquis, being informed of the important commission which she had faithfully executed, would have been glad to reward her, and Lauriane said that she longed to rescue the wretched creature from her evil life. But no one knew what had become of her; they presumed that she had rejoined those of the gypsies who had escaped from the *basse-cour*.

The captured *reitres* had been transferred to Bourges. Their cases were summarily dealt with. Captain Macabre was sentenced to be hanged as a highwayman, rebel and traitor.

The marquis took pity on Bellinde, who was driven frantic by the hardships of her life in prison; he refused to testify against her, that is to say, he declared that she was not in her right mind. She was banished from the city and province, and forbidden ever to reappear there under pain of death.

The Moor was cured, and Lucilio, having witnessed her fortitude in suffering, which she endured with a sort of exalted joy, began to become very deeply attached to her. But he feared lest he should seem mad if he told her so, and their mutual affection, carefully concealed on both sides, spent itself on *the children*, Mario and Lauriane, with a sort of rivalry.

Madame Pignoux was handsomely rewarded, as was her faithful maid-servant. They had escaped harsh treatment by flight. The *Geault-Rouge* had escaped burning, thanks to the eagerness of the enemy to pursue their expedition.

At long intervals they received news of Monsieur de Beuvre. Those intervals were very painful to his daughter. It was the period when the people of La Rochelle and the nobles who had joined them became corsairs on the sea, and formed the audacious project of blockading the mouths of the Loire and the Gironde, in order to levy tribute on all the commerce of those streams. De Beuvre had hinted at a purpose to accompany Soubise in this perilous undertaking.

In her moments of grief Lauriane did not lack loving consolation; but none was so wonderfully ingenious and so untiring as Mario's. His loving heart and his delicate tact found comforting words whose sweet artlessness compelled Lauriane to smile through her tears; she could not resist the temptation to call Mario when the others failed to divert her mind from gloomy thoughts.

She would say to Mercedes:

"I do not know what spirit of light God has bestowed upon that child; but a trivial word from him does me more good than all the kind words of those who are more mature than he.—He is a mere child, however," she would add mentally, "and I am not old enough to love him with a mother's love. Ah! well, I know not how it happens that I cannot endure the thought of ceasing to live with him."

Early in April—1622—they received better news.

De Beuvre had happily thought better of his purpose to accompany Soubise, who had had very bad luck at the Isle of Rié, against the king in person. De Beuvre had confined himself to privateering on the coast of Gascogne—with profit and excellent health, he said.

But this same affair of the Isle of Rié was destined none the less to result unhappily for Lauriane and her friends at Briantes.

The Prince de Condé had hoped that the king would follow his advice and rush madly into danger. The king did not fail to do so; personal courage was the only virtue he had inherited from his father. But Condé was unfortunate: no bullet reached the king; his horse passed the shallows at low tide without encountering quicksands, and his majesty fought valiantly against the Huguenots with no resulting illness or even fatigue.

Moreover, while wielding his sword with ardor, Louis XIII., being wisely advised by his mother, who was wisely advised by Richelieu, opened his ears to suggestions of conciliation and to negotiations tending to put an end to the civil war.

Thus monsieur le prince, whose only desire was to mix up the cards, was sorely annoyed and discontented, and he replied to the letters he received from his government of Berry by honeyed letters overflowing with gall.

Among other acts of retaliation against the Huguenots in his province, although they had, as a general rule, been perfectly quiet, he ordered

Monsieur de Beuvre's property to be sequestered, unless he should return to Berry within three days after the publication of the order.

It would have been very difficult for Monsieur de Beuvre, then at Montpellier, to reach his château in three days. At that epoch it would have required at least twice that length of time to advise him of the measures taken against him.

The lieutenant-general and Mayor of Bourges, Monsieur Pierre Biet, whose habit it was throughout his life to side with the strongest, and who had been a zealous Leaguer in his youth, determined to display his zeal, and decreed, on his own authority, that, Monsieur de Beuvre having failed to appear and explain his absence within the time allowed for such appearance, mademoiselle his daughter, Dame de Beuvre, de la Motte-Seuilly, etc., should be removed from her château and taken to a convent at Bourges, there to be instructed in the religion of the State.

CHAPTER LXIII

It was on a delightful evening in spring that Mario and Lauriane were strolling about the enclosure at Briantes, laughing together in tones as melodious as those of the nightingale, when they saw Mercedes running toward them in consternation.

"Come, come, my beloved lady," she said, throwing her arms about her young friend; "let us try to escape; they shall not take you until they have killed me."

"And what of me?" cried Mario, picking up his little rapier, Which he had thrown on the ground in order to play more freely. "But what is the matter, Mercedes?"

Mercedes had no time to explain. She knew that the outer tower was guarded by the provost's troops; she wished to try to return to the château with Lauriane hidden under her cloak, so that she could escape by the secret passage.

But it was an impossible undertaking, and Mario opposed it when he saw that the inner tower also was guarded.

While they were deliberating, the marquis was in dire distress: he had informed the provost's agents, who exhibited their commissions in proper form, that Madame de Beuvre had gone out in the saddle with his son. But when they demanded his word of honor and he pretended to be insulted by their suspicions, in order to avoid taking a false oath, their suspicions increased, and, while humbly asking his pardon, they stationed guards in the towers in the king's name, and proceeded to make a minute search of the house.

The provost's guard of La Châtre was not so numerous or so well equipped that a large force could be sent to Briantes. Moreover, officers and men alike obeyed their orders with reluctance and were very much averse to offending worthy Monsieur de Bois-Doré. But they were afraid of being denounced to monsieur le prince, who was much dreaded in the city and throughout the province.

So they did their duty conscientiously, hoping that Monsieur de Bois-Doré would threaten and resist; in which case, as *perhaps* they were not in sufficient force, they were all prepared and fully disposed to withdraw,—a not infrequent result of the differences between the provincial executive and recalcitrant provincial nobles.

The marquis realized the situation, and Aristandre gnawed his fists with impatience, awaiting the signal to fall upon the backs of the officers of the law. But Bois-Doré felt that it was a serious emergency, and that it was not simply a matter of thrashing the watch in some trivial dispute.

Monsieur de Beuvre was so deeply compromised that to take up his defence would inevitably be considered an act of rebellion against the royal authority; and under the circumstances, those gates were more effectually guarded *in the king's name*, in the eyes of every patriotic châtelain, than they would have been by a whole army.

Bois-Doré, despite his belligerent disposition, and despite the fact that he was an incorrigible Protestant at heart, had always, since the extinction of the Valois line, looked upon the king as the personification of France; and at this time, when the last efforts of the Reformed religion were on the point of betraying us to external enemies, unintentionally, doubtless, but inevitably, Bois-Doré was inspired by the genuine sentiment of nationality.

However he was resolved not to abandon his friend's daughter at any cost. He knew how the children of Protestant families were persecuted in the convents, and that Lauriane's courageous resistance would doubtless aggravate the harshness of that persecution. This new disaster must be averted by adroit management, and he appealed, by a furtive glance, to the fertile genius of Adamas.

Adamas went to and fro, heaping courtesies on the archers and scratching his head when no one was looking.

It occurred to him to flood the courtyard by opening the gates of the pond on that side, or to set fire to the château by means of a small quantity of firewood piled in the shed, at the risk of having to singe his beard a little in extinguishing it, when he had succeeded in frightening the enemy away; but in the midst of his perplexities Lauriane appeared, calm and haughty, leaning on the arm of the pale and pensive Mario.

The Moor followed them, weeping bitterly. Four of the provost's guards escorted them with due respect.

This is what had happened.

Lauriane had insisted upon being told what the matter was. She had realized at once that any resistance for the purpose of saving her would lay her friends open to the charge of high treason. She was well aware that her father had risked his head, and, when he went away, she had foreseen that her own liberty would be threatened one day or another. She had never mentioned the subject; but she was ready to submit to any fate rather than deny her opinions.

In vain did Mario and Mercedes passionately implore her to say nothing and to remain where she was: she raised her voice, declaring vehemently that she proposed to give herself up; and when the guards who were seeking her drew near the garden, she had already left it and was walking straight toward them.

They hesitated to take her into custody, her self-possession causing them to doubt if it were really she. But she named herself, saying:

"Do not put your hands upon me, messieurs; I give myself up voluntarily. Kindly permit me to go and bid my host adieu; please accompany me."

The marquis was deeply distressed by her appearance; yet he could not but admire the noble girl's great courage.

"Monsieur," he said to the lieutenant of the provost's guard, "you see that I am resigned to the necessity of obeying your commands, since such is madame's desire; but you surely will not be less honorable than she. You will permit me to drive her to Bourges in my carriage, with my son and his governess. I will take but two or three servants, and you can escort us and watch us as closely as you deem best."

So reasonable a request was readily granted, and the family had an hour in which to make their preparations for departure.

Lauriane gave her attention to that duty with wonderful self-possession. Mario, dismayed and dazed, as it were, allowed Adamas to dress him without a word. He was seated when his boots were put on, and seemed not to have sufficient strength to raise his little legs. Lucilio went to him and showed him these words, written in Italian:

"Be brave, follow the example of that brave heart."

"Yes," cried Mario, throwing his arms about his tutor's neck, "I am doing all I possibly can, and I realize what *she* is doing. But don't you think that my father will find a way to set her free."

"If it can be done, do not doubt it, monsieur," said Adamas. "Thank God! Adamas will not leave you, and will think about it every moment. If monsieur le marquis is resigned, it is because there is still some hope."

The marquis took Adamas and Mercedes in his great carriage. Clindor took his seat on the box with Aristandre.

It was agreed that Lucilio, concerning whom the marquis did not feel altogether at ease, should go to Bourges secretly.

"I have it, monsieur," said Adamas to the marquis, when they had passed La Châtre.

"What, my good fellow? What have you?"

"My idea! When we reach Etalié, we will ask leave to rest a moment at Madame Pignoux's. She has a goddaughter of Madame Lauriane's age. We will have them change clothes, and we will take her with us in place of madame."

"But is this god-daughter certain to be there at this time?"

"If she isn't there," said Mario, whose spirits were revived by Adamas's project, "I will put on Lauriane's skirt and scarf and hood; then you can say that I have remained at the inn, whereas she will remain in my place, and she can easily escape from there to Guillaume's or Monsieur Robin's, when we have gone a little way."

"Do everything for the best, my children," said the marquis, "but say nothing to me about it; for it will be very embarrassing not to be able to deny on my word of honor all knowledge of the substitution, and they will certainly require me to do so when it is discovered. So try something else and speak low. I am not listening to you."

"You forget," said Lauriane, "that I will not assent to any plan for my escape. Do not try to invent one, Adamas; and do you yield to the inevitable, Mario. I have sworn to accept my fate."

Lauriane did, in fact, refuse to alight at the *Geault-Rouge*, where the projected substitution might have been effected with some chance of success.

Mario hoped that, when they had gone a little farther, she would change her mind and assent to some scheme; but to no purpose did they argue that the affair might be arranged without compromising the marquis. She was inflexible.

"No, no," she said, "no one will believe that the marquis did not close his eyes voluntarily. Who knows, my poor Mario, that they would not keep you as a hostage until they had recaptured me? And, as for Adamas, he would surely go to prison. That is what I will not have, and I will not consent to escape, willingly or unwillingly; for, if you persist, I will shriek and make an outcry to make sure that I am taken again."

Lauriane's resolution could not be shaken. It was necessary to abandon all hope of rescuing her from captivity, and they arrived at Bourges more discouraged and downcast than when they had left Briantes.

The result of this submissive conduct was most favorable. The lieutenant-general, Monsieur Biet, who had confidently expected that the marquis would ruin himself by rebelling against Lauriane's arrest, was greatly surprised when he appeared before him with her, and requested for her an honorable reclusion, and such consideration as her dignified conduct entitled her to expect.

Monsieur Biet had no choice but to adopt a mild tone, to express his great regret at the rigorous measures adopted, which he attributed to secret orders from the prince, and to consent that Lauriane should be taken to the Convent of the Annunciation, founded by Jeanne de France, aunt of her illustrious ancestress, Charlotte d'Albret. Lauriane had several friends there, and she was allowed to keep Mercedes to wait upon her.

This convent was one of those to which the fiery Jesuit propaganda had not penetrated. The nuns, vowed to a life of meditation, did not threaten Lauriane with a too severe proselytism.

The marquis had a conference with the superior, wherein he was able to predispose her in the young recluse's favor, and he secured permission to see her every day, with Mario, in the parlor, in presence of one of the sisters.

Despite this hopeful prospect, Mario's heart was broken when the heavy door of the convent closed between him and his dear companion. It seemed to him that she would, never come forth again, nor was he free from anxiety concerning Mercedes, who strove to smile when she left him, but who was like a madwoman for a moment when she no longer saw him, and realized that she was doomed, for the first time in her life, to sleep under a different roof.

The result was that she hardly slept at all, nor did Lauriane. They talked almost all night, and wept together, being no longer restrained by the fear of distressing Mario by their grief.

"My dear Mercedes," said Lauriane, as she kissed the Moor, "I know what a sacrifice you make for me by parting from your child for my consolation."

"My daughter," replied the Moor, "I confess that in consoling you I console Mario, since he loves you perhaps more than he loves me. Do not say no; I have seen it; but I am not jealous of you, for I feel that you will make his life happy."

It was impossible to shake the Moor's conviction that that improbable marriage would take place, and Lauriane dared not contradict her, especially at that moment.

Bois-Doré had some doubts concerning the orders said to have been given by the prince with regard to Lauriane. The prince was naturally treacherous, grasping and ungrateful; but he was not cruel, and his aversion to women did not go so far as persecution. Moreover, the marquis had fancied that he could detect some symptoms of confusion in the lieutenant-general's manner when he questioned him concerning the prince's alleged secret orders. He hoped to induce him, by gentle persuasion, to revoke his decree.

He sent a messenger to Poitou to try to find Monsieur de Beuvre and urge him to return at the earliest possible moment, and he took up his abode at Bourges, in order to follow up his plan with respect to Monsieur Biet, and also to keep his eye upon his dear ward.

The messenger was unable to find Monsieur de Beuvre; he had gone to sea again, no one knew where. At the end of two months they had not heard from him.

Lauriane wept for him as for the dead. She was not deceived by the tales the marquis told her to persuade her that he had been seen and that he was well. He pretended to be embarrassed by the presence of the sister, who slept all the time, and to be afraid to show her the letters which supported his statements.

Lauriane adopted the course of remaining calm, in order to tranquillize Mario, whose eyes were constantly fixed upon her with an anxious expression.

CHAPTER LXIV

The year 1622 passed in this way, and the marquis was unable, by prayers or threats, to obtain the prisoner's release on parole.

Monsieur Biet, fearing that he had made a mistake, had obtained authority to imprison Madame de Beuvre, after it was done.

The situation was made much worse by her father's prolonged absence and silence. It became quite useless to deny the reasons therefor. No one could retain any doubt as to what had happened; and Monsieur Biet replied, with a bitter smile, to the marquis's urgent entreaties and reproaches:

"But why does not the gentleman come and get his daughter? She will be restored to him instantly, and so will the management of her property."

Lucilio had settled at Bourges, in the suburb of Saint-Ambroise, under a false name. He saw no one but Mario, who came alone, simply dressed and without ostentation, to take his lessons.

Mercedes, who was allowed to go in and out, served his meals, to which the philosopher probably would not have given a thought, absorbed as he was by his work.

At this juncture it became evident that Monsieur Poulain had changed greatly for the better. He was still at Bourges, engaged in obtaining permission to become an abbot, when Lucilio found himself face to face with him one day in the little garden appurtenant to his humble apartment.

On accosting each other, he and the future abbé discovered that they lived under the same roof.

Lucilio expected to be denounced and harassed. Nothing of the sort happened. Monsieur Poulain took pleasure in his society, and displayed great interest in Mario when he came to take his lessons.

Monsieur Poulain was too shrewd a man not to have reflected profoundly on his past experience, and he realized how little dependence could be placed on the Prince de Condé, for the Archbishop of Bourges refused to make him abbot until monsieur le prince should authorize him, and monsieur le prince seemed in no haste to do so.

Thus our friends led a reasonably peaceful life during this species of exile at Bourges. Indeed, they enjoyed more real security than they had enjoyed at Briantes during their last weeks there.

But the marquis was sadly distressed to have broken up all his luxurious, comfortable and active habits. He lived very simply and quietly, in order not to attract attention to Lauriane in a city where the spirit of the League was by no means extinct, and where the brief but violent reign of the Reformers had left unpleasant memories.

Mario strove to be cheerful in order to divert him, but the poor child was far from cheerful himself; and when he read *Astrée* aloud to him in the evening, he was always thinking of something else, or sighing over those pictures of streams, gardens and bosky groves which intensified the tedium and confinement of his present situation.

So Mario's cheeks were pale, and he became pensive. He worked desperately to perfect his education, and it was a great pleasure to him to keep Lauriane informed concerning his studies, imparting to her his most recently acquired scraps of knowledge. It was an excellent way of killing time in their daily interviews; for there is no more painful restraint than that caused by the impossibility of talking freely before witnesses with the persons one loves.

The Jesuits, who were already to be found everywhere with their fingers in every pie, tried to persuade the marquis to entrust that charming child's education to them. He so contrived his reply as to give them some ground for hope, realizing that it would not be well to have an open rupture with them.

They were not deceived by his craft, and took alarm at Mario's mysterious visits to the faubourg. They followed him, and thereupon were much distressed concerning Master Jovelin. But Monsieur Poulain arranged everything, declaring that he knew Master Jovelin to be an orthodox Catholic, and that he, Poulain, was present at the young gentleman's lessons. The ex-rector feared them more than he loved them, but he was adroit enough to fool them.

Meanwhile the war drew rapidly to a close. The news of the peace of Montpellier arrived, and gave rise to magnificent projects for rejoicing in honor of Monsieur le Prince, on the part of his good city of Bourges. But the projects had to be abandoned; the prince arrived unexpectedly, in very bad humor, feeling that his rôle was at an end.

The king had cheated him: in the first place, he had refused to die; in the second place, he had negotiated the peace without his knowledge. And then the queen-mother had regained some measure of influence. Richelieu had obtained the cardinal's hat, and despite all monsieur le prince's endeavors, was insensibly drawing near to the centre of power.

Condé simply passed through the province and the city. He no longer believed in astrology; he was becoming pious from disappointment. He had made a vow to Notre-Dame-de-Lorette.

He started for Italy without giving the slightest attention to the affairs of the province. Monsieur Biet, feeling that the Huguenots were about to recover liberty of conscience, and that it would ill become him to require Lauriane's release to be extorted from him, went himself to the convent with the marquis, to set her free.

The nuns parted from her with regret, testifying freely to her gentleness and courtesy.

Lauriane had suffered much during those five months of mental constraint; she too had lost color and flesh; she had attended, without a murmur, all the religious services, maintaining a dignified and respectful demeanor, praying to God with all her soul before the Catholic altars, and abstaining from any reflection that might have wounded the saintlike maidens of the Annunciation. But when they urged her to renounce her faith, she bowed, as if to say: *I understand*, and met all the questions that were put to her with an obstinate silence. It was no time for her to assert her liberty of conscience when it might be that her father was prostrate under the headsman's axe. So she held her peace and submitted to their importunities with the stoicism of a sufferer who, with his hands bound, listens to the flies buzzing about his head, unable to brush them away, but unwilling even to wink.

On all other occasions she treated the sisters with the greatest respect, and won their hearts by the most delicate attentions. Luckily, a truly Christian spirit reigned among them. They prayed for her conversion, they prayed for her salvation, and they left her in peace. It was a miracle; elsewhere Lauriane, might, in desperation, have been accused of witchcraft and condemned to perish by earthly flames; that was the last resource when the persecuted heretics had the courage to refuse to be convicted of heresy by their own admissions.

At last, on November 30th, our friends, overflowing with joy and hope, returned to the château of Briantes.

They had received good news from Monsieur de Beuvre. He had written many times; but his messengers had been intercepted or had betrayed their trust. He was to return very soon, and he did, in fact, return. He was welcomed with much feasting and merrymaking; after which they talked of separating.

It was proper that Lauriane should return to her own château, and the bulky De Beuvre felt cramped in the small manor of Briantes. Lauriane could not manifest before her father the slightest reluctance to resume her life with him. Indeed she was conscious of no such reluctance, she was so happy to have him at home again. And yet she felt a sudden and involuntary chill of sadness when she entered the dismal château of La Motte.

The Beaux Messieurs de Bois-Doré escorted her thither, and, at her father's request, were to remain two or three days with her. Mercedes and Jovelin were of the party. It was not therefore the sensation of solitude taking possession of her already; indeed, might they not, were they not certain to see one another almost every day?

This vague apprehension which disturbed Lauriane was a sort of disenchantment, which she did not fully understand. She had always insisted upon regarding her father as a hero; her anxieties at the convent, due to the thought of the perils he had incurred for his faith, had exalted to enthusiasm the conception she had formed of him. She had been forced to abandon her ideal since he had been at home. In the first place, although De Beuvre had complained that he grew stout in idleness, and they had expected that he would return emaciated and exhausted, he was ruddier and more portly than ever. His mind seemed to have grown dense in proportion. His blunt gayety had become a little vulgar. He posed as a sailor, smoked a pipe, swore beyond all reason, forgot to wrap his scepticism in Montaigne's ingenious aphorisms, and at times adopted an air of sly and mysterious satisfaction which was by no means courteous to his friends.

The solution of this last riddle was let fall by him on the day following his return to La Motte, during a conference which we are about to describe.

CHAPTER LXV

They had hunted during the day, then supped, and were sitting about the fire in the large salon, when Guillaume d'Ars, who had been very assiduous in his attentions to Lauriane since the news of the peace, asked leave, with some playful emotion, to make a speech.

They all ceased their games and conversation, and Guillaume, after appealing to Lauriane for special encouragement, which she accorded him without a suspicion of what it was all about, spoke as follows:

"Mesdames"—Mercedes was present,—"messieurs, friends, kinsmen and neighbors, all honored, respected and beloved, I beg you to listen to a story which is my own. In me you see a young man neither better nor worse made than many another; ignorant enough, Master Jovelin will agree; reasonably rich and well-born, but those are not virtues; brave, but that is no subject for boasting; lastly—I pause that some one may kindly eulogize me; for, as you see, I hardly understand praising myself."

"Assuredly," exclaimed the marquis with his customary good-humor, "you are more than you claim, cousin: the flower of the nobility of the province, the mirror of chivalry, and, like Alcidon, 'so much esteemed by those who know you, that there is naught to which your merit doth not entitle you to aspire.'"

"A truce to your insipid nonsense from *Astrée!*" said Monsieur de Beuvre. "What are you aiming at, Guillaume? and why do you come in quest of praise from us, when no one here has any thought of complaining of you?"

"Because, messire, having a momentous request to present to you, I wished to have for advocates all those in whom you place most confidence."

"We all bear witness to your loyalty, courage, courtesy and staunch friendship," said Lauriane. "Now, speak; for there are two women here, that is to say two curious mortals."

Lauriane had no sooner spoken thus than she blushed and regretted her words, for the enthusiastic and slightly fatuous air of the excellent Guillaume suddenly gave her a hint of what was coming.

In truth, it was an offer of marriage which Guillaume, more encouraged by her than she had intended or supposed, laid before her father and herself, invoking anew the support of all those who were present, and blending hyperbole, wit and sentiment in a way which might be considered agreeable and becoming in view of the spirit of the time.

The declaration was somewhat long and involved, as good breeding demanded, although it was none the less outspoken and sincere, and most cordial toward all present.

When his purpose had become manifest, very diverse sentiments were depicted on the faces of his audience. Monsieur de Bois-Doré manifested much embarrassment and extreme displeasure, held in check as much as possible. Lauriane lowered her eyes with an expression of melancholy rather than annoyance. Mercedes anxiously tried to read what was written in Mario's great eyes. Mario had turned toward the wall; nobody could see his face. Lucilio watched Lauriane closely.

Monsieur de Beuvre alone remained unmoved, with no other expression than one of reflection; one would have said that he was making a mental calculation that engrossed his whole attention.

No one spoke, and Guillaume was somewhat confused. But that silence might be considered a sign of encouragement as well as of disapproval, and he knelt at Lauriane's feet, as if to await her reply in an attitude of absolute submission.

GUILLAUME D'ARS PROPOSES MARRIAGE.

"Rise, Messire Guillaume," said the young woman, rising herself in order to induce him to obey her more quickly. "You surprise us with a thought which is quite new to us, and to which we cannot reply as quickly as it was suggested."

"Rise, Messire Guillaume," said the young woman, rising herself in order to induce him to obey her more quickly. "You surprise us with a thought which is quite new to us, and to which we cannot reply as quickly as it was suggested."

"It did not come to me quickly," said Guillaume. "It has been in my mind two or three years. But your youth and your mourning made me fear that I might speak too soon."

"Permit me to doubt it," said Lauriane, who knew by public report that Guillaume had always led a joyous life and had recently sighed at the feet of several more or less marriageable ladies.

"My dear daughter," said Monsieur de Beuvre at last, "permit me to tell you that Guillaume is not telling an untruth. For a long time past, as I know, he has thought of you whenever he has thought of marriage. But, in my opinion, he has decided a little too late to make his desire known to you."

"A little late?" exclaimed Guillaume in dismay; "can it be that you have disposed——"

"No, no!" laughed De Beuvre; "my daughter is neither betrothed nor promised to anyone, unless it be to our *youthful* neighbor, the Marquis de Bois-Doré, or to this solemn personage, the other Monsieur de Bois-Doré, who slumbers yonder while another seeks the hand of his future bride!"

Mario, bewildered and wounded, did not turn. It seemed as if he were asleep; the Moor alone saw that he was weeping; but the marquis rose and retorted with more animation than he usually displayed:

"I will wager, my dear neighbor, that your raillery is intended as a rebuke for our silence, so we will break it. You will forgive me, Guillaume; for, as surely as heaven is above us, I esteem you the best and most loyal man in the world, worthy in every respect to be our Lauriane's happy husband. But, with no desire to injure you in her eyes, I hereby declare that my suit preceded yours, and that I was encouraged by her and her father when I urged my suit."

"You, cousin?" exclaimed Guillaume in amazement.

"Yes, I," replied Bois-Doré, "as uncle, guardian and father by adoption of Mario de Bois-Doré here present."

"Here present? Nay," said Monsieur de Beuvre, still laughing, "for he is sleeping the sleep of innocence."

"As a child should do!" added Guillaume gently.

"I am not asleep!" cried Mario, rushing into his father's arms, and revealing his face all discolored with the sobs he had stifled in his hands.

"Hoity-toity!" said Monsieur de Beuvre, "he says that with his eyes half-closed with sleep!"

"Nay," rejoined the marquis, scrutinizing his child's face, "with his eyes inflamed with tears!"

Lauriane started; Mario's grief reminded her of the scene in the labyrinth, and brought before her mind once more the apprehensions she had forgotten. The child's tears pained her deeply, and Mercedes's glance disturbed her like a reproach.

Lucilio seemed to share her anxiety. Lauriane felt that she held in her hands for a long while, perhaps forever, the happiness of that family which had bestowed so much happiness on herself. She became altogether depressed, and, seeing that the marquis too was weeping, she gave the old man and the young man each an equally affectionate kiss, entreating them to be reasonable and not to borrow trouble concerning a future which she had not yet faced.

De Beuvre shrugged his shoulders.

"You are all very foolish," he said; "and as to you, Bois-Doré, I consider you thrice mad to have fed this poor schoolboy's brain on your absurd romances. You see the result of spoiling a child. He deems himself a man, and wishes to marry, forsooth! at an age when all he needs is the birch."

These harsh words put the finishing touch to Mario's despair; they made the marquis seriously angry.

"You seem to be in the mood for making unnecessarily cruel remarks, neighbor," he said. "The birch has no place in my method with a child who has displayed the courage of a gallant man. I am well aware that he should not marry for several years; but it seemed to me that I remembered that our Lauriane herself did not wish to marry for seven years from that day last year, when, in this very room, she gave me a pledge."

"Oh! let us not speak of that ghastly pledge!" cried Lauriane.

"Nay, let us speak of it and give thanks to God," replied the marquis, "since that dagger was the means of restoring to me my brother's child. Thus it was through your blessed hands, dear Lauriane, that that happiness entered my house; and, if I was mad to hope that you too would enter it, forgive me. The happier one is, the more greedy one is of happiness. As for you, friend De Beuvre, you surely will not deny your encouragement of my idea. Your letters prove it; you said: 'If Lauriane chooses to have patience and not go mad over the thought of marriage until Mario is nineteen or twenty years of age, I assure you that I shall be very glad.'"

"I do not deny it!" rejoined De Beuvre; "but I should be an idiot not to look at the question of my daughter's marriage in both aspects: the future and the present. Now, the future is less secure; who will assure me that we shall all be in this world six years hence? And then, when I wrote as you say, my dear neighbor, my position was not all that could be desired; and I tell you plainly that now it is much better than you imagine. So listen to me, Monsieur d'Ars, and you, marquis, and you above all, my dear daughter. I rely upon secrecy being maintained as to that which I am about to confide to none but persons of honor and discretion. I have doubled my fortune in this last campaign. That was my principal purpose, and I have accomplished it, while serving my cause at the risk of my life. I fought bad men to the best of my ability, and contributed, like others, to the honorable terms of peace which the king grants us. And so, Monsieur d'Ars, if you do me honor by asking for my daughter's hand, it is only by virtue of your name and your personal merit; for I am probably as rich as you. — And do you, friend Sylvain, when you manifest your friendship for me by the same request, understand that your treasure has no power to dazzle me; for I have my own treasure, *three ships upon the sea*, all full of *silver, gold and precious wares*, as says the ballad.

"And so, my dear and noble lords, you will give me time for reflection before replying to you; and my daughter, knowing now that it will not be difficult to find another husband for her, will take counsel with herself and form her own decision."

Thereupon there was nothing more to be done than to say good-night.

Guillaume, like a man of the world, treated Mario's pretensions lightly, but without acrimony or malice; for the child was excited enough to demand satisfaction, and Guillaume loved him too well to care to irritate him to that point. He took his leave with the not unreasonable hope of triumphing over a rival who did not come to his shoulder.

Mario slept poorly and had no appetite the next day. His father took him home, fearing that he would fall ill, and beginning to conclude that it is not well to play with the future of children in their presence. But this tardy repentance did not cure him. His abnormal, romantic brain, which had never ceased to be the brain of a child, could not understand the sound conception of time. Just as he believed that he was still young, so he imagined that Mario was ripe for the kind of love, cold and loquacious, chaste and affected, with which *Astrée* had permeated his mind.

Mario knew nothing of the subtle distinctions of words. He simply felt an intolerable heart-ache, the only deep-rooted and lasting torture.

He said: "I love Lauriane;" and if he had been asked with what kind of love, he would have answered in good faith that there were not two kinds. Pure as the angels, he had the true ideal of life, which is to love for the sake of loving.

As soon as De Beuvre and his daughter were left alone, he strongly urged her to decide in favor of Guillaume d'Ars.

"I did not wish to displease the marquis by declaring my preference," he said; "but his dream is rank madness, and I fancy that you do not care to wear the black cap six years longer, until this little brat has lost all his milk teeth."

"I did not enter into this engagement myself," replied Lauriane; "but I am afraid that you unconsciously entered into it for me with the marquis."

"I would snap my fingers at it, if I had," rejoined De Beuvre; "but that is not the case. So much the worse for the old fool and his cub if they take thoughtless words seriously; one will console himself with a wooden horse, the other with a new doublet; for they are equally childish."

"My dear father," said Lauriane, "it is no longer possible for me to jest about the marquis. He has been more than a father to me, something like a father, mother and brother all together, there has been so much protecting care, motherly affection and pleasant raillery in his manner toward me! And if Mario is only a child, he is not like other children. He is a girl in gentleness and delicacy; and he is a man in courage, for you know what he has done, and, furthermore, that he is very learned for his years.. He could teach both of us!"

"Faith, my girl," cried De Beuvre, puffing himself out, "you dote too much on the Beaux Messieurs de Bois-Doré, and it seems to me that I am no longer of much account in your eyes. You seem to think a vast deal of their grief and nothing at all of my consent, since you turn a deaf ear to me when I speak of Guillaume d'Ars."

"Guillaume d'Ars is a good friend," replied Lauriane, "but he is too old as a husband for me. He will soon be thirty years old, and he knows the world too well; he would soon begin to consider me silly or uncivilized. His suit would have flattered me perhaps before the peace; he would have deserved some credit for offering us the support of his name when we were persecuted. He deserves little to-day, when our rights are acknowledged and our tranquillity assured. He will deserve still less if he persists in his suit, now that he knows that we are richer than we were."

De Beuvre tried in vain to induce her to change her mind. He was exceedingly vexed with her; for, even if their ages had been the same, he would have much preferred Guillaume to Mario. A son-in-law devoted to physical exercise and to the heedless pursuit of pleasure suited him much better than a cultivated mind and an exceptional character.

Lauriane remonstrated, although she used after every sentence the formula: "Your will shall be mine." —But when she said it she relied upon the promise her father had made, since, her widowhood, never to force her inclination.

De Beuvre, who had become more covetous as soon as he became richer—this transformation takes place suddenly in those of mature years,—was sorely tempted to take her at her word and to say: "*It is my will*." —But he was not an unkind man, and his daughter was almost the only object of his affection.

He contented himself with harassing her and depressing her spirits by talking incessantly of those material interests to which she had believed him to be so indifferent when he made his last Huguenot crusade.

She did not give way, but, in order not to wound him, she agreed to show the greatest consideration in rejecting Guillaume's suit, and to receive his visits until further notice.

CHAPTER LXVI

The *Beaux Messieurs* did not return to La Motte for a week. Mario had a slight attack of fever. Lauriane was anxious and wept. Her father refused to take her to Briantes, saying that it was useless to keep illusions alive. There was a slight quarrel between them.

"You will make them think me most ungrateful," she said. "After all the care and attention I received from them, it is my duty to go to nurse Mario. You should at least go there every day. They will say that you have forgotten them, now that we no longer need them. Ah! why am I not a boy? I would ride there every hour in the day; I would be that poor child's friend and companion, and I could show my friendship for him without putting a noose around my neck, or incurring blame!"

At last she induced her father to take her to Briantes. She found Mario almost recovered from his grief and cured of his fever. He seemed to have determined once more to be a child. The marquis was a little hurt by Monsieur de Beuvre's conduct. But they could not remain at odds. The parents gradually entered into conversation as if nothing had happened; Lauriane began to laugh and romp with her innocent lover.

"My dear neighbor," said De Beuvre to Bois-Doré, "you must not be offended with me. Your plan for these children was pure dreaming. See on what excellent terms they are in those innocent games! That is a sign that in the game of love they would be always at war. Remember that a too young husband is not long content with a single wife, and that a deserted wife is jealous and shrewish. Moreover there is another obstacle between the children, which we have not considered: one is a Catholic, the other a Protestant."

"That is not an obstacle," said the marquis. "They can be married at the same church, reserving the right to return to the one they prefer."

"Oh! yes, that is all very well for you, you old unbeliever, who belong to both churches, that is to say, to neither; but for us— —"

"For you, neighbor? I don't know to what communion you belong; but I believe implicitly in God, and you don't believe in Him at all."

"*Perhaps*! *Who can say*?" as Montaigne says; "but my daughter is a believer, and you cannot induce her to give way."

"She would not have to give way. Here, she was always free to pray as she chose. Mario and she used to say their evening prayer together, and they never thought of disputing. Besides, Mario would be all ready to do as I did."

"Yes, to say as you did in the days of the good king: 'Long live Sully and long live the pope!'"

"Lauriane would be no more obstinate in her Calvinism, be sure of that!"

Bois-Doré was mistaken. The more frankly De Beuvre avowed his scepticism, the more earnest was Lauriane in her disinterested attachment to the Reformation. De Beuvre, who knew it well and who was seeking an opportunity to create obstacles, raised the question during dinner. Lauriane stated her views in mild language, but with remarkable firmness.

The marquis had never discussed religion with her or before her. In fact, he never discussed it with anyone, and found the half-Gallic, half-pagan divinities of *Astrée* quite reconcilable with his vague notions concerning the Deity. He was distressed to see Lauriane take up the cudgels in that way, and he could not resist the temptation to say to her:

"Ah! you bad girl, you would not be so obstinate in your opinions if you loved us a little more!"

Lauriane had not detected her father's purpose. The marquis's reproach made it clear to her. It was the first reproach he had ever addressed to her, and she was deeply grieved. But the fear of irritating her father prevented her from answering as her heart prompted. She looked down at her plate and held back a tear that trembled on her eyelid.

Mario, who seemed entirely engrossed in preparing little Fleurial's dainty dinner, spied that tear, and said abruptly, in a grave, almost manly tone, in striking contrast to the puerile occupation of his hands:

"We are making Lauriane sad, father; let us say no more about it. She has a brain of her own, and she is right. For my part, if I were in her place I would do as she does, and I would not abandon my party in misfortune."

"Well said, my little man!" said De Beuvre, impressed by Mario's intelligent air.

"And it suggests to me," said the marquis, "that we are above such profitless discussions. My son already has the free spirit of noble minds, and he would never be the one to dispute Lauriane's opinions."

"Dispute them, no indeed," said Mario; "but——"

"But what?" queried Lauriane eagerly; "you do not mean that you would share them, Mario, even through affection for me?"

"Ah! if that were the case," exclaimed De Beuvre, once more struck by a sudden thought, "if the child, with his name and his wealth, should decide to espouse our cause heartily, I do not say that I would not advise Lauriane to wear her black cap some time longer."

"Then it is all right!" said the marquis; "when the time comes——"

"No, no, father!" interposed Mario with extraordinary vehemence; "that time will never come for me. I was baptized a Catholic by Abbé Anjorrant; I was brought up in the idea that I ought never to change; and, although he did not ask me to take any oath to it when he was dying, it would seem to me as if I should disobey him by leaving the church in which he put me. Lauriane has set me the example and I will follow it; we will remain as we are, and it will be all right. That will not prevent me from loving her, and if she doesn't love me, she will do wrong and be a bad girl."

"What do you say to that, my child?" queried De Beuvre; "doesn't it strike you that he is the sort of little husband who, when he saw you burning, would say: 'I feel deeply grieved, but I can do nothing, because it is the pope's will?'"

Lauriane and Mario disputed like the children they were; that is to say, their cheeks grew red as fire. Lauriane sulked; Mario did not move an inch, and finally exclaimed with much heat:

"You say, Lauriane, that you would degrade yourself if you should change. Then you would despise me if I changed, would you not?"

Lauriane realized the justness of the retort, and said no more; but she was piqued, like a woman with whom her lover makes conditions, and her glance said to Mario: "I thought that you loved me more than you do."

When she was riding home with her father, he did not fail to say to her:

"Well, my child, do you not see now that Mario, that charming youth, is a Papist of the old stock, like his own father, who served the Spaniard against us? And some day, ashamed of his old uncle's inanity, he will make war on us! Then what will you say, when you see your husband in one camp and your father in the other, shooting bullets at each other, or fighting hand to hand?"

"Really, father," said Lauriane, "you speak as if I had evinced a desire to remain a widow; but I have never determined upon that. I cannot see, however, why Monsieur d'Ars is not equally exposed to the evil fate which you predict. Is not he a Catholic and a devoted partizan of the royal power?"

"Monsieur d'Ars has no will of his own," replied De Beuvre, "and I will answer for it that we shall be able to bend him to all our purposes, on every occasion. More bigoted men than he have changed sides when the prospects of the Reformation seemed bright."

"If Monsieur d'Ars has no will," rejoined Lauriane, "so much the worse for him; he is no man; and yet he is a man in years!"

Lauriane was not mistaken. Guillaume was a weak character; but he was a handsome fellow, a pleasant neighbor, brave as a lion, and very generous to his friends. He was mild and easy-going with the peasantry, and allowed himself to be robbed without paying the slightest heed; but he followed the example of the nobles of his time: he allowed the peasantry to wallow in ignorance and poverty. It seemed to him a very fine thing that Lauriane's vassals were neat and well-fed, and very amusing that Bois-Doré's were stout; but when he was told that, at Saint-Denis-de-Touhet, the peasants died like flies during the epidemics; that at Chassignoles and Magny they did not know the taste of wine and meat—hardly that of bread; and that, in the Brenne country, they ate grass, while in other even more unhappy provinces they ate one another, he would say:

"What do you expect to do about it? Everybody cannot be happy!"

And he did not exert his mind beyond its powers to find a remedy. It had never occurred to him to live on his estate, as Bois-Doré did, and to share his well-being with all those who were dependent upon him. He passed as much time as he could at Bourges and Paris, and aspired to a rich marriage, in order that he might lead a more joyous life than ever, with a woman whom he would probably make perfectly happy on condition that she had no more brain and sensitiveness than he.

He was the type of his caste and his epoch, and no one thought of blaming him.

On the other hand, Lauriane was considered a fanatical heretic and Bois-Doré an old imbecile. Lauriane herself did not judge Guillaume so severely as we do, but she felt that he lacked pith and substance, and she experienced unconquerable ennui when, she was in his company. At such times the days passed at Briantes would come back to her like a delightful dream. Well might she have said: *Et in Arcadia ego!*

However, she had no idea of becoming Mario's wife. In her inmost thoughts she remained his older sister, proud of him and striving to emulate him; but she found no suitor to her liking, although many a one came forward as soon as her father was seen to be purchasing additional estates. By dint of making involuntary comparisons between her father, who was so practical and selfish, who criticized her so often in regard to her charities, and the excellent Monsieur Sylvain, who always lived himself and caused everybody about him to live as in a fairy tale, she conceived a dislike for cold reason, and became in secret the most dreamy and romantic maiden on earth, according to Monsieur de Beuvre and her other relations of both religions. In private, they laughed at her and at what they called her ridiculous love for a baby in arms.

By dint of hearing it said that she was in love with Mario, Lauriane, being persecuted to some extent in her own home, was driven, as it were in spite of herself, to look upon that love as possible. So it was that she admitted the idea of it when Mario was fifteen.

But she speedily rejected that idea again, for Mario at fifteen did not seem as yet to distinguish between love and friendship. He was respectful in his manner toward her, and at the same time familiar in his speech after the fashion of a well-bred brother. He did not say a word which could lead her to think that passion had revealed itself to him. Sometimes, it is true, he flushed deeply when Lauriane suddenly appeared in some place where he did not expect her, and he turned pale when some new project of marriage for her was broached in his presence. At least, Adamas so informed his master, and Mercedes confided the same observations to Lucilio. But it may be that they were mistaken. The boy was growing rapidly and reading a great deal; perhaps he had pains in his head and limbs.

We will say but one word concerning this period, when Mario was fifteen years of age and Lauriane nineteen. Their placid existence and tranquil relations were so happily monotonous that we can find no traces thereof in our documents concerning Briantes and La Motte-Seuilly.

We find there, however, mention of the marriage of Guillaume d'Ars to a wealthy heiress of Dauphiné. The nuptials were celebrated in Berry, and it does not appear that Lauriane's rejection of his suit had displeased honest Guillaume, for she was of the party, as were the Bois-Dorés.

A year later, in 1626, the lives of our characters are more clearly outlined. That was the epoch of the baptism of Monseigneur le Duc d'Enghien—afterward the great Condé—which hastened the course of events for them.

This baptism took place at Bourges on the 5th of May. The young prince was then about five years of age. The splendid festivities in connection with the ceremony attracted all the nobility and all the bourgeoisie of the province.

The Marquis de Bois-Doré, who had at last secured the salutary indifference, if not the dangerous favor of Condé and the Jesuit faction, yielded to the wishes of Mario, who was curious to see a little of the world, and to his own inclinations, which led him to exhibit his heir under more favorable circumstances than in 1622, when he was in a very painful and disquieting situation.

CHAPTER LXVII

When his mind was once made up, Bois-Doré, who could do nothing by halves, employed Adamas's genius and industry for a whole month in superintending the preparation of the splendid costumes and sumptuous equipages which he proposed to exhibit before the court and the city.

The supply of horses and gorgeous accoutrements was replenished; they made investigations concerning the new styles. They exerted themselves to eclipse all rivals. The old nobleman, still erect on his legs and straight of back, still becurled and anointed, still in good health and young in fancy, chose to be dressed in the same fabrics cut in the same style as his *grandson's*. So Mario was called at court, because the prince, seeking to jest pleasantly with Bois-Doré, and forgetting the degree of kinship between the Beaux Messieurs, asked him if it was from economy that he dressed his grandson in the clippings of his own clothes. Mario understood the great vassal's contempt, and felt more of a royalist than ever.

Lauriane also had expressed a wish to see a very great fête for the first time in her life. As her father had taken no part in the new uprising of the Huguenots, and, moreover, as a new treaty of peace had been signed within three months, they could appear at Bourges without risk. It was agreed that they should all go together.

Magnificent banquets, banners with Latin distichs and anagrams in honor of the little prince, regiments of children, in brave array and exceedingly well drilled, for his escort, the singing of motets, speeches by the magistrates, presentation of the keys of the city, concerts, dances, a play given by the Jesuit college, angels descending from triumphal arches and presenting rich gifts to the young duke—that is to say, to monsieur his father, who would not have been content with sweetmeats,—manœuvres by the militia, ceremonial functions and merry-makings—all this lasted five days.

They saw many great personages there.

The comely and famous Montmorency—whom Richelieu afterward sent to the scaffold—and the Dowager Princesse de Condé—called the poisoner—represented the godfather and godmother, who were no others than the King and Queen of France. Monseigneur le Duc received baptism in the *chrémeau*—a little cap trimmed with precious stones—and a long dress of cloth of silver. The Prince de Condé wore a gray coat all stamped with gold and silver.

The Beaux Messieurs de Bois-Doré were invited by Monsieur Biet to take their places on the platform reserved for the higher nobility, not because they were among the best friends of the little court, but because of their rich attire, which did honor to the spectacle.

Mario's beauty attracted even more notice than his costume.

Lauriane heard the ladies—notably the little prince's youthful and lovely mother—call attention to the beautiful boy's charms. She felt disturbed for the first time, as if she were jealous of the glances and smiles of which he was the recipient.

Mario paid no heed to them. He looked at the princely child with curiosity. He was ugly and of sickly aspect; but there was much intelligence in his eyes and resolution in his gestures.

On the 6th of May, as our friends were preparing to depart, De Beuvre led the marquis aside.

They had been sojourning at the house of a friend.

"Look you," said he, "we must have done with this, and come to some decision."

"Have a little patience. The horses will soon be ready," replied Bois-Doré, thinking that he was in haste to start for home.

"You do not understand me, neighbor; I say that we must make up our minds to marry our children, since that is their idea and our own. I must tell you that I am about to make another journey. I came here only to make arrangements with certain people who assure me of excellent opportunities in England, and if I must entrust my Lauriane to you once more, it will be quite as well that she should be married to your heir. It is an excellent chance for him; for my vessels are in a fair way to multiply, so I am told, and the peace will simply double the opportunities of Anglo-Protestant piracy. So that my daughter might have aspired to better men than you, as to name and wealth, but not as to heart; and as the trouble of taking care of her will interfere with my taking proper care of my business, I desire, on resuming my freedom of action, to place my Lauriane in good hands. So say yes and let us hasten matters."

The marquis was staggered by this proposition, which. Monsieur de Beuvre had seemed little inclined to receive favorably during the past four years, if it had been made to him. But it did not require much reflection to convince him of the impropriety of this plan, and of Lauriane's father's selfish heedlessness. Bois-Doré was often heedless himself, often injudicious; but he was a father in the truest sense, and Mario in love and married at sixteen seemed to him to be in a more perilous situation than Mario romantically and conjugally inclined at eleven.

"You cannot mean it," he replied; "let our children be betrothed, if you please; but as to marrying them, it is altogether too soon."

"That is what I meant," said De Beuvre. "Let them be betrothed, and do you take my daughter with you once more. You can watch over the lovers, and in two or three years I will return for the wedding."

Bois-Doré was romantic enough to yield; and yet he hesitated. He had forgotten all about love, about its tempests at all events. But a glance from Adamas, who pretended to be arranging the luggage, and who was listening intently with both ears, reminded him of the flushes and pallors he had noticed on Mario's face, which might be the manifestation of suffering carefully concealed.

"No, no," he said. "I will not put my child beside the fire; I will not expose him to the risk of burning up or disobeying the laws of honor. Abide in your château, neighbor, and let us be prudent. You are rich enough. Let us exchange oaths, without the knowledge of our children. Why deprive either of them of sleep? Three years hence we will make them happy without perplexity or self-reproach."

De Beuvre realized that ambition and greed had led him to make an absurd suggestion. But he had become obstinate and choleric. He lost his temper, refused to give his word, and decided to take his daughter to Poitou, to her kinswoman the Duchesse de la Trémouille.

Mario nearly swooned when, as they were about entering the carriage, he was informed that Lauriane would not return with them and was going away for an indefinite period. His father had tried to lighten the blow; but De Beuvre insisted upon dealing it, either to test the boy's sentiments, or to have his revenge for the lesson in prudence he had received with a bad grace from the least prudent of men. Lauriane, who knew nothing as yet— her father having told her simply that they were to remain a few days longer at Bourges,—rushed downstairs when she heard the marquis's pained exclamation at the sight of Mario pale and swooning. But Mario soon recovered, declared that he had had an attack of cramp, and jumped into the great carriage with his eyes closed. He did not wish to see Lauriane, whose tranquillity, down to that moment, wounded him to the lowest depths of his heart. He supposed that she knew everything, and had decided, without regret, to part from him forever.

The marquis longed to remain, to have an explanation with De Beuvre. He had the courage to refrain, when he saw how brave Mario was: whatever the result, the young man had reached an age when separation for a few years had become necessary.

Mario, expansive as he was on all other subjects, opened his heart to no one, and affected the most perfect serenity during the journey.

At Briantes the marquis questioned him adroitly, Mercedes imprudently. He held his ground, saying that he loved Lauriane *much*, but that his grief would affect neither his reason nor his work.

He kept his word. His health suffered a little; but he assented to all the measures that he was urged to adopt in that regard, and he soon recovered.

"I hope," the marquis would say sometimes to Adamas, "that he will not be too sentimental, and will forget that wicked girl who does not love him."

"For my part," said the sage Adamas, "I hope that she loves him more than she seems to do; for if our Mario should lose the hope that keeps him alive, we should have cause for anxiety!"

In 1627, that is to say the next year, the château of Briantes was threatened anew with disaster. It was proposed to raze its stout walls, its little bastions and its fortified towers.

Richelieu, being definitely established in supreme authority, had decreed and ordered the destruction of the fortifications of cities and citadels throughout the kingdom. This excellent measure, construed most broadly, extended to "all fortifications constructed within thirty years, about the houses and châteaux of private individuals, without the express permission of the king."

Briantes was not in that category; its defences dated from feudal days and were useless against cannon. The sheriffs and magistrates of La Châtre, displeased at having to shave themselves, as Adamas the ex-barber said, would have been glad to shave all the noble lords, their neighbors. But Bois-Doré, feeling the necessity of protection against bands of adventurers and highwaymen, maintained his rights and forced them to be respected. He was too much beloved by his vassals to fear that they would act like those of many other nobles, who voluntarily posed as executors of the great cardinal's orders.

The measure was very popular and at the same time very sweeping. It was hunting down the spirit of the League in its feudal lairs. But the orders were carried out only in Protestant neighborhoods, and that bold decree remained upon paper, like many of Richelieu's bold conceptions.

Berry escaped by showing its claws, as always. Monsieur le Prince did not allow a stone to be removed from his fortress of Montrond; the châteaux of the great and petty nobility remained standing, and the great tower of Bourges did not fall until the reign of Louis XIV.

Bois-Doré had hardly recovered from this excitement when he was assailed by another, more serious yet less alarming.

"Monsieur," said Adamas to him one evening, "I must needs regale you with a story which Monsieur d'Urfé would have put in the form of a romance, for it is most pleasant."

"Let us have your story, my friend!" said the marquis, pulling his lace cap over his bald skull.

"It relates, monsieur to your virtuous druid and the fair Moor."

"Adamas, you are becoming a joker and a satirist, my good man. No calumny, I beg you, concerning my excellent friend and the chaste Mercedes!"

"Why, monsieur, where would be the harm if those two worthy persons should be united by the bonds of matrimony? Do you know, monsieur, that this morning, as I was arranging the learned man's library—he will allow nobody but me to touch his books, and, in truth, it requires a man with some little learning—I saw the Moor stealthily kiss a bouquet of roses which she places on his table every morning while he is breakfasting with you. Then she suddenly saw me, and, turning as pale as the scarf she wears on her head, she fled as if she had committed some great crime. I have suspected something, monsieur, for a long time, a very long time. All this friendship, all these little attentions of hers—I was sure that they would lead them both to love."

"To be sure," said the marquis. "But go on, Adamas!"

"Well, monsieur, the discovery made me laugh loud and long, not in mockery, but with satisfaction, for one is always pleased to guess or surprise a secret, and when you are pleased, you laugh. And so Master Jovelin, returning to his room, asked me mildly, with his eyes, why I was laughing so heartily, and I told him, innocently enough, to make him laugh too—and also, I confess, to see how he would take it."

"And how did he take it?"

"His face shone like a sunbeam, exactly like a pretty girl's; and one cannot but believe that happiness remakes a man; for his face, with its great mouth and great black moustache, lighted up like a star, and he seemed to me as beautiful as he is sometimes when he is playing his sweet-toned bagpipe."

"Very good, Adamas, you are training yourself to be a fine speaker. And then?"

"Then I went out, or rather I pretended to go out; and, on looking back through the partly open door, I saw dear Lucilio take up the flowers, kiss them passionately, and put them in his doublet, flowers, thorns and all, as if he took pleasure in being pricked and feeling the soft petals at the same time. And he paced the floor, pressing that love-token to his breast with both hands."

"Better and better, Adamas! What next?"

"Then the Moor entered by another door and said to him:

"'Is it time to call Mario for his lesson?'"

"What was his reply?"

"He said no with his eyes and his head; so that I could see that he wished to detain her. She started to go away, thinking that he was busy with some of his monkey-tricks; for she acts with him, monsieur, like a servant who has no hope of pleasing her master. But he knocked on the table to recall her. She went back. They looked at each other; not long, for she soon lowered her lovely black eyes and said to him in Arabic, at least I judged so from her manner:

"What is your wish, master?"

He pointed to the goblet in which she had placed the roses; and she, seeing that they were not there, said:

"'It must be that sly creature Adamas who took them away, for I never forget them.'"

"She said that?"

"Yes, monsieur, in Arabic. I could guess at every word! Then she ran to fetch more flowers, and he followed her to the door like a man fighting against himself. He went back to his table, put his head in his hands, and, my word for it, monsieur, he found the noblest sentiments imaginable in his heart to reconcile his love with his virtue."

"But why should he fight so against it?" cried the marquis; "does he not know that I should be overjoyed to have him marry that beautiful, good woman? Go, bring him to me, Adamas; he retires late and will still be at work. Mario is asleep, and this is the most propitious moment for discussing so delicate a subject."

CHAPTER LXVIII

The good marquis had no difficulty in confessing Lucilio.

He frankly admitted that he had adored the Moor for a long while and that for some time he had fancied that his love was returned. But he summed up the situation with his concise pen.

In the first place he was afraid of attracting persecution which he had thus far escaped in France only by a miracle. Then, when it had seemed to him beyond question that Richelieu, despite all his warfare against the Reformed religion, had adopted as an inflexible policy the maintenance of the Edict of Nantes in favor of liberty of conscience in every form, he had decided to await Mario's marriage to Lauriane or to some other woman who had won his heart. Whatever his dear pupil's frame of mind might be, whatever hope or regret, placid expectation or secret excitement, he did not choose to set before him the selfish and perilous spectacle of a marriage for love.

The marquis approved his friend's generous forethought; but he found an expedient.

"My excellent friend," he said to him, "the Moor is close upon thirty, and you have passed your fortieth year. You are still young enough to attract each other, and your ages are well balanced; but, without offence, you are no longer boy and girl, to leave blank pages in the book of your felicity! Make the most of the happy years that still remain. Marry. I will travel with Mario for a few months, and while we are absent I will tell him that I alone conceived the idea of a marriage of reason between Mercedes and you. I will invent some pretext to explain why you could not wait until our return, and when he sees you again, his mind will be accustomed to the new condition of affairs. Marriage always has a sobering effect, and then I trust to you to conceal the joys of the honeymoon behind the thick clouds of prudence and self-restraint."

So it was that the marquis took Mario to Paris. He showed him the king and his court, but at a distance; for society had changed greatly in the fifteen years that worthy Sylvain had been living on his estates. The friends of his youth were dead, or had withdrawn, as he had, from the hurly-burly of the new society. The few great personages still on the stage with whom he had formerly had some acquaintance, hardly remembered him, and, except for his antiquated attire, would not have recognized him.

Mario's attractive and modest manners were observed however: the *Beaux Messieurs* were warmly welcomed in some houses of distinction, but no one suggested taking them any higher; and indeed neither of them desired very earnestly to approach the pale sun of Louis XIII.

Mario was terribly disappointed when he saw the fainthearted son of Henri IV. ride by, and the marquis had discovered in that face no encouragement to pursue his design of obtaining the royal confirmation of his title of marquis.

New edicts appeared every day against the usurpation of titles; edicts little respected, for the nobles, old and new, continued to assume names of domains of very doubtful authenticity. Their obscurity protected them. Bois-Doré was forced to recognize that he had no better refuge than that.

Furthermore, he could not avoid the discovery that in Paris nobody was a *beau monsieur* who was not of the court. To be sure, in their daily drives and on Place Royale, more or less people turned to gaze at the strange contrast between his painted face and Mario's deliciously fresh complexion; and for some time the goodman, thinking that he was recognized, smiled at the passers-by, and put his hand to his hat, ready to welcome overtures which no one thought of making. That gave him an air of dazed hesitancy and vulgar affability which aroused laughter. The ladies who sat under the young trees in the Cours-la-Reine, or walked back and forth fan in hand, said to one another:

"Who is that tall old fool, pray?"

And if those ladies were of the society in which Bois-Doré had reappeared, or bourgeoises of the quarter where he lodged, sometimes there would be one who would reply:

"He is a nobleman from the provinces, who prides himself on having been a friend of the late king."

"Some Gascon, I suppose? They all saved France! Or some Béarnais? They were all foster-brothers of our dear Henri!"

"No, an old ass from Berry or Champagne. There are Gascons everywhere."

So it was that honest Sylvain was quite effaced in that forgetful, ostentatious crowd, strive as he would to appear to advantage there. He said to himself with some vexation that it was better to be first in one's village than last at court. It is certain however that, with a little impudence and scheming, he could have pushed Mario ahead as so many others were pushed; but he dreaded some affront on the score of his problematical marquisate.

He resigned himself therefore to play the part of the provincial boor, and would have suffered terribly from ennui, had not Mario, who was always studious and intelligently artistic in his tastes, taken him to see the monuments of art and science which were the principal attractions of the capital of the kingdom in his eyes.

The pleasure and profit which the young man derived from them consoled the old man in some measure for what he called in his secret thoughts an abortive journey.

He did not tell Mario of all his disappointments. He still cherished the hope of discovering his mother's family and acquiring thereby a fine Spanish title, an inheritance of some sort. He had written many times to Spain to make inquiries and to furnish information concerning Mario, in case the said family should display any interest. He had never received any but vague, perhaps evasive replies.

At Paris he determined to go in person to the Embassy. He was received there by a sort of private secretary, who informed him, in substance, that, in compliance with his frequent requests they had at last elucidated a mysterious affair. The young woman who had eloped and disappeared did in fact belong to the noble family of Merida, and Mario was the issue of a secret marriage, the validity of which might be contested.

The young woman had left no claim to any fortune, and her family were by no means anxious to recognize a young man reared by an old heretic, only partially purged of his heresy.

The marquis, deeply incensed, determined to stop there and to repay the contempt of those haughty Spaniards with oblivion. It had cost his pride dearly enough to besiege the doors of an embassy which he, as a former Protestant and a good Frenchman, bitterly detested.

And yet he was sad, and confided his distress to his inseparable Adamas.

"Of a surety," he said to him, "the pleasantest and most honorable life is that of the provincial nobility. But, while it is suited to those who have fought and suffered, it may become burdensome and even shameful in the case of a young heart like Mario's. Have I reared him with the greatest care, have we made of him, thanks to his precocious talents, an accomplished gentleman, fit for any station, only to bury him in a country manor, on the pretext that he has no need to make his fortune, and that he is tender-hearted and humane? Should he not have a little taste of war and adventure, and by some brilliant deed win that marquisate which the great cardinal's ideas of universal levelling may take from him any day? I know that the child is very young, and that we have lost no time as yet; but his inclinations seem to tend in the direction of study, and I ransack my wits to determine how he will find a way to distinguish himself in that direction."

"Monsieur," replied Adamas, "if you think that your son will be more of a cripple than you in battle, you hardly know him."

"I do not know my son?"

"Well, no, monsieur, you do not know him: he is a mysterious creature who loves you so dearly that he never dares to have an idea to perplex you or a trouble for you to share. But I know what is in the bag: Mario dreams of war as much as of love, and the time is near at hand when, if you do not divine his ambition, you will have him either sick or melancholy on your hands."

"God forbid!" cried the marquis. "I will question him on this subject to-morrow!"

In such a matter, when a man says to-morrow, it means that he is inclined to shirk, and the marquis did in fact shirk. Paternal weakness fought a great battle with paternal pride, and won the day. Mario was not yet strong enough to endure the fatigues of war; and, furthermore, the war with England or Spain to which all indications pointed, seemed to be postponed for a brief space by Richelieu's mighty efforts to create a French navy. There was no need of haste; there was plenty of time; the opportunity would come soon enough!

So they returned to Briantes late in the autumn and found Lucilio married to Mercedes.

Mario, on being informed of this event in Paris, manifested more satisfaction than surprise. He had felt for a long while, in the burning air which his Moor involuntarily breathed upon him, as well as in Lucilio's gentle melancholy and in the adroit and affectionate language of his bagpipes, the waves of passion which sometimes set his own blood on fire. His heart felt as if it were caught in a vise at the thought of happy love; but he had extraordinary control over himself. As his father lived only in his life, he had at an early age accustomed himself to conceal his emotions from him; and, when Adamas reproved him for keeping his thoughts too much to himself, he would reply:

"My father is old; he is wrapped up in me as a mother is in her child. It is my duty not to shorten his days by causing him anxiety, and heaven has entrusted to me the mission of making him live a long while."

Lauriane was living in Poitou, and they rarely heard from her. She wrote in an affectionate and respectful tone to the marquis, but she hardly mentioned Mario's name, as if she dreaded to remind him of herself.

By way of compensation she wrote in the most affectionate terms of the Moor, Lucilio, and the faithful retainers of the family. It seemed that her affection, held in check with those who had the first claim upon it, instinctively took its revenge with the others. She announced several times, with a sort of affectation, that there were divers projects of marriage under consideration, and that she would soon inform them of her decision, desiring, she said, to make a choice that would be agreeable to the marquis, whom she looked upon as a second father.

The strange feature of these alleged marriage projects was that she recurred to them year after year, as if they were constantly abandoned and revived, without imparting anything of interest to her friends as to her choice; as if her real purpose were to say to them: "I do not marry because I am not so inclined; but do not for one moment think that I am reserving myself for you."

Such was, in fact, her purpose in writing these letters, and her state of mind may be thus described:

When he took her away from Berry, intending soon to part from her, Monsieur de Beuvre had inflicted a cruel wound upon her heart by inventing a fable to the effect that the marquis and his heir, when consulted by him at Bourges, had met his advances very coldly. Mario had shown himself a very fervent Catholic on that occasion; he had sworn that he would never enter into a *mixed* marriage.

Lauriane should have distrusted a father in whom the thirst for gold had penetrated to the very entrails, and who, being in haste to go away, was determined at any price to persuade her to marry promptly. She refused to marry in anger and without due consideration; but she promised to reflect upon it, and in her heart proudly abandoned the ungrateful Mario. She had loved him at Bourges — really loved him for the first time after years of placid friendship. And that first love of her life, almost before it was admitted, hardly revealed to herself, she had had to blush for in very shame, and to crush it without a sign of weakening!

She had some suspicions; but, while her father did not swear that he exaggerated nothing, he could at least give her his word of honor that he had proposed their betrothal to the marquis, and that he had evaded the proposal on the pretext that Mario was still too young to have the idea of love suggested to him. Lauriane was too pure to realize the risks she might have run by returning to Briantes. She remembered that, at the moment of parting from her, Mario, who was said to be ill, had shrugged his shoulders and turned his head away, saying:

"You make too much ado about a little cramp. I have no pain now."

So she said again to her father what she had said to him with all sincerity some time before, that she had never looked upon that marriage as a possibility; and she encouraged him to go away, as he desired to do, promising him that she would marry any suitable aspirant who did not inspire aversion in her.

But such an aspirant did not appear. All those whom Madame de la Trémouille presented to her failed to please her. She found in them the positivism which had invaded her father like a passion, but she found it in the form of cold and somewhat cynical selfishness. The halcyon days of the Reformation were passing away, like the social structure of the preceding century. The Reformed religion was heroic only under cruel persecution, and Richelieu, crushing the remains of the party by the inevitable logic of events, bore no resemblance to a persecutor. France said to the Protestants by his mouth: "Confine yourselves to religious liberty; let politics alone. Turn your faces with us against the enemies without the realm!"—The Protestants proposed to become a republic; they became a Vendée.

Save the French Puritans—that redoubtable, heroic, indomitable party, which stood at bay and immolated itself at La Rochelle two years later—all French Protestants were at this time inclined to adhere to the principle of French unity; but many had determined not to give in their adhesion until after a victory which should secure favorable and lasting terms for their party.

Now, among those who reasoned well, but who were about to be led on to reason ill and to choose between a foreign alliance and final extermination, the nobility were generally speaking less pure in their purposes than the bourgeoisie and the common people. They made reservations in their own interest; those most highly placed insisted upon being purchased, and translated their craving for religious liberty into a craving for offices and money.

Lauriane was intensely indignant at these numerous defections which were announced every day, or which awaited their turn in shameful anticipation. She had formed a more chivalrous idea of the honor of the party. She was forced now to recognize the fact that her father, whose greed had so humiliated her, was simply doing a little more tardily what most men of his age had done all their lives, and what most young men were eager to do in their turn. Still, Monsieur de Beuvre was one of the best; for he had no idea of betraying his flag. He simply made haste to make his bargain before the flag was dragged in the dust.

It was possible that Lauriane might fall in with an exception to the general rule. There were exceptions, for she herself was one. She did not fall in with them, perhaps because she was so pensive and distraught that she did not know how to look for them.

Youth and beauty are justifiably proud. They wait to be discovered and reveal naught themselves, because they dread to have the appearance of offering themselves.

CHAPTER LXIX

Although we have hitherto done our utmost to follow our characters step by step through the ordinary life of the *stay-at-home nobility*, which our authorities enabled us to study with some care, we are forced now to pass over a brief interval of time, and to seek the Beaux Messieurs de Bois-Doré far from their peaceful domain.

It was in 1629, the first day of March, I believe. Mont Genèvre, covered with snow, presented a scene of extraordinary animation upon both slopes, and even to the very opening of the ravine called the Pas de Suse.

The French army was marching upon the Duc de Savoie, that is to say upon Spain and Austria, his trusty allies.

The king and the cardinal climbed the mountain in spite of the intense cold. The cannon were dragged up through the snow. It was one of those scenes of grandeur which the French soldier has always acted so magnificently amid the sublime grandeur of the Alps, under Napoléon as under Richelieu, and under Richelieu as under Louis XII., without diverting himself with attempts to dissolve the rocks, as Hannibal's genius is said to have done, and without other artifice than intrepid determination, ardor and cheerfulness.

In one of the paths trodden through the snow parallel with the road, two horsemen happened to be ascending side by side the precipitous slope of the mountain on the French side. One was a young man of some nineteen years, of robust frame and with a grace of movement most pleasant to behold under the becoming warlike costume of the age. So far as colors were concerned, the young man was dressed in accordance with his own fancy. His equipment and his weapons, as well as his isolation, indicated a gentleman making the campaign as a volunteer.

Mario de Bois-Doré—the reader will assume that it is he whom I am describing—was the comeliest cavalier in the whole army. The development of his youthful strength had in no wise diminished the wonderful charm of his noble and intelligent face. His expression was like an angel's in purity; but the sprouting beard reminded one that this youth with the divine glance was but a simple mortal; and that young moustache faintly outlined the curve of a smile, somewhat indifferent, perhaps, but with a cordial kindliness showing through its melancholy.

Magnificent brown hair, of a soft shade and curling naturally, framed the face to the neck, and fell in a heavy braid—the *cadenette* was more in vogue than ever—below the shoulder. The face wore a delicate flush, but was pale rather than ruddy. The exquisite distinction of manners and dress was the principal characteristic of that figure, which did not attract the glance, but from which the glance found it difficult to detach itself when it had rested upon it.

Such was the impression of the horseman whom chance had brought side by side with Mario.

The last-mentioned horseman was about forty years of age; he was thin and sallow, with regular features, very mobile lips, a piercing eye, and an expression of cunning tempered by a disposition to serious reflection. He was dressed in rather a problematical costume, all in black, and in a short cassock, like a priest on a journey, but armed and booted like a soldier.

His bony, active horse easily kept pace with his companion's ardent and impetuous steed.

The two horsemen had saluted each other without speaking, and Mario had slackened his pace to allow the other, as his senior, to ride first. The traveller seemed to appreciate that scrupulous courtesy, and declined to pass the younger man.

"In truth, monsieur," said Mario, "our horses seem to keep step, which fact proves the good-will of both, for I have difficulty in keeping mine to a pace which does not leave all the others behind, and I have had to give my companions a long start, in order not to reach the top of the pass before them."

"That which is a fault in your noble beast is a good quality in mine," replied the stranger. "As I almost always travel alone, I go my way without giving anyone reason to blame me for fatiguing my horse. But may I ask you, monsieur, where I have had the honor of seeing you? Your amiable face is not altogether strange to me."

Mario looked closely at him and said:

"The last time that I had the honor of seeing you was at Bourges, four years since, at the baptism of Monseigneur le Duc d'Enghien."

"Then you are really the young Comte de Bois-Doré?"

"Yes, Monsieur l'Abbé Poulain," replied Mario, putting his hand once more to his plumed hat.

"I am overjoyed to find you as you are, monsieur le comte," rejoined the rector of Briantes; "you have grown in stature, in attractiveness, and in merit as well, I can see by your manners. But do not call me *abbé*; for I am not one as yet, alas! and it is possible that I may never be."

"I know that Monsieur le Prince has always refused to assent to your appointment; but I thought— —"

"That I had found something better than the Abbey of Varennes? Yes and no. While awaiting the opportunity to assume some title, I succeeded in leaving Berry, and chance attached me to the fortunes of the cardinal, in the service of Père Joseph, to whom I am devoted body and soul. I can say to you, between ourselves, that I am one of his messengers; and that is why I have a good horse."

"I congratulate you, monsieur. Père Joseph's service can call for no work that a patriotic Frenchman may not do, and the cardinal's fortune is the destiny of France."

"Do you really mean what you say, Monsieur Mario?" queried the priest with an incredulous smile.

"Yes, monsieur, on my honor!" the young man replied, with an accent of sincerity which overcame the diplomatic priest's suspicions. "I do not wish Monsieur le Cardinal to know that he has two cordial admirers in my father and myself; but do us the honor to believe that we are loyal enough to desire to serve the cause of the great minister and of the fair kingdom of France, with our hearts and bodies, as well as you, if we can."

"I believe in you implicitly," replied Monsieur Poulain, "but I have less faith in monsieur your father! For example, he did not send you to the siege of La Rochelle last year. You were still very young, I know; but younger men than you were there, and you must have chafed at having to miss the glorious rendezvous of all the young nobility of France."

"Monsieur Poulain," rejoined Mario, with some severity, "I thought that you were bound to my father by the ties of gratitude. All that he was able to do for you he did, and if the Abbey of Varennes has been secularized for the benefit of Monsieur le Prince, you can not blame my father, who was largely defrauded in that affair."

"Oh! I do not doubt it!" exclaimed Monsieur Poulain; "give me the Prince de Condé of all men to tangle up accounts! and I blame him and him alone. As for your father, monsieur le comte, let me tell you that I still love and esteem him infinitely. Far from having any thought of injuring him, I would give my life to know that he had devoted himself without mental reservation, to the Catholic cause."

"My father does not need to devote himself to the cause of his country, monsieur! I mean to say that he warmly embraces the cardinal's cause against all the enemies of France."

"Even against the Huguenots?"

"The Huguenots are no more, monsieur! Let us leave the dead in peace!"

Monsieur Poulain was impressed anew with the dignified expression of that sweet face. He felt that he was not dealing with an ambitious and frivolous youth, like others with whom he was familiar.

"You are right, monsieur," he said. "Peace to the ashes of the men of La Rochelle, and may God hear you, to the end that they may not come to life again at Montauban and elsewhere. Since your father has recovered so fully from his religious indifference, let us hope that he will, if need be, permit you to march against the rebels in the South."

"My father always has permitted me to follow my own inclination; but understand, monsieur, that it will never lead me to march against Protestants, unless I see that the monarchy is in great danger. Never will I draw the sword against Frenchmen, from ambition or vainglory; never can I forget that that cause, once glorious, now brought low, placed Henri IV. on the throne. You were reared in the spirit of the League, Monsieur Poulain, and now you are fighting against it with all your strength. You have changed from the wrong to the right, from the false to the true; I have lived and I shall die in the path upon which my feet were placed: loyalty to my country, detestation of intrigues with the foreigner. I am entitled to less credit than you, having never had occasion to change my views; but I promise you that I will do my best, and that while respecting freedom of conscience in others, I will fall with all my strength upon the allies of Monsieur de Savoie."

"You forget that they are the allies of the Reformed religion to-day."

"Say of Monsieur de Rohan! Thereby Monsieur de Rohan is consummating the ruin of his party; and that is why I said to you: Peace to the dead!"

"Well, well!" said Père Joseph's trusted agent, "I see that, like the excellent marquis, you have a romantic mind, and that you will be guided, according to his example, by sentiment. May I, without indiscretion, inquire for the health of monsieur your father?"

"You will soon see him in person, monsieur. He will be glad to see you. He is riding ahead, and we shall overtake him within a quarter of an hour."

"What do you say? Monsieur de Bois-Doré, at seventy-five or eighty years of age— —"

"Takes the field against the enemies and assassins of Henri IV.! Does that surprise you, Monsieur Poulain?"

"No, my child," replied the ex-Leaguer, now become, by the force of events, a continuator and admirer of the policy of the Béarnais; "but it seems to me that he is a little late in setting about it!"

"What would you have, monsieur? he did not choose to take the field all alone; he waited for the King of France to set the example."

"Faith," said Monsieur Poulain with a smile, "you have an answer for everything! I long to salute the marquis's noble old age! But it is impossible to trot here. Pray tell me of a man to whom I owe my life: Master Lucilio Giovellino, otherwise called Jovelin, the great bag-piper."

"He is happy, thank heaven! He has married my dearest friend, and they are doing us the favor to take charge of our house and our property during our absence."

"Your dearest friend? Do you refer to Mercedes, the beautiful Moor? I should have supposed that you preferred to her—with feelings of a different nature, it is true—a younger and even lovelier friend."

"Do you mean Madame de Beuvre?" rejoined Mario, with a frankness in striking contrast to Monsieur Poulain's insinuating curiosity. "I can readily answer you as I would answer the whole world. She is, in very truth, a person whom I loved fervently in my childhood, and whom I shall respect all my life; but her affection for me is very placid, and you may question me concerning her without reserve."

"Is she not married yet?"

"I have no idea, monsieur. As we have been travelling for several months, we have little news of our friends at a distance."

Monsieur Poulain scrutinized Mario by stealth. He had the tranquillity of a broken heart, but not the prostration of a hopeless soul.

"Do you not know," said the rector, "that Monsieur de Beuvre was with the English fleet before La Rochelle?"

"I know that he was killed there, and that Lauriane has no one but herself to depend upon."

"She was in Poitou when the Duc de Trémouille, after the desertion of the English, went to the king's camp to abjure his heresy."

"She did not accompany him there!" said Mario, hastily. "She asked permission to share the captivity of the heroic Duchesse de Rohan, who refused to submit; and, having failed to obtain that favor, she was preparing to return to Berry when we left our province."

"I knew all that," said Monsieur Poulain, who seemed, in truth, to be well posted upon all subjects.

"If you did not know it," Mario replied, "I should not regret having told you. Surely you would not furnish the Prince de Condé with a new pretext for confiscating Madame de Beuvre's property?"

"No, indeed!" replied the rector laughing outright, with a sort of cordiality. "You reason well, and a man may, without great risk, be as frank as you are, when he knows his companions. But have entire confidence in me, for I have broken entirely with the Jesuits, at my risk and peril!"

Monsieur Poulain spoke the truth.

A few moments later he was in the Marquis de Bois-Doré's presence, and the interview was very civil—almost friendly—on both sides.

CHAPTER LXX

The marquis did not need to convoke the ban and arrière-ban in order to raise a small troop of volunteers. His best men, sure of being well rewarded, had followed him enthusiastically.

The intrepid Aristandre took a keen personal delight in the idea of thrashing messieurs the Spaniards, whom he detested in memory of Sancho; the faithful Adamas rode a gentle palfrey in the rear-guard, and carried in his saddle-bags his master's perfumes and curling-tongs, nothing more!

Save for a touch of the tongs to what little hair was still left on his neck, and a little scented water for his own enjoyment, the marquis was as simple in his toilet as he had formerly been dazzling. No more wigs, no more paint, almost no lace, embroidery and purl; simply an ample doublet of woolen cloth, with open sleeves, short-clothes of the same material extending below the knee, boots fitting tight to the leg, with plain linen ruffles falling over the tops, a broad unembroidered neckband, and over the whole an immense, thick fur-lined cloak—such was the costume of the Beau Monsieur de Bois-Doré.

The metamorphosis can be explained in a few words.

Mario had fought a duel to discipline an impertinent knave who in his presence had made sport of the marquis's plaster mask, black hair and innumerable bows and buckles. Mario had dealt severely with his adversary—it was his first affaire!—but Bois-Doré, being informed of the episode after it was over, did not choose to expose his son to a repetition of it. Suddenly, and without a word to any one, he abandoned his dye and his wig one day on the pretext that Monsieur de Richelieu was justified in proscribing luxury, and that everyone should set a good example. Being thus resigned to appear old and ugly, he heroically appeared before his family. But to his great surprise they all uttered an exclamation of pleasure, and the Moor artlessly said to him:

"Ah! how handsome you are, master! I thought you much older than you are!"

The fact is that the marquis was exceedingly well preserved under his mask, and was extraordinarily handsome considering his great age.

He did not know—he was not likely to know—what infirmities were. He still retained his teeth; his ample, bald forehead was furrowed by graceful wrinkles, without a trace of malice or hatred; his moustache and royale, white as snow, stood out against his yellowish-brown complexion, and his great eye, keen and laughing, still shone mildly through his long, bushy, bristling eyebrows.

He was still erect as a young poplar, and stiff in proportion; but he no longer shrank from placing his foot in Aristandre's powerful hand to mount his horse. Once in the saddle, he was as firm as a rock.

Thereafter he received so many sincere compliments upon his beautiful old age, that he changed his whole system of coquetry: instead of concealing his age, he exaggerated it, representing himself as eighty years old although he was but seventy-seven, and taking the keenest pleasure in astonishing his young comrades-in-arms by his tales of the old wars, long buried in the archives of his memory.

On the 3d of March—that is to say on the second day after the meeting of the Beaux Messieurs de Bois-Doré with Monsieur Poulain—the royal vanguard, consisting of ten or twelve thousand picked men, camped at Chaumont, the last village on the frontier. The volunteers, having no materials for a camp, passed the night as best they could in the village.

The marquis tranquilly retired in the first bed that came to hand, and fell asleep like a man inured to the trade of war, who knew how to make the best of the hours of repose, to sleep for one hour when he had but one, and for twelve, to provide against emergencies, when he had nothing better to do.

Mario, intensely excited and impatient to fight, sat up with several young men, volunteers like himself, with whom he had become acquainted on the road.

It was in a wretched inn, the common room of which was so crowded that one could hardly turn about, and so filled with tobacco smoke that men could not recognize one another.

While the regular troops were as sedate and silent as the most rigid community of monks, the bands of volunteers were merry and uproarious. They drank and laughed and sang obscene songs, recited erotic or amusing verses; they talked of politics and love-making; they quarreled and embraced.

Mario sat by the fireplace dreaming, amid the uproar. Close beside him stood Clindor, become as stout-hearted a youth as his master, but somewhat awed to find himself surrounded by the nobility. He took no part in the noisy conversation; but he was burning to muster courage to do so, while Mario's reverie was cradled by the tumult, which neither tempted nor annoyed him.

Suddenly Mario saw a creature of most extraordinary aspect enter the room. It was a small, thin, dark girl, dressed in an incomprehensible costume; five or six skirts of brilliant hues, each one shorter than the next below; a waist glistening with tinsel and spangles, a quantity of multi-colored plumes in her crimped and curled hair, innumerable necklaces and gold and silver chains; she was covered with bracelets, rings, and glass ornaments, to her very shoes.

That strange creature was of no age. She might have been a precocious child or a worn-out woman. She was very small, ugly when she chose to smile and talk like other people, beautiful when she flew into a temper, which latter seemed to be with her a constant necessity or a normal condition. She insulted the inn-servants because they did not serve her quickly enough, swore at the troopers because they did not make room for her, clawed those who tried to take liberties with her, and retorted with indescribable blasphemy upon those who made sport of her absurd costume and her savage humor.

Mario was wondering with what purpose so shrewish a creature had introduced herself into such company, when a stout woman with a pimply face, absurdly bedizened with wretched gewgaws, also entered the room, laden with boxes like a mule, and called for silence. She had some difficulty in obtaining it, but at last delivered in French a sort of announcement, overflowing with hyperbolical laudation of her companion, the incomparable Pilar, Moorish dancer and infallible soothsayer, possessed of all the learning of the Arabs.

That name Pilar aroused Mario from his lethargy. He examined the two gypsies, and, despite the change that had taken place in them, recognized in one the pupil, victim and executioner of the miserable La Flèche; in the other the ex-Bellinde of Briantes, the ex-Proserpine of Captain Macabre, now styling herself Narcissa Bobolina, lute-player, dealer in laces, and on occasion mender and plaiter of ruffles.

The company assented to an exhibition of the talents proclaimed. Bellinde played the lute with more energy than correctness, and the dancer, for whom they made room by climbing on the tables, gave a display of epileptic agility, her extraordinary suppleness and energetic grace winning frantic applause from an assemblage already much excited by wine, tobacco and discussion.

Pilar's success with those inflamed imaginations simply intensified Mario's disgust, and he was about to retire; but he had sufficient curiosity to listen to the predictions which she was beginning to make on general subjects, while waiting for someone to ask her to reveal the secret of his future.

"Speak, speak, young sibyl!" was the cry on all sides. "Shall we be lucky in war? Shall we force the Pas de Suse to-morrow?"

"Yes, if you are in a state of grace," she replied disdainfully; "but as there is not a man among you who is not covered with mortal sins as with blotches of leprosy, I am sorely afraid for your soft white skins!"

"Stay," said someone, "we have here a chaste and gentle stripling, an angel from heaven, Mario de Bois-Doré! Let him begin the test and question the soothsayer."

"Mario de Bois-Doré?" cried Pilar, her sparkling eyes becoming dull and lifeless. "He is here, you say? where? where? Show him to me!"

"Come, Bois-Doré," they shouted on all sides, "do not hide your face, but hold out your hands."

Mario came forth from his corner and showed himself to the two women, one of whom darted forward to grasp his hand, while the other turned her head away as if to avoid being recognized.

"I saw you, Bellinde," said Mario to the latter; "and as for you, Pilar," he added, withdrawing his hand, which she seemed to wish to put to her lips, "look at *my lines*, that is enough."

"Mario de Bois-Doré!" cried Pilar, suddenly losing control of herself, "I know them well enough, the lines in your fatal hand! I studied them carefully enough long ago. I never told your fortune; it is too cruel and too unhappy."

"And I know your science," retorted Mario, shrugging his shoulders. "It depends on your whim, your hatred, your folly."

"Very well, put it to the test!" cried Pilar, more and more incensed; "and if you do not believe in my science, do not fear to listen to your sentence. To-morrow, my pretty Mario, you will sleep on your back, on the edge of a ditch; but to no purpose will your lovely eyes be open and staring, you will never again see the light of the stars."

"Because there will be clouds in the sky," observed Mario, undisturbed.

"No, the weather will be fair; but you will be dead!" said the sibyl, wiping the cold perspiration from her forehead with her hair. "Enough! let no one else question me! I shall say things that are too harsh to all of you here!"

"You will take back your words, you wicked she-devil!" cried the young man who had procured for Mario the pleasure of this agreeable prophecy. "Do not let her leave the room, friends! These infernal witches lead us into death by the confusion they sow in our minds. They are the cause of our losing, in the face of danger, the confidence that saves. Let us compel her to swallow her words and to confess that she said them from pure deviltry."

Pilar, supple as a snake, had already glided from the room. Some ran after her. Bellinde fled by another door.

"Let them go," said Mario. "They are two venomous beasts whose story I will tell you some other time. I am not at all disturbed by the prediction; I have paid for my knowledge of what that noble science is worth!"

They pressed Mario with questions.

"To-morrow," he said, "after the battle, after my threatened death! Permit me now to go to see if my father is carefully guarded by his people; for I know one of those women, perhaps both of them, to be quite capable of seeking to injure him."

"And we," replied his young friends, "will make a circuit of the village to be sure that there is no band of thieving, murdering gypsies in hiding anywhere."

They made the circuit with great care. It seemed quite useless, the regular camp having sentries posted and vigilant patrols who covered all the neighborhood to a considerable distance. They learned from the villagers that the two women had arrived alone on the preceding day and lodged in a house which they pointed out. They declared that the women were then in the house, and Mario did not consider it necessary to set a watch upon them. It was enough in his judgment, to guard the house in which his father was.

The night passed very quietly; too quietly for the liking of the impatient young gentlemen, who hoped to be awakened by the signal for battle. But they were disappointed. The Prince of Piedmont, brother-in-law of Louis XIII., had come on behalf of the Duc de Savoie to open negotiations, and the conferences effected a suspension of hostilities to the great dissatisfaction of the French army.

The following day passed in feverish suspense, and the gypsy's prediction, having come to naught, ceased to alarm Mario's friends.

The two vagabonds had packed up and passed through the vanguard on their way to France, there to ply their wandering trade. There was no fear that they would be allowed to retrace their steps. The cardinal had issued the strictest orders that all women and children, and especially women of disorderly lives, should be rigorously excluded from the camp-followers. Lewd women, gypsies, dancing girls and sorceresses were threatened with death if caught within the lines.

During the evening of the 4th of March, Mario was called upon to narrate the adventures of big Bellinde and little Pilar. He did it in a clear and simple way that drew upon him the attention of all who were present. Hitherto his modesty had prevented him from attracting notice: his interesting narrative, and the touching, natural, and at the same time entertaining way in which he told it caused his delighted comrades to forget the pleasures of the gaming-table and the advanced hour.

He might, had he chosen, have told the whole story of his life; but an indescribable feeling of timidity made him omit any mention of Lauriane's name.

CHAPTER LXXI

It was after midnight when they separated. Each group repaired at once to the more or less execrable lodgings it had secured, and Mario was standing with Clindor at the door of his own lodgings, when a vague shadow, crouching on the threshold, rose and came toward him.

It was Pilar.

"Mario," she said, "do not be afraid of me. I have never injured you, and I have no reason to wish your old father ill. I do not espouse Bellinde's hatred of you."

"Does Bellinde still hate my father?" said Mario. "Has she forgotten that he saved her from being hanged as Captain Macabre was?"

"Yes, Bellinde has forgotten it, or perhaps she never knew it; but it is too late to tell her of it, and she doesn't hate anyone now."

"What do you mean?"

"That I have done to her what she wanted to do to you."

"What was that? Tell me!"

"No, Mario, it's of no use; you would not love me any more for it; and you hate me now, I know."

"I hate no one," replied Mario; "I hate evil, and evil instincts horrify me. You have retained yours, unfortunate girl! I knew it yesterday, when you took a frantic delight in trying to disturb my mind. You will never succeed, you may as well understand that and leave me in peace; it is better for you that I forget you."

"Listen, Mario," exclaimed Pilar half aloud, in a choking voice. "This is not the way to treat me. Really, it is not, if you love anyone on earth! for I love you and I have always loved you. Yes, in the days when we were equally poor, sleeping on the same heather and begging on the same road, I was in love with you. I was born so; I cannot remember a single day in my whole life when I was not consumed by the passion of love or hatred. I never had any childhood! I was born of flame and I shall die of flame, a genuine spark from the stake! What does it matter? Even so, I am worth more to you than your Lauriane, who has always despised you and who will never love anything but her old heretics—luckily for her! Yes, luckily for her, I tell you! for I know all about both of your lives. I have been twice in your province, and one day I passed close to you without your recognizing me. You tossed me a small coin. See, here it is at my neck, concealed under my necklaces as my most precious treasure; I made a hole in it, and I wrote your name on it with the point of a knife. It is my talisman. When I no longer have it, I shall die!"

"Come, come," said Mario, "enough of this nonsense! What do you want now? Why did you return here at the peril of your life, and why did you wait for me at this door? Give me back that coin, and take these gold pieces which you may need."

"Keep your gold, Mario; I do not need it; I wish to keep and I shall keep your pledge, although you blush to know that your name is written on my breast. I have come here to tell you my story, and you must listen to it."

"Tell it quickly then; it is very cold and I am sleepy."

"I wish to tell it to you alone, and your page is listening. Come outside the walls with me."

"No, my page is sleeping against the door. Speak here, and make haste, or I leave you."

"Listen then, I shall soon have told it all. You know that my father was hanged and my mother burned!"

"Yes, I remember that you often told me so. Well?"

"Well, La Flèche brought me up to torment me. It was he who broke my bones to make me more flexible, and carried me about in a cage to make me ill and frantic. He exhibited me like a wild beast that bites everybody."

"But you took a horrible revenge upon him, did you not?"

"Yes, I suffocated him with sand and stones and dirt, when he was calling: 'Help! I am thirsty! I am thirsty!'—One of his arms still moved, and he tried to choke me with it. But, at the risk of my life, I forced what life he had left down his throat. Didn't I owe him that? Wasn't it my right? You would have saved him perhaps, and he would have paid you like Bellinde, who, but for me, would have succeeded in poisoning you all yesterday, you and your father and your servants, in order, so she said, to fulfil the prediction I had made before witnesses, and to protect my fame as a soothsayer."

"And then you——"

"I owed her that, too! Listen, listen to my story! After avenging myself on La Flèche, I hid in the pavilion in your garden. I had seen that you were angry with me, and I was waiting for your anger to pass. I thought that you would look for me, that you would be anxious about me, and would keep me in your château to love me. But toward evening, you came there with your Lauriane, and you told her that you hated me and I heard every word! Then I dropped a stone on her to kill her, and I hid myself. But you thought the stone had fallen of itself and you left me there.

"I passed the night there, dying with cold and hunger. I was in a frenzy of rage; that kept me up. I cursed you both; I cursed myself for having offended you. I meant to let myself die; but I had not the courage, and as I wanted nothing more of you, whom I believed that I hated, I went to Brilbault to get Sancho's money, which La Flèche had made me steal two or three months before, at La Caille-Bottée's house.

"In those days I didn't know the value of money, and I hated La Flèche so bitterly that I gave it all back to Sancho, who had hidden it so carefully that he was able to manage the gypsies with promises and a few crowns from time to time. But I knew where he had buried his treasure, and there was a good deal of it left; a good deal to me, at least, I needed so little. I divided it into several parts and hid them in different places.

"I had taken it into my head that I could live alone without being dependent on anybody, and wander all over the world at will, child that I was! But I soon got tired of it, and as I happened to fall in with Bellinde, who was flying from the country, with her head shaved and in a miserable plight, I told her that I had some little hidden treasures, but was very careful not to tell her where they were! Oh! how she flattered me, tormented me, made me tipsy and questioned me even in my sleep, trying to find out! She never lost the hope of extorting my secret from me; that is why she became my mother and my servant, always fawning on me and betraying me. Ah! yes, she betrayed me shamefully! She sold me, she abandoned me when I was still a child; and when, later, I realized and felt my shame, I swore that I would be revenged upon her when I no longer needed her. Now, the crows are feeding oh her flesh, and it was a righteous deed, God knows!"

"You are a wretched, horrible girl!" said Mario. "Now have you finished?"

"Now, I want you to love me, Mario, or I will avenge myself on your Lauriane, whom you still love, I know that; for you didn't choose to speak of her to your comrades in the inn just now. Oh! I was there too, hidden in the garret, where I heard all the evil you said of me."

"Since you heard all, how can you be mad enough to ask me to love you?"

"I am not mad! One can pass from hatred to love, I know by my own experience. You abhor and adore at the same time. Besides, you admitted that I had fine eyes now, and slender arms, and a sort of diabolical beauty. That is what you said at the inn just now. And many of those gentlemen offered me the night before money to buy other silk skirts and other earrings, because, beautiful or ugly, I had turned their heads. But I want nothing from them and nothing from you! I still have money hidden in Berry, and I can go there when I choose. Beware, Mario! Your Lauriane will answer to me for you. Take me with you, or renounce her."

"As you confess your evil purposes so boldly, I arrest you," said Mario.

He tried to seize her, being determined to turn her over to the camp authorities; but he seized nothing but her scarf: the girl herself, fleeter and more unsubstantial than the clouds driven by the wind, eluded him and vanished. He pursued her and might have caught her, for he too knew how to run; but he had hardly turned the corner when the bugles sounded boots and saddles; it was the signal of departure for the long-expected battle.

Mario forgot the wild threats that had excited him and hastened to his father, who was hurriedly dressing.

At daybreak the whole army was on the march.

"The Pas de Suse is a gorge about a quarter of a league in length, in some places less than twenty paces wide, and obstructed here and there by fallen rocks. The tergiversation of the Prince of Piedmont had had no other purpose than to delay the advance of our army for a few days. The enemy had used the interval to good advantage in strengthening their position.

"The gorge was intersected by three strong barricades protected by bastions and ditches. The cliffs commanding it on each side were alive with soldiers, and protected by small redoubts.

"Lastly, the cannon of Fort Tallasse, built on a neighboring mountain, swept the open space between Chaumont and the entrance to the gorge. It was one of those positions where it seems possible for a handful of men to check the advance of an army.

"Nothing, however, could check the *furie française*." [10]

So many accomplished historians have described this glorious action, that we shrink from attempting the task after them; it is not our business to write history according to official facts, but to seek it in episodes that have been overlooked. That is why we shall follow the Beaux Messieurs de

Bois-Doré through the carnage, and not allow ourselves to be dazzled by the majesty of the picture as a whole. An additional reason for adopting this course is that they had little leisure to contemplate it themselves.

It was a magnificent scene: a combat of heroes on a sublime stage!

The first cannon-shot awoke echoes of intense excitement in Mario's heart. How he passed the first barricade, whether upon a winged horse or "upon the fiery breath of the god Mars himself;" how he forgot his sworn promise to his father not to leave his side, he never knew. All the passion of his soul, all the fever in his blood, ordinarily restrained by modesty and filial love, produced a sort of volcanic eruption within him.

He even forgot for a moment that his father was following him into the very midst of the fray, and, in order not to lose sight of him, was exposing himself to no less risk.

Aristandre was there, it is true, stationed like a marble wall about his master; but Mario, when the fighting was most desperate, turned more than once to look for the old man's gray plume, which towered above all the rest, and each time, as he saw it waving still, he thanked God and trusted to his lucky star.

The whole affair was carried through so impetuously that it did not cost France the lives of fifty men. It was one of those miraculous days when every man has faith, and when nothing is impossible.

The position carried, Mario was galloping along the Suse road in pursuit of the fugitives, among whom was the Duc de Savoie in person, when he saw a masked horseman riding toward him at full speed on his right.

"Halt, halt!" he shouted; "the king's service before everything! Take my despatches! I know you; I trust you!"

As he spoke, the horseman slipped from his horse in a swoon, while the horse himself, utterly exhausted, fell on his knees.

Mario was the only one of the young men who had the self-restraint to renounce the opportunity to display his prowess farther; he leaped from his horse and picked up the sealed package which the courier had dropped.

But as he was about turning back toward the royal camp, a party of armed men, who seemed not to have taken part in the action, and who were evidently pursuing the messenger without regard to where they were going, suddenly appeared at Mario's right and rode toward him, shouting in Italian that his life would be spared if he surrendered the package without giving the alarm.

Mario shouted for help with all his strength. No one heard him. His father was still far behind, his companions already far ahead. He fired his carbine to attract attention, and, to avoid wasting his shot, aimed it at his assailants, one of whom rolled in the dust. Mario did not wait for the others. He had remounted, and rode away like an arrow, amid a hailstorm of bullets, some of which lodged in his hat, others in the bank by the road.

He heard a tumult behind him, yells, shots. He paid no heed and did not turn.

He had not seen the messenger's face or recognized his voice. He regretted having to abandon to the enemy a man who might be useful. But if was of the utmost importance to save the despatches, and it was only by a miracle that he saved them.

His retrograde course surprised those whom he met; At a short distance from the royal headquarters, he met his father, who was alarmed to see him pass thus without stopping, and supposed that he was wounded and that his horse was running away.

But Mario shouted: "Nothing! nothing!" and vanished in a cloud of dust.

At first he was turned away from the king's tent; he at once determined upon his course of action and hastened to the cardinal's.

The cardinal had already been exposed to so many attempts at assassination that it was no easy matter to obtain access to him. But the despatches which Mario waved above his head, and the excellent young man's winning countenance suddenly inspired the great minister with entire confidence. He summoned him to his presence and took the package, which Mario, in his haste, did not think to present to him with one knee on the ground.

[10] Henri Martin, *History of France.*

CHAPTER LXXII

The cardinal read the despatch.

It contained some good news: perhaps a report of the small number of troops that Gonzalez of Cordova had before Casal; perhaps of a conspiracy of the queens against the power which saved France.

Whatever it may have been, the cardinal folded the despatch with a shrewd smile and looked up at Mario, saying:

"Propitious fate has ordained everything so well to-day, that it has chosen an archangel for messenger. Who are you, monsieur, and how does it happen that you are the bearer of such a despatch?"

"I am a volunteer," Mario replied. "I took this despatch from the hand of a dying man, which was held out to me in the midst of our pursuit of the enemy. He said to me: 'The king's service before everything.'—I could not obtain access to the king, so I thought I would seek access to your eminence."

"So you thought that it was all the same, in the sense that the king can have no secrets from the minister?"

"I thought that he should have none," replied Mario, calmly.

"What is your name?"

"Mario de Bois-Doré."

"Your age?"

"Nineteen years."

"Were you at La Rochelle?"

"No, monseigneur."

"Why not?"

"I do not care to fight against those of the Reformed religion."

"Are you one of them?"

"No, monseigneur."

"But you approve of them?"

"I pity them."

"If you have any favor to ask of me, do it quickly, for time is precious."

"Give us days like this often, that is all that I ask," replied Mario; and, in his eagerness not to waste the cardinal's time, he took his leave without observing that His Eminence was inclined to speak further with him.

But other duties demanded the great minister's attention. He turned to something else and forgot Mario.

On the following day, as they were pitching their camp at Suse, Mario thought that he saw Monsieur Poulain pass dressed as a countryman. He called him, but received no reply.

Monsieur Poulain was in hiding, according to his custom. Being regularly employed upon secret missions, the ex-rector showed his face as little as possible in certain localities, and never appeared openly in the presence of the eminent personages who employed him.

While the king—that is to say the cardinal—was receiving the Duc de Savoie's submission at Suse, which ceremony necessarily lasted several days, the marquis was reposing after his excitement.

Although Richelieu's campaigns in nowise resembled the partizan warfare of his youthful days, Bois-Doré had borne himself as tranquilly as if he had never left the battle-field; but it had been a rude shock to him to see Mario subjected to that test. In the first place, he had been afraid that Mario would not come up to his hopes; for, since the terrible night of the attack upon Briantes and Sancho's death, Mario had often exhibited much repugnance for bloodshed. Sometimes, indeed, when he saw how little interest he took in the siege of La Rochelle, which excited all the youthful minds in their neighborhood, the marquis, although well satisfied with his principles, had been somewhat afraid of his prudence. But when he saw him rushing upon the Spaniards and climbing over the redoubts in the Pas de Suse, he thought him far too rash, and asked pardon of God for bringing him there. At last, however, he had recovered confidence, and, upon learning of the episode of the despatch, he wept for joy and chattered with pleasure in the bosom of the faithful Adamas.

Adamas attracted attention in the town by his arrogant airs and his utter contempt for everybody except Monsieur le Marquis and Monsieur le Comte de Bois-Doré. Aristandre was well pleased to have killed many Piedmontese, but he would have liked to kill more Spaniards. Clindor had not behaved badly. He was terribly frightened at the beginning, but he said that he was all ready to go through it again.

But Mario, amid the gratification of all his dear ones, was oppressed by profound disquietude. Although he despised vain predictions, and had passed through his baptism of fire without thinking of them, he trembled at the recollection of a foolish threat, and Pilar appeared again and again in his dreams, as the spirit of evil, in the guise of an invisible and intangible enemy. He learned, to his cost, that the weakest adversaries may, by a perseverance of hatred, become the most formidable. He had Lauriane constantly before his eyes; it seemed to him that she was threatened by some terrible danger. He took his fears for presentiments.

One morning he returned to Chaumont, as if for exercise. He inquired for the little gypsy to no purpose. He rode over to Mont Genèvre, and learned that a woman's body had been found there on the morning of the 3d of March. At first they had thought that she was frozen to death; but when they buried her they noticed that her lips and her neckerchief bore the marks of burning, as if she had been forced to swallow some corrosive poison. The mountaineers who gave Mario this information proposed to show him the body. They had buried it in the snow temporarily, the ground being frozen so hard that a grave could not easily be dug.

Mario at once identified the body as Bellinde's. So Pilar had told the truth. She had disposed of her companion; she might by the same means dispose of her rival.

Mario returned to Suse at full speed and told his father the whole story.

"Let me go to Briantes," he said. "Await me here to continue the campaign, if it is to be continued. If a definitive treaty is signed, you will know it in a few days, and will join me at home, without haste and without tiring yourself. I can go more quickly alone, quickly enough to arrive before that detestable creature, who has neither the means nor the power to travel by post."

The marquis consented. Mario instantly made his arrangements to start the next day with Clindor.

During the evening Monsieur Poulain visited them, with the utmost precaution. He was in most excellent spirits, and, at the same time, most mysterious.

"Monsieur le marquis," he said to Bois-Doré, when he was alone with him and Mario, "I owed you much before, and I shall owe my fortune to your amiable son! The valuable despatch of which I was the bearer, and which he succeeded in saving, assures me a less dangerous and more honorable place in the confidence of Père Joseph, that is to say, of the cardinal. I have come to pay my debt, and to inform you that your sole ambition is gratified. The king confirms your claim to the marquisate of Bois-Doré, on the sole condition that you shall construct somewhere on your domains a house to which you shall give that name, and which shall, by royal letters patent, be made transmissible to your heirs and their descendants. His eminence hopes that you will continue to serve in his army, if the war continues, and he will avail himself of his first leisure moment to summon you to his presence, in order to congratulate you upon the courage and devotion of the *old man* and the *child*; I ask your pardon, those were his words. Monsieur le cardinal noticed you both in the charge, and he afterward inquired your names. He was also particularly gratified with you, monsieur le comte, because you asked him simply for more fighting as your reward. I had the honor to appear before him in my humble person, and to tell him the story of my perils and your own, not forgetting that, at eleven years of age, you killed with your own hand your father's murderer; and lastly I reminded him that he was indebted for the receipt of news that was no less advantageous than agreeable to him to this same child, who is as shrewd and intelligent as he is brave. So you have a good start, Monsieur Mario. Humble as I am, I will help you forward with all my strength if opportunity offers."

Despite the marquis's very earnest desire to present Mario to the cardinal, Mario refused to await the uncertain fulfilment of the promise of an audience.

Having warmly thanked Abbé Poulain—he told them under his breath, with a smile, that they might call him so thenceforth,—Mario, happy in the joy of his father and Adamas because of the famous marquisate, threw himself on his bed, slept a few hours, embraced his old friends once more, and started for France at daybreak.

Mario attempted to travel too fast. Although he had an admirable horse, he thought that he would do better to travel by post at full speed, and his own strength failed him. He had received a slight wound in the affair of the Pas de Suse, and had carefully concealed it; the wound became inflamed, he was attacked by fever, and when he reached Grenoble fell helpless on his bed. Clindor, in dismay, discovered that he was delirious.

The poor page ran to fetch a doctor. He was not skilful; he irritated the wound still more by his remedies. Mario was very ill. His impatience and disappointment at being thus delayed aggravated his condition. Clindor decided to send a messenger to the marquis; but he lost his head and sent him to Nice instead of to Suse.

One evening when he was weeping in desperation on the landing outside the room in which Mario lay helpless, he thought that he heard him talking to himself and hastily entered the room.

Mario was not alone; a slender, pale-faced creature, dressed in red, was leaning over him as if to question him.

Clindor was afraid. He thought that the devil had come to torment his poor young master's last moments, and he was trying to remember some formulas of exorcism, when by the dim light of the night lamp he recognized Pilar.

His fear increased. He had overheard her conversation with Mario at Chaumont. He knew therefore that she loved him to frenzy. He believed that she was entirely under the influence of Satan, and fear produced its accustomed effect upon him, that is to say it made him brave; he threw himself upon her, sword in hand, and nearly wounded Mario, whom Pilar exposed as she avoided the blow.

He was not able to strike a second time; Pilar disarmed him, he knew not how, jumping upon him so quickly and unexpectedly that he was forced to fall back.

"Be quiet, stupid idiot that you are!" she said; "I did not come here to injure Mario, but to save him: don't you know that I love him, and that his life is mine? Do what I bid you do, and in two days he will be on his feet."

Clindor, not knowing which way to turn, and realizing that the charlatan whom he had summoned made the patient worse with each new prescription, yielded to Pilar's ascendancy. Despite the fear she caused him, she acted upon his will by virtue of a fascination which he did not admit, but which he could not shake off. At times he trembled to entrust Mario's life to her, but he obeyed, saying to himself that he was bewitched by her.

In Mario's case the fever was simply a result of nervous irritation: a day of repose would have cured his wound. But the physician had applied a healing ointment which produced the effect of poison throughout his whole system.

Pilar washed and purified the wound. She possessed those *secrets* of the Moors to which the Christians of Spain had recourse as a last resort. She administered powerful antidotes. The purity of the patient's blood and the wonderful equilibrium of his constitution seconded the effect of the remedies. He partly recovered consciousness that same night; and on the following morning he was no longer delirious. In the evening, although terribly weak, he felt that he was saved.

In his transports of joy, Clindor unconsciously made a declaration of love to the clever gypsy. She paid no heed whatever. She concealed herself behind the head of the bed so that Mario might not see her. She was well aware that her appearance would agitate him.

Two days later, Mario felt so fully restored that he ordered Clindor to look about for a post-chaise which he could purchase, so that they might continue their journey. Clindor, seeing that it was too soon, pretended that he could not find one, whereupon Mario bade him bring horses for them to ride.

Clindor was driven to despair by his persistence; Pilar interposed. Mario nearly fell ill again with anger when he saw her and learned that he owed his life to her. But he soon became calm and said to her in a mild tone:

"Whence do you come? where have you been since you made those threats?"

"Ah! you are afraid for *her*!" rejoined Pilar with a bitter smile. "Set your mind at rest; I have had no time to go thither. I will not go, if you will cease to hate me."

"I will, Pilar, if you abandon all thought of vengeance; but, if you persist in it, I shall hate you as much as I hate the life I owe to you."

"Let us not speak of that for the moment; you can safely remain quiet and not return to your province, since my presence with you is a guaranty that everything is well."

Therein Pilar touched the crucial point of the situation. Mario restrained his impatience and consented to remain at Grenoble until he should be fully cured. He had to consent also to allow Pilar to wait upon him. He could not dream of turning over to the strong arm of the law the woman who had just saved his life and whom it was his duty to try to convert from her evil ways by gentleness. He dared not irritate her by displaying his contempt, and despite the unconquerable repugnance she inspired in him, he was reduced to the necessity of being perturbed in mind when she was long absent and of rejoicing when she returned.

This state of affairs became intolerable after two or three days. Pilar, incapable of any sort of moral reasoning, was determined to be loved; she described her passion with a species of wild eloquence, saying and believing that it was chaste, because it was not governed by the senses, and sublime, because it had all the fervor of an unbridled imagination and a wilful temper. She heaped curses upon Lauriane and bitter reproaches upon Mario, exhibiting her mad passion shamelessly before poor Clindor, who took fire beside that volcano.

Mario soon wearied of the absurd rôle he was compelled to play. In vain did he try to transform that nature, incapable as it was of loving the right for the right's sake, or even of conceiving that Mario or anyone else on earth could so love it.

"If you did not love that Lauriane so madly," she said to him with appalling frankness, "you would entrust me with your vengeance; for she always has despised you and always will."

CHAPTER LXXIII

Mario was able to leave his bed at last, and one evening he went out alone, starving for fresh air and liberty, to test his strength, being fully determined to continue his journey even though he must procure Pilar's imprisonment until further notice, or though he must allow her to accompany him in order to hold her in subjection.

Meditating upon the most advantageous plan to adopt, he walked slowly toward the Convent of the Visitation, aimlessly, as if attracted by its elevated site. Suddenly he found himself face to face with a person who stopped in front of him. He too stopped. It was as if they were both irresistibly forced to look at each other.

To judge from her appearance and her manner, the stranger was a woman of noble rank, richly dressed, short and slender, pale, but young and beautiful, so far as he could see through the black mask which women of refinement wore when walking.

She wore a widow's cap and was dressed in black throughout. Her flaxen hair was arranged in two graceful masses over her hair. She was entirely alone. No companion, no servant before or behind her.

The graceful and modest charm of her carriage had impressed Mario at a distance. As she approached, her light hair and black attire had made his heart beat fast. At a little distance he put away the illusion; face to face, he was agitated and uncertain.

The same perplexity seemed to assail the masked lady. At last she passed on, returning Mario's salute.

Mario walked a little way, not without turning several times; he walked a little farther and stopped again.

"At the risk of being discourteous and receiving a sharp rebuke, I propose to find out who that woman is!" he said to himself.

He retraced his steps, walking rapidly, and found himself again face to face with the masked lady, who also had turned back. They both hesitated, and were very near passing a second time without speaking. At last the lady determined to break the ice.

"I ask your pardon," she said with some emotion, "but unless I am deceived by a striking resemblance, you are Mario de Bois-Doré?"

"And you are Lauriane de Beuvre?" cried Mario, intensely excited.

"How does it happen that you recognized me, Mario?" said Lauriane, removing her mask. "See how I have changed!"

"Yes," said Mario, beside himself with joy, "you were not half so lovely before!"

"Oh! do not feel compelled to be gallant to that point," said Lauriane. "My father's death, the sufferings of my party, and the downfall of all my hopes have aged me more than the years have done. But tell me of yourself and yours, Mario!"

"Yes, Lauriane; but take my arm and let us go to your home; for I must speak to you, and unless you are under proper protection here, I will not leave you."

Lauriane was surprised at Mario's excited air; she accepted his arm and said to him:

"I could not, if I would, take you to my present home. It is the convent which you see yonder on the plateau. But you can escort me to the gate and on the way we will tell each other all about ourselves."

Being urged to tell her story first, she told Mario that after the fall of La Rochelle, having failed to obtain permission to share Madame de Rohan's imprisonment, she had attempted to return to Berry. But she had learned in time that the Prince de Condé had given orders to arrest her again in case she should make her appearance there.

An old aunt, her only remaining relation and faithful friend, was superior of the Convent of the Visitation at Grenoble: she was a former Protestant, who had been consigned to that institution when very young, and had allowed herself to be converted there. But she had retained a very great sympathy for the Protestants, and she urged Lauriane most affectionately to come to her for shelter and protection until the end of the war in the South. Lauriane had found some repose and much affection there. She had been no more persecuted there than by the nuns at Bourges. From consideration for her aunt, they had even pretended not to know that she was a heretic, and she was allowed to go out alone and masked, to carry alms and consolation to the divers unfortunate Protestants living in the suburbs.

"Lauriane," said Mario, "you must not go out any more; you must not show yourself in public again until I tell you. It is due to the interposition of Providence that you have not been met and recognized by an invisible and dangerous foe. Here we are at the gate of the convent; swear by your father's memory that you will not pass through this gate again until you have seen me."

"Shall I see you again then, Mario?"

"Yes, to-morrow. Can you receive me in the parlor?"

"Yes, at ten o'clock."

"Do you swear that you will not go out?"

"I swear it."

This time Mario was overjoyed to see the gate of the cloister close between Lauriane and himself. He considered that she was safe there if Pilar did not discover her. He carefully explored the immediate neighborhood of the convent, to satisfy himself that he had not been followed and watched by her. He knew that she was capable of sacrificing the whole community in order to reach her rival.

He returned to his apartments and did not find her there. Clindor had not seen her since his master went out.

All Mario's anxiety revived. He was going down to the street when he heard an uproar which made him quicken his pace. He saw Pilar being taken to prison by a party of archers. She uttered piercing shrieks, at once heart-rending and savage; and when she saw Mario, she held out her hands to him imploringly with a despairing expression which shook his resolution for a moment.

"Ah! cruel!" she cried, "it is you who cause me to be cast into a dungeon as the reward of my love and my care! Infamous wretch! you wish to be rid of me. Curse you!"

Mario, without replying, questioned the leader of the squad in whose custody she was.

"Can you tell me," he said, "whether you propose simply to imprison her for the night as a vagrant, or whether you have arrested her on suspicion of some crime or misdemeanor?"

He was informed that she was accused of a misdemeanor. The physician who had treated Mario with such ill success, irritated to find that he had been cured by an adventuress, accused her of breathing upon her patients, in terms which were equivalent in those days to a charge of unlawfully practising medicine, which charge was likely to have far more serious consequences then than in our day, since the question of witchcraft could always be raised, a crime which the most learned magistrates took seriously and punished with death.

"Whatever may happen to her," said Mario to himself, "it is most important that this dangerous girl should lose track of Lauriane, whom perhaps she has already discovered."

On the following morning he hurried to the convent.

"Now," he said to his friend, "we may breathe freely, but we cannot go to sleep over the volcano."

And he told the whole of his strange adventure with the gypsy.

Lauriane listened attentively.

"Now," she said, "I understand everything. Let me tell you, Mario, why I was so deeply moved when I saw you yesterday, and why I had the assurance to speak to you without being certain that I recognized you. Also, why I hesitated the first time, thinking that I was deceived by my imagination. A week ago, I received an anonymous letter full of insults and threats, in which I was told that you had been killed in the battle of the Pas de Suse. I was overwhelmed by that news. I wept for you, Mario, as one weeps for a brother, and I wrote a letter to your father and sent it instantly to the mail carrier. Little by little, however, reflection led me to doubt the truth of the suspicious intelligence I had received, and when I met you I was on my way to the town, to ascertain, if possible, the names of the nobles who were killed in that battle. I had resolved, if yours was among them, to go to your father and try to sustain him and care for him in that terrible trial. I surely owed him that, did I not, Mario, for all his kindness to me in years gone by?"

Mario gazed at Lauriane; he could not tire of contemplating her altered features, her eyes inflamed by grief and tears, the traces of which seemed very fresh.

"Ah! my Lauriane," he cried, kissing her hands, "so you have retained a little affection for me?"

"Affection and esteem," she replied; "I knew that you had refused to fight against the Protestants."

"Ah! I will never do that! and yet I never told my principal reason! I can tell it to you now: I would not run the risk of firing upon your father and your friends. Lauriane, I always loved you dearly; why were your letters to my father always so cold with respect to me?"

"I, too, can speak with perfect frankness now, my dear Mario. My father, when we went to Bourges the last time, four years ago, had the strange idea of affiancing us to each other. Your father rejected, as he was bound to do, the suggestion of so ill-assorted a union; and I, a little humiliated by my poor father's thoughtlessness, informed you several times of marriage projects, to which I gave but slight consideration in the melancholy situation in which I then was. At the same time I was cold to you in words, my dear Mario, and perhaps somewhat humiliated by the thought of the presumption which you would naturally attribute to me. Let us smile to-day at all that past misery, and do me the justice to believe that I do not entertain the slightest thought of marriage. I am twenty-three years old; my time has gone by. My party is crushed, and my fortune will be confiscated whenever it suits the Prince de Condé's caprice. My poor father is dead, stripped by the hazard of war of the property he had amassed in his maritime expeditions. So I am neither rich nor beautiful nor young. I have but one cause of rejoicing: it is that I can live hereafter not far from you, without being suspected of aspiring to anything except your friendship."

Mario listened, trembling and bewildered.

"Lauriane," he said impetuously, "you show your disdain of my name, my youth and my heart when you speak of the tranquil bond of friendship which it would be easy for you to resume. But it is for me to say: It is too late. I have always loved you reverently, and I do not think that my love is any less reverent because I have loved you more passionately since I lost you and since I have found you again. I, too, Lauriane, have suffered keenly! But I have never despaired altogether. When I had carefully concealed my grief, in order not to allow myself to languish and die, God sent me, in His merciful compassion, gusts of hope in Him and of faith in you.

"'She knows, she must know that it would kill me,' I would say to myself; 'she will love me, she will not love another, because of her kindness of heart if for no other reason! I am only a child, but I can soon and very quickly make myself worthy of her, by working hard, by keeping my heart pure, by having courage, by making them happy who will love me, and by fighting gallantly when there comes a righteous war': for this one is righteous, is it not, Lauriane, and your heart cannot be so changed that you love the Spaniards to-day?"

"No, surely not!" she replied. "And it was because Monsieur de Rohan insisted upon this mad, disgraceful and desperate alliance that I awaited the result of events here, and took no deeper interest in them."

"You see, Lauriane, that nothing separates us now. If I am not the good and learned man that I would like to be, I believe at all events that I know as much and can fight as stoutly as most of the young men of twenty-five to thirty years, with whom I came in contact in the army. As for my affection, Lauriane, I can answer for its lasting so long as my life shall last. I am entitled to no credit for it, for I was born loyal, and from childhood it has been impossible for me to consider any other woman than you lovely and lovable; I placed my heart in your keeping the first day that I saw you. I have never become accustomed to living apart from you, and I have never passed a single day at Briantes without sitting down to dream of you, instead of playing and amusing myself, whenever I left my studies for an instant. What I thought, what I said to you eight years ago, in the famous labyrinth, I still think and I say to you again to-day.

"I cannot live happily without you, Lauriane! In order to be happy, I must see you always. I know that I have no right to say to you: 'Make me happy!'—You owe me nothing! but perhaps you will be happier with me than you were with your poor father, or than you are now, alone, persecuted, and obliged to conceal yourself. I do not need that you should be rich; but if you are bent upon being rich, I will enforce your rights as soon as peace is assured; I will defend you against your enemies. Married to me, you will have absolute freedom of conscience; and under my protection you can pray as you choose. We will not fight for our altars, as the King and Queen of England are doing at this moment. If you must have a title, why I am bemarquised for good and all. Whether you are still beautiful or not, I do not know, I never shall know. I see that you have changed. You are paler now and thinner than when you were sixteen years old; but in my eyes you are much lovelier so, and if you had never been lovely, it seems to me that I should have loved you no less dearly.

"If therefore a woman's happiness consists in being beautiful in the eyes of the man she loves, love me, Lauriane, and you will have that happiness. Listen, Lauriane, and let me speak to you as in the old days. I have been submissive and brave down to this day; do not deprive me of my strength; if you wish to wait still longer and know me as a friend and a brother, I will wait until you trust me. If you wish me to go back to the army—and, in truth, such is my desire—come to the camp as my father's ward and adopted daughter. I will see you only when you choose, not at all if you insist, until you accept me for your husband. But do not leave us again; for, with or without your love, we are and desire always to be your family, your friends, your defenders, your slaves, whatever you wish us to be, provided that you permit us to love you and serve you."

Lauriane pressed Mario's loyal hands in hers.

"You are an angel," she said, "and it requires courage on my part to refuse you. But I love you too well to chain your brilliant destiny to mine, melancholy, as it is, and alas! complete; I love your father too well to be willing to cause him this sorrow."

"My father? you doubt my father?" cried Mario, beside himself. "Ah! Lauriane, do you not understand that your father deceived you! Say that you do not love me, that you have never loved me!"

At that moment there was a violent ringing at the gate of the convent, and a moment later the Marquis de Bois-Doré rushed into the parlor and embraced Mario and Lauriane in turn.

He had not received Clindor's message, but Lauriane's letter; and as the treaty was signed and he was returning to Berry, he had come to the convent to take her home with him. He was greatly surprised to find Mario there, thinking that he had already returned to Briantes.

The situation was explained to him; then Mario, still intensely agitated, said to him:

"You arrive in good time, father. Lauriane here thinks that you do not love her!"

A second explanation ensued. The marquis perceived Mario's agitation and grief, and he smiled.

Lauriane suddenly understood that smile.

"Dear marquis," she cried, blushing and trembling from head to foot, "give me back the letter I wrote you when I thought that your son was dead! Give it back to me, I insist; do not show it."

"No, no," replied the marquis, handing the letter to Mario with a sly expression; "he shall never see it, unless he snatches it from my hands— which he is quite capable of doing, as you see!"

CHAPTER LXXIV

The letter was short and disconsolate; Mario had soon devoured it with his eyes, while Lauriane hid her face on the old man's shoulder.

Lauriane, in the first outburst of bitter grief, had written the marquis that she had always loved Mario since their separation and should wear mourning for him all her life.

"For now," she said, "I feel for the first time that I am really widowed!"

"You are not, you never will be, my Lauriane," said the marquis, removing her little black cap for a moment. "I have never desired any other daughter than you, and we will go home and prepare for the wedding at Briantes."

I leave you to imagine the rejoicing at the old manor at the simultaneous return of the Beaux Messieurs de Bois-Doré, Lauriane, Adamas, Aristandre, and even Clindor, who, the better to destroy the spell cast upon him by the gypsy, hastened to pay court to all the village maidens.

The marriage of Monsieur Sylvain's beloved children could not be celebrated publicly until Lauriane had made submission to the king and obtained her pardon, for she had proclaimed herself a rebel in a moment of desperation; and, despite Monsieur Poulain's influence, the king remained inflexible so long as the *War in the South* lasted.

It was short and bloody. It was the last gasp of the party as a political faction.

"Upon the ruins of that demolished party, Richelieu caused the son of Henri IV. to swear to maintain the religious liberty proclaimed by his father." [11]

Thereafter they could safely present to Louis XIII. the Marquis de Bois-Doré's petition in behalf of his daughter-in-law. To that end Mario went in person to Nîmes, where the king had made a triumphal entry with Richelieu. Monsieur de Rohan had gone to Venice.

Mario obtained a decree restoring his wife's estates in despite of monsieur le prince, who was sniffing eagerly at them, and likewise restoring her liberty without condition or reservation. The cardinal received him and rebuked him mildly for having taken no part in that war. Mario requested another opportunity to fight in Italy, and the cardinal, as he dismissed him, said in an undertone, with a most affable smile:

"I promise you the opportunity, but say nothing about it unless you wish me to fail!"

Mario found the Abbé Poulain at Nîmes, thoroughly exhausted and delighted to have a few weeks of repose. He had assisted Mario so cordially, that the young man invited him to come to Briantes, and they set out together, the priest congratulating himself upon the prospect of celebrating the marriage of the young people.

They started on an intensely hot day. It was early in July. The country which they rode through had been laid waste by the war and not a tree, not a cottage was standing.

By the king's command the troops had ravaged the territory around all the rebellious cities, in order to starve the inhabitants.

"We are passing through a conflagration," said Monsieur Poulain to Mario; "the sun treats us as we treated this poor soil, and I verily believe that our clothes will take fire."

"Really, monsieur l'abbé," said Clindor, who loved to mingle in the conversation, "there's a very unpleasant smell of something burning!"

"I believe that some house is still burning behind yonder hill," said Mario; "do you not see smoke?"

"There is very little of it," said the abbé; "some little hovel, I presume. I confess, monsieur le comte, that I am weary of so much misery. I used to hate the Huguenots; now that they are down, I am like you, I pity them. I witnessed the Privas affair. Well, I have had enough of it, and I defy the greatest gluttons of vengeance to say that they are not surfeited with it."

"I should say as much!" said Mario with a sigh; "but listen to those shrieks, monsieur l'abbé; there is somebody in great distress. Let us go to see."

Behind the hill where the smoke was ascending, they heard shrieks, or rather one long, piercing, heart-rending shriek. The appalling duration of that distant cry, which seemed to be uttered by a child, made a profound impression on the abbé. Clindor could not believe that it was a human voice.

"No, no," he said, "either that is a shepherd's pipe, or somebody is killing a kid."

"It is a human being expiring in torture," said Monsieur Poulain; "I know that frightful music only too well!"

"Let us hasten then!" cried Mario; "we may be in time to save an unfortunate fellow creature. Come, come, monsieur l'abbé! The peace is signed; no one has the right to torture Huguenots!"

"It is too late," said the priest, "the sounds have ceased."

The shrieks had suddenly ceased and the smoke had disappeared. Perhaps they were mistaken. However, they urged their horses and soon reached the top of the hill.

Thereupon they espied, in the valley beyond, and much farther away than they had supposed, a group of peasants bustling about a half-extinct fire. Before they came within ear-shot, the men had dispersed. A single old woman remained near the smoking ashes, which she was turning over with a fork as if in search of something. Mario arrived first at the spot, where his nostrils were assailed by an acrid, intolerable odor.

"What are you looking for there, mother?" he said; "what have you been burning?"

"Oh! nothing, my fine gentleman! nothing but a witch who gave us the fever with her look whenever she passed. Our men made an end of her, and I am looking to see if she didn't leave her secret in the ashes."

"What? her secret?" said Mario, disgusted by the sang-froid of that harridan.

"You see," replied the old woman, "she had something around her neck that glistened, and she lost it struggling when they put her in the fire. Then she shrieked: 'I have lost it, I am lost myself!' — It must have been an amulet to protect her from a violent death, and I would like to find it."

MARIO FINDS PILAR'S TALISMAN.

*"Look" said Mario, picking up a coin with a hole in
it, which he saw shining at his feet, "is this it?"*

*"Yes, yes, that's it, my fine gentleman! Give it to me
for the trouble I had keeping the fire burning."*

"Look," said Mario, picking up a coin with a hole in it, which he saw shining at his feet, "is this it?"

"Yes, yes, that's it, my fine gentleman! Give it to me for the trouble I had keeping the fire burning."

Mario threw the coin far away, impelled by a feeling of unconquerable horror. He had read upon it a name carved with a knife. It was Pilar's talisman. Naught else remained of her save that testimony of her fatal love, a few charred bones, and the disgusting odor of burned flesh with which the atmosphere was heavy.

Overwhelmed with horror and pity, Mario rode rapidly away, refusing to give Clindor, who questioned him closely, the key to the riddle; and, during a considerable part of the journey, he was unable to shake off the painful impression produced by that shocking incident.

But when they drew near the manor, we can readily believe that he had forgotten everything, and thought only of the joy of seeing once more his dear betrothed, his beloved father, his loving Mercedes, his paternal tutor Lucilio, the sage Adamas, and the heroic charioteer,—all those loving hearts who, while spoiling him to the best of their ability, had succeeded as by a miracle in making him the best and most charming of mortals.

The wedding festival was magnificent. The marquis opened the ball with Lauriane, who, being happy and at peace once more, seemed not a day older than the handsome Mario.

[11] Henri Martin.